# Nightmares & Sin

## Sin

### Monstrous Hearts Series

## Quell T. Fox

FLUFFY FOX PUBLISHING

Published by Fluffy Fox Publishing, an imprint of Fluffy
Fox, LLC
PO Box 5433, Fall River, Massachusetts 02723-0408

Nightmares & Sin is part of the Monstrous Hearts Series; a series dedicated to the villains. The authors in this series have dedicated their time to make sure villains get love too. This is the overall theme you will find in these books.

They can be read and enjoyed in any order.

**Disclaimer: There are dark themes in this book that are not meant for everyone. This include kidnapping, blood play, and knife play.**

# CHAPTER ONE

## Kaine

I tip my head back as I bring the shot glass to my lips, opening my mouth and pouring in the familiar liquid. It burns my throat as it goes down, a welcomed and delicious feeling. I slam the glass down on the table in front of me just as Maxen lets out a whoop and throws his fist into the air before bringing his other arm around my shoulder and giving me an excited shake.

"That's my boy!" he shouts, jabbing his finger towards my opponent who is fighting to sit straight in his chair across the table from us.

"Give up?" I ask with a smirk, feeling almost none of the effects of the alcohol even though I believe that last one was shot eleven.

The young college kid across from me scoffs and I know what his answer will be. These dumbass kids never know when to give up, and it's one of the reasons I play this game almost every weekend. It's a sure source of entertainment.

It should be boring, knowing exactly what's going to happen, but I love the control of it. Forcing the morons to push their limits, never give up. I love watching the fire in their eyes slowly dwindle down as the booze takes over before it extinguishes completely and they topple over to the floor in a mess of their own excrements.

I've been doing this for so long I can tell you almost exactly how the night will end, just by the attitude of my opponent and his shitbag friends. Some pass out, some throw up, hell, one guy was even rushed to the hospital to have his stomach pumped—good on him for not giving up.

They're all told not to do this, not to go against me. I'm undefeated. Everyone who parties at this bar on a Friday night knows that. Yet, the frat guys around here are all too stubborn to say no.

"Pour another," the guy across from me says, his words slow but filled with determination. Everyone around us quiets down, and the only thing that can be heard is the jukebox blasting an old Bon Jovi hit and the clank of billiard balls coming from the back room. Everyone's eyes dart from him to me, all wondering what I'll say. Will I allow it? Will I keep going?

Of fucking course I will.

The poor guy.

I've never said no before. Why would tonight be any different?

Maybe I should feel bad for the kid... or any who think they have a chance, but I'm pretty sure I was born without an ounce of compassion—being a demon will do that to you.

I raise my arms out to the sides, a smirk turning up my lips.

"Do as the man says."

A mix of cheers and gasps erupt around our table, drowning out the background noise. Everyone who is gathered, eagerly waiting to see what happens next. At this point, it's turned into more of a "how many before they drop" competition, instead of the "who can outdrink who" that it started out as. I've even seen a few people placing bets on the number of shots instead of who the winner will be. After all the long months of me doing this, you'd think no one would take me on, but humans are cocky and straight-up stupid. Sure, they don't know what I am, but that shouldn't matter. If I've been undefeated for this long, why would that suddenly change?

Humans and their fucking egos.

Just as the person we like to call our referee is finished pouring the shots—one for me and one for the guy that is sure to throw up after this one—screeching erupts towards the entrance, and the crowd of people hovering around us turn their heads in that direction. I follow along, because damn, do I love a good fight, and that's exactly the type of energy swirling around this place right now.

The music is loud, top of the notch speakers booming out an old classic rock song that really shouldn't be as popular as it is, but I can still make out the shouts of a woman through the pounding bass. Confusion settles in for a moment, but as the crowd starts to part, and a red-faced girl, who looks to be about the same age as the loser across from me, stomps towards us, I put two and two together.

The *girlfriend.*

Oh, how I love when this happens.

I lean back in my chair, crossing my arms over my chest, and wait for the show, attempting to not look too excited but I can't hide it. I bite on my bottom lip to stop my grin from widening.

"Andrew Brian Lewis!"—Ah, a three-namer? How fitting—"You get your ass up and outside right this minute. We're going home!"

It takes Andrew, whose eyes are barely open at this point, a long moment to catch on to what is going on. His eyes are hazy as he blinks them open, looking around to find where the familiar voice is coming from. When he finally turns in the right direction, glazed over eyes landing on the girl, he breaks out into a smile. As she begins to shout at him again, clearly showing who wears the pants in that relationship, his smile turns into a frown. "Go away, Rhonda," he says in a bored tone, trying to shoo her but his arm looks more like a limp noodle than something with bones in it.

"So help me, Andrew, if you don't—"

She's cut off as Andrew's face morphs into a sickly green. The crowd catches on and takes a few steps back and just in enough time. Andrew turns and blows chunks all over his girlfriend who shrieks in disgust, annoyance, and embarrassment. Seemingly the only person who didn't get the memo that turning green means someone is about to barf.

*So, you were wrong*, Maxen says to me through our mind link. The one all demons have the ability to use, but most keep shut off. There aren't many demons who like someone enough to allow them in, but Max and I are different.

I shrug. *It happens from time to time.*

Though I plan to not make a habit of it. I could argue that if the girl hadn't of showed up, he would have taken that last shot before everything came back up, but I know it's pointless. If Maxen is anything, it's a good discussionist, if that's even a word. If not? Well, he's good at making his freaking point. Which sometimes can be exhausting, other times entertaining.

I get to my feet, everyone stepping back to give me the room I need to stretch.

They treat me like a god around here. Bringing me drinks when I need one, not getting too close, not speaking to me unless spoken to... It's a nice change from how things are back home. In Hell.

Oh, and did I mention this was my third game of the night?

Sitting for that long makes my back ache, so a good stretch is just what I need. These humans up here really don't know how to live if this is the shit they sit in. As I raise my arms above my head, I feel the bones popping into place and I groan in satisfaction.

As everyone slowly starts to make their way out of the bar, since closing is in about twenty minutes, the show is over, and it now reeks of sour orange chicken, I nod my head to Andrew's blond-haired friend, the one who was cheering him on all night.

"Be sure the tab gets paid, yeah?" He clenches his jaw, clearly annoyed at the situation, as I pick up my last shot and toss it back.

I can't blame him. If Max pulled that kind of shit, he'd be on his own. I'm all about being my best friend's wingman, but there is a line. And because I am the cocky asshole that I am, as I pass by, I slap Andrew's friend on the back in that friendly type of way I see all the college kids doing. "Have a lovely night." I grin.

He jerks out of my hold, pulls his wallet from his back pocket, and stomps over to the bar. I guess twenty-four shots, plus whatever else they drank could total up to a decent bill, but that's the bet you take when you play the game. Besides, all these college kids have trust funds, so I don't know why he's grumbling about something that will surely go on daddy's credit card.

"Another great win, as usual," Max says excitedly as we step out onto the sidewalk, the cool breeze rustling my hair. He's buzzing with energy, as he usually is after such a thrilling night. Even though everything worth any amount of fun is closing shortly, the streets are still bustling with people.

"I swear these college kids are getting dumber as the days go on," I drawl, pulling out a cigarette and putting it to my lips.

"Maybe we should switch it up? Check out a biker bar or something. I bet it would be more of a challenge."

I roll my eyes. "Challenge? No. But I bet it would have a better show. More fighting, more entertainment. It's worth a shot." I shrug.

"Ah, I see what you did there," Maxen says, grinning at my pun. "Oh, fuck me!" He whistles as we pass by a group of girls who barely look legal. They all giggle and bat their lashes at him. He slows his pace before turning around and walking backwards. "What are you ladies—"

I cut him off by grabbing his arm and yanking him back, lighting my cigarette with my free hand at the same time. "Sorry, ladies! My buddy here is a little drunk and—"

"Oh, we don't mind!" the petite blonde girl says, cocking her head to the side and running her tongue along her plump bottom lip. My underwear has more material than the outfit she's wearing, and that says a lot, considering I wear fitted briefs.

I raise a brow, holding Max back and shoving the lighter into my pocket. "Yes, well, I do. Herpes and all that. You know how it is. *Ciao!*" I wiggle my fingers at them and move quicker, their scoffs and swears echoing into the night.

My grip on Max's arm tightens and I pull him after me. "Are you really trying to get another case of Chlamydia, you moron? Those girls are fucking hookers."

He groans, running his hand through his dark hair. "I'm fucking starving."

"Didn't you just feed yesterday?" I ask.

"Those demon girls just don't do it for me anymore. Besides, drinking depletes it."

A grin crosses my lips as I meet his desperate look. He always needs a feeding after a night of letting off so much energy. "Then let's go hunting."

# CHAPTER TWO

## BEXLEY

I knew picking up this shift at the café was a mistake. I never work Friday nights because I hate dealing with all the drunken assholes who come in after the bars close. The tips are great since more than half the idiots who come in here are drunk as fuck. Too inebriated to notice what kind of bill they're giving me and walk out throwing a, "keep the change" over their shoulder or they're just drunk enough that they can't keep their small dicks in line and try to butter me up with a big fat tip.

Spoiler alert: the only kind of fat tip I like is one that's on the end of a long, thick—

"Bexley! Break is over!" Ginger shouts. I let out a frustrated growl. I was only able to milk an extra two minutes of my break. Ginger keeps track of me like a housewife who thinks her husband is cheating on her with his secretary. You'd think she were the owner or something.

Oh, wait. She's just fucking him.

I get to my feet and push the five-gallon bucket of icing back into its corner with my foot. Shoving my phone into my back pocket, I walk out of the storage room that doubles as our break room. My entire body deflates as I see the line literally going around the building.

I was gone for fifteen—okay, *seventeen*—minutes. How the hell did this happen?

"Get in gear, Bex, bars just closed," Rachel says as she walks past me. She is allowed to talk to me this way or any other way she wants. She's my best friend and roommate. If the other one pulled this shit? We'd be fighting.

I make my way over to the counter, taking my place behind the register. I'm no stranger to dealing with rushes, I normally work the morning shift and it's just as busy, only the customers are a lot less active since they're half asleep and not buzzing with alcohol coursing through their veins. Instead, the melatonin is still lingering and they're more pleasant.

I hip check Ginger who is in the middle of taking someone's order, a man who is so far gone he doesn't realize he's now talking to a different girl. Ginger glares but continues to write on the cup as I punch the order into the register.

"That'll be $7.79," I say with a tired smile. He hands me a twenty as he sways on his feet, letting out a burp that has me gagging and hoping my nose hairs don't fall out.

"Keep the shange," he slurs, blinking slowly and moving to the pickup end of the counter.

It's going to be a long fucking night.

The rush finally dies down a little after three in the morning. Why Fucking Derrik insists on keeping the place open until four is beyond me. We should be able to close as the rush dies down, but nope. The asshole has to keep us here until the streets are empty and so much more creepy. Of course, that's only because his precious employee of the month gets to use his fancy BMW to drive herself home.

He doesn't give a flying fuck about Rachel and I, who both have to walk back to our apartment on the dangerous NYC streets. I mean, obviously, we call an Uber, but he doesn't know that.

We're sitting in one of the empty booths, both having a coffee knowing we still have some time before we make it back to our warm and comfortable beds.

"Derrik said it was cool if I leave," Ginger announces loudly as she walks into the dining area from the back room, dressed like a hooker, purse on her elbow, keys in hand. I fucking hate this girl.

"Can I ask you a question before you go?"

She stops right at the door, hand on the handle, and turns to me with an eyebrow raised.

"What are you going to do when Fucking Derrik moves on to the next employee?" Rachel gasps and holds back a laugh as Ginger's mouth drops open.

"You're such a bitch, Bexley." She scoffs and continues out the door.

"You know you're getting written up, right? I bet she's gonna go suck his dick extra hard until he signs the fucking form."

"Won't be the first time." I find the straw, but all I get are slurping sounds. "Ugh," I groan. "This coffee fucking sucks anyway. It's like, defective or something."

"Maybe when you're employee of the month, you can offer anal and have him buy a new brand."

"Ew!" I shout, pulling out my straw and tossing it at her. It hits her in the forehead and falls to the table. "Not happening. I don't even want to think about it." I shiver at the thought. I've been working here for three years now. The *employee of the month* Rachel and I speak of isn't an actual employee of the month, it's just the employee that Derrik has decided to fuck for the time being.

Like, have some self-respect. If you're going to fuck your boss, at least make sure he's a lawyer or a doctor or something. A café owner? Ridiculous.

The bell above the door ringing has Rachel and I both looking up. Instantly, my chest warms at the two men who just walked in. Tall, dark, and tattooed. The kind who will fuck you and never call you again—my favorite. I'm at the point in my life where I enjoy the bad decisions I make, and the last thing I want is to settle down.

I turn back to Rachel, lowering my voice to a whisper. "Who would ever want to touch Derrik's dick, when something like *that* is running around the streets?"

"Actually, we were walking. I prefer to do my running in the morning."

"And I don't run at all."

Rachel's eyes widen and her face splits into a *haha, you got caught* grin. I purse my lips and take a deep breath. I turn in my seat, planting my arm on the back of the booth.

"Got super hearing, do ya?"

The one with bright silver eyes grins, while the other smirks devilishly. My panties all but combust inside my jeans.

"It's a gift," the one who has bright blue eyes says in a more rugged tone.

"Or a curse," I mumble, getting to my feet.

"Depends who you ask," one of them says as I make my way around the counter.

*Just shut up while you can, Bex.*

Once I'm behind the counter, I plaster a smile on my face, trying to pretend that little introduction didn't just happen. Both guys walk up to the counter and look over the menu as I ignore the crude gestures Rachel is making behind their backs. Sure, I'd totally suck these guys off, as she's suggesting I do, but that is beside the point.

"Welcome to The Coffee Club," I greet as cheerily as my tired, slightly embarrassed body will allow. "What can I get for you?"

The one with silver eyes looks down at me, running his tongue along his bottom lip, and I self-consciously tuck some hair behind my ear. I don't normally cower in the presence of hot guys... but these two are next level. And they look like they could be brothers... which for some fucked-up reason, I find so much more sexy than it should be. Only during sleep deprivation would I be thinking of getting tag teamed by two super hot, tattooed brothers.

That's a total fucking lie. I'd fantasize about these guys railing me during any state of mind.

They're nearly the same height, both with dark as night hair, bright eyes—though different colors—wide shoulders, thick arms, narrow waists... and the list goes on. Hell, they even match. Both in dark jeans and a black T-shirt that is hugging every muscle on their delicious bodies that it could pass for a second skin.

"I can't seem to find what I'm looking for," the silver-eyed guy says, tilting his head to the side as he reads the menu board. The other is typing something out on his phone, his lips turning up into a smirk at his friend's—or brother's?—words.

"Uh, well do you know what it's called? We do have a secret menu..."

"I believe it's called a *Bexley*." He looks down at me lazily, a smirk resting on his full lips. The other huffs out a laugh and my eyes widen.

"How—"

He points to my boob and I look down.

*Fucking duh, Bex!* The goddamn name tag.

"Okay, you got me." I run my hand over my face. "Listen, it's almost time to close and I'm exhausted. So what can I make for you?"

"Is that not part of the menu?" he asks, feigning innocence.

His lines are cheesy as all hell—like, all the extra cheese piled into one heap—but... fuck if I don't want more of them. I cross my arms over my chest, boosting up my boobs just a bit.

"As a matter of fact, it is," I say, mocking excitement. "However, it's the most expensive item on the menu and I doubt you could afford it. Maybe you should find something in your price range. A nice latte? Perhaps a cappuccino?"

I catch Rachel throwing me two thumbs-up, egging me on.

The blue-eyed guy reaches into his pocket and pulls out a black credit card, sliding it across the counter with one finger on top. "This should cover it." He winks at me.

My jaw drops. Are these guys really trying to *buy* me? The wink has my knees weakening, but they are not getting away with this that easily.

"I'm not a hooker, nor will I pretend to be one, even if you guys are hot."

"Perhaps for free then?" Silver eyes grins.

I blink at the two guys, both of who are now staring me down with humor etched on their faces, a delicious heat hidden behind their eyes. Rachel is nodding eagerly in the background, but my mouth is going dry, brain free of the snappy comebacks it's usually full of.

As tempted as I am to say *yes, please fucking take me home. Do what you want to me. Rail me. Make me call you daddy*—*at the same time...* I don't. Because even though I am all about their fine asses, I don't appreciate the cocky attitude they have. The cheesy lines were cute... but flashing the money around? No thanks.

"Are you guys getting coffee or not? If not, the door is that way."

I raise my arm to point towards it just as the bell rings and in walks a man who is just as gorgeous, yet completely opposite looking of the two in front of me.

The two guys at the counter look like they could be convicts of the most delicious nature, the one who just walked in could pass as a super sexy priest... or something else that would be the opposite of a convict. He's tall like these two, only his skin is fair, hair is blond, and his eyes are a bright caramel brown, almost gold.

What is going on around here tonight?

The guys at the counter stiffen as this new customer steps up behind them. The one with the blue eyes slowly turns and I watch the muscle in his jaw tick. "Following us again? What's wrong, no one wants to play with you? All your pals in bed all ready?"

So they know each other? Why do hot people hang out with hot people?

I pull the front of my shirt away from my chest a few times to get some air. It's getting stuffy in here and I'm starting to sweat.

"Just wanted to check-in, is all. How are things back home?" New guy's voice is soft and smooth, and I think I could listen to him speak for the rest of my life. It's soothing, like a sweet caress to my most intimate parts. I clench my legs together and try to clear the fog that's invaded my head.

"Oh, you know, hot and torturous, as always."

As blue eyes continues with their passive-aggressive banter, the silver-eyed one turns and smiles at me in a way that makes me wish I could disappear. Or drop all of my clothes and bend over the counter. Either would suffice.

"So, how about my offer?"

"Thanks, but I'd rather get tar and feathered on Fifth Avenue."

"That's a bit dramatic, don't you think?" He places his palms flat on the counter and leans forward. I get this most intoxicating scent of spice and something sweet... it's doing all kinds of things to my insides that it shouldn't be.

"Oh, honey, you haven't seen nothing yet," he says in a low, tantalizing tone.

I keep my cool and do my best to not word vomit all the dirty thoughts of what I want to do with them. To them. But in my book, being an arrogant ass won't get you a damn thing.

He opens his mouth to spew another cheesy-ass line, I'm sure, but the newcomer speaks up instead.

"If you won't be ordering anything, please move aside so paying customers can."

I smile sweetly and shoo silver eyes with a few flicks of my wrist. "He's not wrong. Paying customers only." I point up to the small sign on my left that's been there for as long as I can remember. Yeah, Derrik is *that* kind of dick. Puts a café in an area loaded with college students, set up charging stations and special laptop tables, but only allows them to stay if they buy an obscenely overcharged cup of coffee.

He lets out a chuckle and taps his friend with the back of his hand, who is now glaring at the blond guy. "Come on, let the baby order his coffee before he throws a tantrum." He and his friend move to the side, pretending to look over the pastry case, though I know they're just buying time. They aren't going to give up. They aren't giving off any creepy Piggy Pickton vibes, but this is NYC, so who the hell knows.

"Welcome to the Coffee Club, what can I get for you?" I ask as the man steps forward, shooting a much kinder smile than I've done all night.

He smiles brightly. "Hello, there. Could I please get a vanilla chai latte in the largest size you have?"

"Of course, babe, anything you want," I say to him as I punch it into the computer. "You catch more flies with honey," I murmur under my breath as I start to work on the latte. And just as I'm placing the cap on it, I have a wonderful idea. The perfect way to get back at the hot jerks who think women should kiss the ground they walk on.

Just as I'm handing the nice guy his change, I tilt my head to the side and ask, "So where are you off to tonight?"

His eyes widen the slightest. "Uh, just heading home..." He takes his change, drops the coins and three one-dollar bills into the tip jar, then pushes the rest of the bills into his wallet.

"Well, I was thinking—"

"Don't do it," the blue-eyed, now angry, man growls.

"Excuse me?" I say. My words tremble at the tone of his voice, and how dark his eyes have gone.

"Don't mind them," the blond one says. "They aren't accustomed to not getting what they want. I'm afraid I have plans this evening; however, if you're in need of an escort to your place of residence, I'd be glad to give you one."

Well, it wasn't what I was hoping for, but it'll do.

# CHAPTER THREE

## MAXEN

"This is unacceptable," Kaine growls as he paces the street. We've stopped a few blocks away from the café because this wrath-filled bastard is unable to keep his cool and just let shit go.

"It's not the end of the world, Kaine. We can find someone else." I run my hand through my hair, watching as he turns. "Let's ju—"

"That is not the point!" he shouts, continuing to stomp the ground with heavy boots as he walks along the glass front stores. I roll my eyes, thankful the streets are mostly clear over here. All I need is for someone to pass by and look at him the wrong way.

Dealing with a demon of Wrath is not always fun, but it can lead to an entertaining night. Just not when I'm hungry.

"I'm perfectly fine with finding food elsewhere." I offer. I could get a hooker for all I care. At this point, I'm tired and my stomach is rumbling, but not in the way human food can fix. No, I need the other thing. The thing that feeds my nonexistent soul.

"That good for nothing prude. I swear if he—" Stopping mid-sentence, he freezes in place. "He will not do this. I will not allow that piece of shit angel to take a thing from me!" he roars.

I raise a brow as he spins and heads back towards the café.

Fuck off, this is not good.

Nope, not at all, considering all the hatred leaking out of him. It's a normal occurrence, but it's abnormally potent right now.

Wrath demons and angels hate each other more than most. In fact, Kaine's kind just tends to hate everyone. It's surprising how well he and I get along, though he can be quite a pain in the ass most of the time. But aside from their intuition to hate one another, Kaine and August have been at war for years. Kaine took a particularly keen hatred for him for no reason other than "I don't like his face." Which of course makes complete sense... to a crazy person.

"Where are you going?" I call after him, dropping my head. I just wanted to find something to eat!

Oh, how this night has changed course. When he doesn't stop and doesn't respond, I go after him, knowing it's time to put my babysitting pants on. It wouldn't be the first time he's done something stupid, and I've become rather good at handling the situations, but something in my gut tells me this is going to be different. That this... is something on a whole new level. Nothing we can't handle though. That's the benefit of having Hell at your back, I suppose. They do anything to cover up their secret of existing to the humans, but it could get us sent into a torture chamber for years since we aren't supposed to be up here. Nothing that hasn't happened before, of course, but I'd rather not.

Just as I suspected he would, Kaine stops in front of the café and reaches for the handle. When he pulls and it doesn't budge, he lets out a deep growl that I swear shakes the entire street. Before I can reach him and tell him how stupid he is being, he rears back his fist and punches straight through the glass, shattering it. The noise pierces my ears, as the hundreds of pieces fall to the ground.

"Fucking Wraths!" I growl to myself.

I pick up my pace, going from a walk to a sprint as the screaming starts.

As I reach the store, he is already inside wreaking havoc. I catch sight of him just as he throws a punch to August's face, which is already bleeding. If I don't get a hold on this situation, it's going to be bad because once those girls realize that angel will start to heal on his own, it'll only be downhill from there. So much more of a mess to clean up.

No way in fuck can we find a witch at this time of night to fix this.

August grunts as he hits the ground, landing in the shattered glass, Kaine kicking him in the ribs. A sickening crunch can be heard, and the girls shriek from the corner behind the counter, hugging each other tightly. They're both in shock, but I'd rather that than them trying to call the police.

I guess I spoke too soon because the friend seems to shake out of it and pulls out her phone just as the thought leaves my head.

"Don't!" I shout, racing behind the counter to take the phone. I snatch it from her hand and shove it into my back pocket. "Don't. I will handle it." I look to Bexley and give her a stern look, letting her know she better not try to pull some shit like that either.

And the night was going so well...

Another crunch has me turning and I find August's arm bending in a way it should not.

I groan. "Fucking dick..." I mumble.

"Do something!" Bexley shouts angrily. "Fucking do something before I call the goddamn cops, you psychopath!"

I point my finger at her. "Don't even think about it," I growl but she only glares back, threat in her eyes. It makes my cock twitch, and I'm almost tempted to snatch her up myself and drag her into the back room to feast on her pussy that is no doubt as beautiful as her face.

Ignoring my need, I rush around the counter and reach Kaine, gripping his shoulder I pull him away. He throws a punch at me that I dodge, but I catch his eyes glowing, and that is not a good fucking sign. He uses my moment of shock to his advantage and turns his attention back to August with another swift kick to the gut.

"What the fuck." This mess is worse than I thought it would be.

I stand on the side, waiting for my in, and when Kaine stands still to run his cut and bloody hand through his hair, I pounce, getting him in a bear hug and pulling him away, wrestling him towards the door. Only when I step out, I trip on the fucking frame that is still in place, and we both stumble to the ground. I land hard on my side, my shoulder burning with pain, and Kaine gets away from me.

He gets to his feet quickly, looks down at me with glowing eyes, and says, "That girl is coming with us."

"Kaine!" I shout in protest, scurrying to get up. My arm hangs limply at my side, and I know it's dislocated. This fucking piece of shit... I look from it to Kaine, who is already back in the store, and realize I don't have time to pop it back into place.

I lunge forward, trying to stop whatever is about to happen, but it's too late. Kaine is around the counter, wrapping his arm around a terrified Bexley. He yanks her away from her friend and disappears. That asshole!

I stop in place to take a breath and the movement has my shoulder aching. Gripping it with my other hand, I quickly shift around and pop it back into place. It burns for a few seconds but then it's healed and I feel nothing. If I'd have been fed, it would have done that all on its own, almost as soon as it happened.

August is stirring and I offer him a hand to pull him up. He's a bloody, swollen mess. If he were human, he'd need an ambulance, but I know he'll be perfectly fine in five minutes.

"Handle this one." I point to the friend behind the counter who has tears streaming down her face and is pressed up against the corner, eyes wide in fear. "Kaine just took that girl back to Hell." August takes my hand and I help him up, his face already looking better but his arm is still a mess. "You need help with that?" I ask, looking to his arm. He just shakes his head and waves me off.

I pull the friend's phone from my pocket and hand it to him.

"Go," he says. "That girl better be back here tomorrow or else this is going to get bigger than just you and me."

"I'll find you tomorrow." I nod, not happy about having to work with this sickening sweet angel but knowing I don't have a choice in the matter. When I said Hell does a lot to cover shit up, it was true, but that usually means death, and this poor café barista does not deserve that because Kaine can't control his temper. I also don't want to get thrown in the Pit over a night of partying in NYC. Handling this ourselves just makes the most sense.

Sure, demons take humans back to Hell all the time. There is a whole process... but not one step of that was followed tonight, and if we don't get this situation under control, we're both going to be sent to the Pit to live out the rest of our days.

"You have one day, Maxen." August holds up a finger. "Just one."

# CHAPTER FOUR

## BEXLEY

The need to vomit turns in my stomach as my head spins. I feel as if I was dropped into a black hole, falling into a dark abyss with no idea where I am going or how I got here. Like I'm Alice falling down that damned rabbit hole, only this is going to be much, much worse.

What terrifies me the most, is how this feeling of falling just continues on for what feels like forever with no end in sight.

Is this death?

Am I dead?

What the hell happened to me?

The confusion and overwhelming feeling of being sick is what keeps my panic at bay, as if I'm in shock and am not sure how to process what is going on. Like my brain is trying to save me from completely freaking out.

My eyes are open, yet I can't see a thing. I blink them a few times, hoping it'll change and I'll somehow see something... anything. But all I see is nothing. Just darkness.

The only thing I hear is a slight whistling sound that makes entirely no sense. It reminds me of the wind, but I feel nothing on my skin.

It's now, as I focus on my body and the nothing I feel, I realize there is something around my waist. I reach down to find an arm banded across my lower belly. I follow it to an elbow, then up to a shoulder, and realize someone is holding me.

I open my mouth to let out a scream, but a hand quickly slaps over my mouth, silencing any noise I was about to release.

Tears form in my eyes at that moment, as my body, for some crazy reason, still chooses to stay calm and not freak the fuck out like I know I should be doing.

My head spins so much I have to shut my eyes before I actually do throw up, though it doesn't do much of anything since I couldn't see in the first place. For half a second, I'm thankful there is a hand covering my mouth as a gag makes its way up my throat. And if they felt my reaction, they don't act like it because their hand stays firmly planted.

I talk myself down from panic and sickness, repeating that it'll all end soon. I'm on the verge of wishing for death over all of this.

Maybe I'm drunk. Or maybe this is a dream. Whatever it is, hopefully when I open my eyes it *will* all be over.

My back is stiff and my head is pounding as I wake from the weirdest dream I've ever had. I groan and rollover. Something hard beneath me is what makes me shoot my eyes open, thinking maybe I fell off the bed in the middle of the night. I don't think I've fallen out of bed since I was five, but stranger things have happened.

Only, when I open my eyes, nothing makes sense.

Panic slithers up my spine as every hair on my body stands straight up.

I look around the room and find two dully lit lanterns hanging by the door, the only bit of light I find.

A dungeon... Dark, bare, and damp.

Pushing myself up into a sitting position, I lean against the jagged stone wall behind me. My hair snags on a few sharper rocks and gets yanked out as I try to position myself in a way I am somewhat comfortable and hopefully less vulnerable. My hand goes to my head to scratch the area that now tickles from the hairs being pulled out. Glancing around, I continue to blink away the bit of blurriness from my eyes. There are no windows, only one door on the wall to my right. Across from me, lining the bottom of the wall is a large puddle. My eyes trail upwards to find where it's coming from and all I find is a large wet spot on the ceiling. Some sort of leak.

"Where am I?" I ask myself, trying to rack my brain for any memory or thought of how I got here but find nothing.

Not a single thing other than that weird dream where I was falling through the darkness.

I look over my body as best I can in the dim light and find no wounds, no bruises, nothing.

I push up to my feet and stagger, leaning onto the wall for help. My knees shake as I make my way towards the door. There is only a pull ring and no knob which makes me believe there is no lock. I reach for it, the metal cold under my hand, and I yank on it without hesitation. It swings open easily and I stumble back, falling hard onto my ass.

I expected it to be heavier. I cry out as a sharp pain travels from my left ass cheek all the way up my spine.

"Fuck," I groan. "I think I broke my ass!" I shift to my side and rub it to soothe the ache, though it does just about nothing.

Pushing myself up once again, this time even more carefully, I make my way back to the door with a limp. Popping my head out, I find a long corridor that is just as sad and bare as the room I am in. Lanterns are also placed along the walls, but they aren't doing much to help with the ambiance.

"Does this place not believe in windows?" I murmur to myself.

Looking from left to right, I notice the left side of the hallway ends not too far off, but the other side looks to have another corridor or something veering off of it farther down, so that's the direction I choose.

Staying close to the wall, I keep my hand out, brushing it along the dirty stone just in case I lose my balance and trip again. My legs are still weak, and my back and ass hurt from the fall.

As I get closer to what looks like another hallway, the one I noticed from the room, I hear voices, so I slow down and come to a complete stop.

"There is no excuse for your actions."

"I know that."

"What do you suppose we do? We can take care of getting the human topside, but the angel? How do we know he won't say anything?"

*Angel?*

"We kill him."

"I love a good killing as much as you do, but that's just stupid. For one moment, can you see past that anger of yours and think clearly? This is both of our heads on the line."

"I know that!"

The voices sound familiar, but I can't place where I know them from.

Nothing about this place is sitting right with me—where is my fight or flight mode? Clearly, broken like many other parts of me, including my tailbone.

"We must speak with Huran."

"Already did."

"And?"

"And he said he will no longer be helping us with our issues!"

I roll my eyes. That guy has an attitude problem. I make my way closer to the corner and peek my head around the side.

Two very tall and very beautiful men are the owners of the voices. One is pacing, a hand in his dark, unruly hair. The other is leaned against the wall, arms over his chest. Both are covered in tattoos and sinfully delicious. So, me being me, and having no common sense and every gut instinct demolished, I round the corner and head straight for them. The one leaning against the wall sees me first, his eyes going wide.

"Kaine?" he says, barely moving an inch.

"What?" the pacing one growls. I continue to get closer to them, and neither of them moves.

"I thought you said the girl was spelled."

"She was."

"Then why is she out of the dungeon?"

"She—what?" He freezes and looks toward the man against the wall who raises his hand, pointing towards me. He turns and his eyes also widen when he sees me, now only about thirty feet from them. Normally, I'd have been to them a lot quicker, but I'm in pain and trying not to push it. And as I keep limping their way, I'm thankful I don't trip and fall, especially since my ass is still sore. Totally something that would happen to me.

He lets out a deep growl. "Oh, I am going to *kill* Marionette!"

"Hiya, boys." I hold up a hand and give a quick wave. "So, sorry to interrupt but I seem to be lost."

"Lost?" the one leaning against the wall asks, sounding as if he doesn't know what the word means. This close up I notice he has gorgeous silver eyes that make my insides swirl with lust.

*Not the time, Bex.*

"Yeah. I have no idea where I am. You know? *Lost.* But I'd like to go home."

"Home?" he repeats my word as if he speaks another language and if I hadn't heard him speaking English myself, I'd think that were the issue. The other is mumbling to himself with small growls in between, fingers going a mile a minute against his phone screen.

"Uh, yeah?" I look from him to the other guy, who is now staring at me as if I kicked his puppy. "My home. Place of residence? Abode? Casa? Shall I ke—"

"Fucking unbelievable!" he shouts, turning to face the silver-eyed guy. "Handle this. I need to find that stupid cunt of a witch."

I raise a brow as I watch him disappear around another corner farther down the hall.

"He's pleasant." I smile, turning my gaze back to the guy leaning against the wall.

He huffs out a laugh. "Quite. And you've caught him on a good day." He gives me a curious look. "So, you have no idea how you got here?"

"Nope." I shake my head.

"And that doesn't concern you?"

"Well, I guess? I mean, I've lived in NYC my whole life so not much scares me anymore. I'm assuming you haven't taken me to murder me, since I'd probably have been tied up for that, but I assume by your lack of shock at seeing me that you're the reason I'm here. There wasn't a lock on the door, so I wasn't being held captive, only placed in the room of someone who has no manners. And you're not attacking me now, so..." I let my words trail off.

"Interesting assessment." His words come out slow and almost impressed.

"Thank you. So... are we waiting for him to get back, or?"

He smirks as his eyes darken a few shades, causing my belly to twist in delight. This man is awfully sexy and it's a little scary how much I want to drop my pants for him right now in the middle of this strange and dirty hallway.

"Oh, there is no need. I can show you exactly where you need to go."

He turns, placing his hand on my lower back as he guides me back from where I came.

# CHAPTER FIVE

## MAXEN

I place my arm on her lower back, the urge to touch her overwhelming. I'm still starving because I haven't been able to eat. I prefer to feed in a more comfortable place—like a bed—but this will have to do. There is also a rule with Kaine and I that when we hunt, we do it together and share the prize. But, well, he fucked up tonight and while he tries to rectify that situation, I may as well get what I can.

I'm hungry and that's partially his fault at this point.

I saw the way her eyes devoured me as she walked over, saw how she couldn't take them away from me as she stood there. I won't have to use much of my power to get this one to drop her pants and that's always the best part. The more they are willing, the better it tastes. Though, it has to be a genuine want for *me*. The need to see my body, feel my lips on them, and my cock in their pussy. Not just the need to get fucked. No, it's all about me. I need to be the one they want.

Me, me, me.

Sure, anything will work. But why eat Chuck eye when there is a Filet Mignon right in front of your face?

It just doesn't make sense.

I lead her down the hall, already feeling the taste of her in my mouth as her need grows. Sweet and succulent. Hell, maybe I won't have to use my power at all. And the best thing about that? Not only does it taste better the less it is tainted with my magic, but it keeps me fuller for longer.

Then it's all about fun and not necessity. And who doesn't like to overindulge?

"I believe this is the way I came?" she says, and I finally hear a bit of nervousness in her voice. The smallest shake.

"It is. There is a waiting room at the other end of the hall. Once my friend returns, we will make sure you get home safely."

"Can't you just tell me where to go?"

I stop abruptly, holding her tight to my side so she is forced to stop. I look down at her and smirk. "Where we are, sweetness, is way worse than any darkened alley in New York City."

She raises a brow. "Wow. I must have really had a rough night."

"The worst."

As we make it to the end of the hall, I push through the door on the right. It is nothing fancy, just an old office used by guards when we have actual prisoners down here—which is uncommon since the Wrath King prefers to send people to the Pit without giving them a trial. Unfair? Absolutely. But his place, his rules. And that's how it is when living in Wrath. I shouldn't spend most of my time here, but Lust gets boring after a while. Wrath keeps me on edge.

Besides, Kaine is here so it's pretty much my home. I go where he goes.

"So, I can wait here?" She looks around the room, eyes settling on the old blue couch.

"Uh-huh."

"And when your friend gets back, you'll... bring me home?" She swallows hard as she looks back at me, eyes lifting to meet mine. I move forward, reaching for a strand of hair that's hanging over her face, and tuck it behind her ear.

"Yep," I say in a low whisper.

Her pupils dilate and her lips part.

I pull my hand away slowly, dragging my thumb along her jawline, stopping on her chin before tilting it up. Her eyes widen just a fraction, but she's basically putty in my hands

27

and I haven't done a damn thing. She just... wants this. And I am all too eager to take it. My stomach twists as I get a whiff of her arousal. I'm keenly aware of her shifting body as she clenches her thighs together. Little does she know it's pointless. I only plan on spreading them apart and burying my face between them.

"Will your friend come too?" she asks breathlessly.

I smirk. "Oh, he'll be coming all right. Just not with us."

I step forward and she steps back. Sliding my fingers down the column of her neck, I drag them over her shoulder, down her arm, and then hook my hand around her waist and pull her close. She leans into me, pressing her warm body against mine, squeezing my erection between us. I let out a low groan.

So fucking hungry.

I could devour her over and over and over and still want more.

When she runs her tongue along her bottom lip, I'm a fucking goner. My eyes go to that plump lip and all sense is gone. I blame it on the starvation, but really, I'm not so sure. Kissing is not something I normally do; it's pointless. It gives me nothing, feeds me in no way at all. Kissing is an act of affection, and sex for me isn't about that. But something about this girl... I want to kiss every inch of her perfectly curved body, run my tongue along her silky smooth skin. So I lean forward and brush my lips against hers, reveling in the feel of them. Pillow soft, slightly moist... I kind of like this.

"The fucking slag is topside for tea. Tea!" The voice pulls me back to reality and my mouth from hers. I groan as my cock throbs, needing release more than I need to eat. My fingers dig into her skin, wishing Kaine would shut the fuck up and get out but I know it's no use. The moment is gone. And I know that for sure when she steps out of my embrace and clears her throat.

*Perfect timing, dickhead.* I glare at him, and he glares right back.

"Now isn't the time for fucking!" he shouts out loud, instead of saying it through our mind link.

I raise a brow and move towards him, sure to keep my voice low. "Do you not recall me saying I was fucking hungry? And it's your damn fault I haven't eaten yet. In about two seconds, I'll put your Wrath anger to shame."

"Oh, you'll survive, you pussy," he sneers, eyes going dark.

It takes everything in me not to rear my fist back and slam it into his face. He moves then, which saves him, cause if I had to look at him for another second, I'd have knocked his block off, willed him to heal, and then done it again. I pull in a deep, steadying breath, knowing if I don't eat soon some poor soul will mistake me for a fucking Wrath demon, and not the lustful incubus I am. Which will only cause more problems than we already have. Kaine needs to get his shit together so that doesn't happen.

# CHAPTER SIX

## BEXLEY

"So, it's time to go home now?" I stare at the back of the man who I was just way too physically close to. Like, way too close.

Sex is not something I've ever been shy about. I have no problem admitting I have needs and enjoy the now-and-again one-night stand or random hook-up. Sometimes the real thing is better than the drawer full of toys I have. Though sometimes the real thing is a douche named Dylan and totally unsatisfying. But no risk, no gain.

Something tells me this tall hunk of man meat in front of me knows how to please a girl—and well. Toe curling, turning my body into J-ello kind of sex. Just his fingers brushing across my skin nearly had me coming. Hell, even when I do it myself it takes much longer than that. After a long moment of the blue-eyed guy still pacing, huffing and puffing, the silver-eyed one turns around with a smile that almost looks genuine.

"Yeah, I'll take you home now."

"The fuck you will!" the other one growls.

"Excuse me?" I choke, my body going cold with full-on fear for the first time since I've been here.

"She needs to go home," Silver eyes says to the other. "For more than one reason."

"No!" he shouts. "She's fucking staying!"

"Kaine," the other one warns. I glance to the blue-eyed one, thankful I finally have a name for him. *Kaine.* That's fitting since he looks like an asshole.

Kaine stomps forward towards the other guy and only stops when their chests touch. They look as if they're having some sort of conversation in their head, but that's nuts, right? People can't do that.

"August will not lay a hand on her," Kaine growls in a low voice.

"August?" I ask, moving forward. Did they bring me here to protect me? Was someone after me? Did they... save me?

Silver eyes glances at me before moving his eyes back to Kaine, who then turns to me with a smile. The first one I've seen on him. It's devilishly handsome. Dangerous. The kind that makes me want to drop to my knees and—ugh, why am I like this?

"Yeah, the guy who tried to take you," he says in a softer tone, though it's somehow no less menacing.

The other guy's eyes widen just a fraction before he straightens his back and looks to me. Kaine takes a few steps forward and starts to speak. "See, we found you on the street with this guy, August, we know. He's been known to do some terrible things to women, and when we saw you stumbling beside him, Max and I knew we had to step in. Brought you here to let you sleep it off." He leans in closer, pausing right by my ear. The heat of his skin is felt on mine, and I hold my breath. "It's why you feel so awful and can't remember anything. Rohypnol." He steps back and shrugs.

I look to Silver eyes—uh, Max—whose expression is tight and otherwise unreadable.

"Is that true?" I croak. He stares at me for a long moment and when he doesn't say anything, Kaine turns towards him.

"Go ahead, Maxen. Tell her what happened."

Max's eyes don't leave mine. Two bright silver orbs practically glowing, mesmerizing.

"It's true," he finally says, pulling his eyes from me and quickly moving out of the room.

Kaine turns to face me, and I throw my arms around him. "Thank you," I whisper. His body is stiff for a moment, but then his arms slide up my hips and around my waist. He holds me tight, hugging me like I'm a long-lost love and not some girl he just saved on a whim from being in the right place at the right time. My belly flips and my panties soak at the feel of his hard, warm body pressed against me.

I mean, a thank you blow job could be in order, right? I'm seriously contemplating the idea when he pulls away and takes my hand. "Come. I'll show you to where you'll be staying until we get things sorted."

How can I say no to that? I move beside him, eager to see a more comfortable place. This certainly can't be where he lives. I probably should have alarm bells going off, but they're conveniently silent.

I'm not due into work for a few days, maybe a vacation is what I need?

I tell myself it's the vacation I'm looking forward to and not getting these two hotties in bed.

The entire walk to Kaine's home is strange beyond words. He led me up the stairs and then outside, which is blanketed in darkness. The moon is a dark red color, hanging full and high in the sky. The rest of my surroundings—dark trees, bare bushes, wrought iron fences, small stone buildings—make me feel like I'm in an old ass, haunted cemetery and not New York City. There are weird sounds coming from every which way, and I can't tell if they're human or animal, and it's hot out here. Like... really hot.

I consider stopping Kaine and asking him to bring me home now, but after knowing how good he feels against me, I'm holding onto the chance of maybe getting laid first. I mean, what does it matter? I may not remember how I got here, but I remember enough to know I have nothing to go home to other than an empty apartment.

Though, I should let Rachel know... Shit. I don't know how long it's been since I've been gone but if she doesn't hear from me, she'll be concerned for sure. Which is what makes me realize my cell phone is missing.

"Uh, do you have a phone?" I ask. "I think I lost mine." We're walking down a cobblestone path towards a giant building that very closely resembles a castle. I'm starting to wonder if this is some kind of prank and I'm on the set of a TV show or a movie. He can't possibly live here, can he?

He starts up the stairs, still holding my hand. "I do. You can use it once you're inside. Or try to, anyway."

"Try?" I stop, and once he realizes it, he does too.

"There is no service here."

I glance around. Tall, dark trees loom over me, but other than that, I see nothing. A loud screech sounds off and I flinch, grasping onto Kaine's arm. It sounded human, but maybe it was just a wild animal. Fisher Cat, maybe? Is it mating season?

"Where exactly is *here*?" I ask quietly.

"Detroit," he says nonchalantly.

"What?!" I shriek, pulling away from him. "How did I get all the way to Detroit?"

"Relax, I'm kidding," he says with a grin.

"Oh." I glance away, feeling silly for overreacting. Obviously, it was a joke. He couldn't possibly have taken me all the way to Detroit without me knowing. How would they have brought me ten hours away without anyone noticing they were hauling around an unconscious female? Though I do enjoy a good true crime podcast and I'm pretty sure people have done worse...

Kaine holds his hand out again, and I look around once more, still not a clue as to where I am, but assuming it must be upstate New York. I turn back to him, look over his handsome face, and feel not a single ounce of negativity from him, so I take his hand and allow him to lead me the rest of the way up the cement steps.

"Where is Max?" I ask once we reach the top, wondering if I'll get to see him again before I leave. He did say they'd both be bringing me back, but he seemed upset when he left.

"He's around. I'm sure he'll be back soon." He pushes open one of the large wooden doors and moves to the side, allowing me to step in. I do so cautiously, no idea what I'm walking into. I've never been in a castle before...

Once I'm in, I look up and my mouth drops open.

# CHAPTER SEVEN

## BEXLEY

What on God's green earth is this?

I glance up at the ceiling that is at least a mile away. Stepping into the room, my feet echo off the marble floor and my gaze stays upwards. This place looks big on the outside but not this big.

Not—four, five, six... *six* floors tall!

The staircase wraps upwards and against the wall of the cylindrical room I'm in. The balusters are made out of something the exact color of a ruby—I only know that because it's my birthstone—while the handrail is black. The floors, steps, and walls are an ash gray, and if it weren't for the deep red accents here and there, I'd think I've gone colorblind.

"Everything okay?" Kaine whispers, his fingers brushing along the back of my arm as he comes up to my side.

"Peachy," I respond breathlessly, still glancing around at the room that looks like something out of a dark fairytale.

He nods his head towards the right.

"We can take the elevator. I hate walking up the stairs."

"Can't imagine why."

As he leads me to the elevator, I take in everything in this room that we pass. I take back what I said about the dark fairytale and change it to horror film. Everything is old but expensive. Faded but sparkling clean. The chairs could pass for electric chairs while the statues are most likely haunted. I wouldn't be surprised if I happened upon a dybbuk box. Now that thought terrifies me more than anything else.

We reach the elevator and Kaine presses the button. The door opens immediately, and my eyes shoot into my hairline.

The entire interior of the elevator is a gaudy blood-red. The walls are velvet and the floor is carpeted. As I step in, I also notice the ceiling is a mirror and I don't hide my frown.

"Awful, I know," he says, shooting me a grin, as he presses the button for floor six. I'm grateful he did not make me walk up that many stairs.

"It's not so bad..."

He narrows his eyes at me, taking a step forward and completely invading my space. "Don't lie to me," he says in a low voice. My breath catches in my throat and I almost choke. "I'll know if you do."

I back up, but he takes another step. I move again and my back is against the wall, chest heaving. The fear is back, but only barely. Just a flicker of it. I have no idea who this man is and he's got me boxed against the wall inside of his house. Then I remind myself that I'd know if he were a bad guy... Wouldn't I? I'm a good judge of character. I'd like to say it was always that way, but that's not true. It took years of me choosing the wrong people to know who the right ones are. Yes, I still like doing stupid things sometimes, like those random one-night stands and hanging around in hopes of having a threesome, but I'm not careless about my choices anymore.

"I was just trying to be nice," I say.

"Well, don't." He brushes some hair away from my face, fingers lingering on my skin, and my eyes fall shut. "Truth is always best."

He steps back the second the elevator stops, and I grip the wall to steady myself, opening my eyes. The door opens and he steps off, glancing back at me. "You coming?"

*Yeah, I almost did, thanks.*

I step out and follow him down a hallway that's decorated similarly to the main room we entered in—minimal color with haunted items here and there. We pass an archway and I look over the banister and into that foyer. He leads me down a few corridors, and I swear this place must be made of magic or something because there is no way the house is this big.

Finally, we reach a hallway that has two large double doors at the end and nowhere else to go, so I assume this must be where I'm staying. Seems a little elaborate if he plans to take me home soon, but what do I know? Also, I'm pretty sure if I needed to escape from this place, I'd end up dying of starvation from getting lost.

He pushes the doors open and I'm brought into a bedroom that's the size of my apartment back home.

Directly in front of me is a large four-poster bed, bigger than I've ever seen. It's all black—frame, sheets, pillows, everything—and up on a small dais. To the right is what looks like a small living area, a large picture window covering most of the wall, and a fashionable couch that looks like it's never been used. To the left is two doors, both closed, so I have no idea where they lead to.

"You can have my bedroom while you're here," Kaine says, turning to face me.

"Is this really necessary? I thought you were bringing me back today?"

"Are you in a rush?"

Not really, but this is weird... isn't it? It should be, so why isn't it?

I open my mouth to speak when there is another high-pitched screech, this time it causes me to flinch. I turn towards where it came from and realize it's attached to a girl. Then I realize it wasn't a screech at all, just her annoying voice.

"I've been looking for you everywhere."

She's thin, blonde, and big-boobed. I glance from her to Kaine, scrunching my nose up.

Why am I not surprised? Why is it the hot guys always go for the girls who look like fucking barbie dolls or runway models?

Fucking gross.

My stomach sours, knowing that's the jealousy talking. Not a clue why, since I barely know this guy and have absolutely no claim to him, but for some reason, I don't like knowing he talks to other girls.

"I'm busy," he says with a finality that has even me wanting to leave.

She makes her way into the room, ignoring his words, but then she spots me. Her lip curls up in disgust.

"Who the fuck is this?" She places a hand on her bony, exposed hip. She has on a navy-blue spaghetti-strap crop top and leather pants that look way too good on her... though, they'd look better if she gained a few pounds.

"None of your business, now get out," Kaine responds, and my throat goes dry.

"No way! We have plans," she pouts.

"Consider them officially canceled." He moves towards her, gripping her by the elbow and dragging her towards the door, and giving her a little push out. "Bye." He closes the door, but it doesn't cut off the ear-splitting shriek she lets out before stomping away.

"You should probably go spend time with your girlfriend," I say, crossing my arms over my chest and pursing my lips.

He takes a deep breath before turning towards me.

"Jealous?" he asks, his eyes darkening.

"Pfft. Of what? I don't even know you."

"But you want to. I can smell your arousal."

My eyes widen. Smell... my arousal? What the hell does that mean?

He saunters over to me, stopping inches away. He looks down at me, jaw clenching.

"Don't worry, baby, it's fucking divine." His arm slithers around my waist and he tugs me to his body. His warmth envelopes me and I fall into it like I've known him forever. Like he isn't a complete stranger who could be lying to me, and like this is where I've been meant to be my whole life.

His face is buried in my neck, nose running along my skin, and he inhales deeply, breathing out with a low growl that sends shivers right to my toes. My fingers tangle in his shirt, needing something to hold on to as my knees start to tremble.

How did he go from being this rageful asshole to this guy I can't control myself around? Is this some sort of fucked-up Stockholm bullshit? Or the opposite of that, I suppose, since he's my savior and not my captor, right?

The door of the room swings open, and Kaine grunts out in annoyance. I push myself away from him, once again unsure of why I keep reacting to the guys this way.

*They're strangers, Bex, get your shit together.*

Yeah, he's hot, but I need some damn self-control.

I straighten out the wrinkles in my shirt, staring at my feet, worried it's that girl again. He didn't deny it was his girlfriend... which now makes me angry for a few reasons.

One, I don't want him to have a girlfriend. Two, why the fuck is he hitting on me—because he most certainly is—if he has a girlfriend?

That's probably the kind of guy he is. Because guys with perfect bodies, faces, and voices aren't nice guys. They aren't the ones who treat you right and marry you. They're the ones who make you feel special then fall off the face of the earth. Or knock you up and then let you know they need to go home to their girlfriend and twins.

Yeah, I'm pissed.

"Everything up top is fine, but we don't have much time."

I look up, recognizing that voice. It's Maxen.

"We have all the time in the world, Max," Kaine responds, hopping on the bed and leaning against the headboard, crossing his ankles. "You're in a better mood. Did you finally eat?"

"Yeah, if you can call it that," he says, stepping into the room and shutting the door behind him.

"Should've waited. I told you I'd get you fed."

"As much as I would have loved to enjoy the meal you've so inconveniently provided, we have more pressing matters to attend to."

"Do we?" Kaine rests his arms behind his head, looking more relaxed. "Cause I'm pretty sure all is well down here."

Max opens his mouth to talk, but I cut him off.

"Actually," I say raising my hand. "I would like to know when I'll be on my way home."

Max looks to me and then to Kaine with a waiting expression. "Yeah, Kaine. When we leaving?" He crosses his arms over his chest.

"Actually, baby, I was hoping you'd want to stay for dinner." He turns his head towards me. "I hate traveling on an empty stomach."

"Dinner?" I glance towards the window. "It's dark as fuck. What is it, like three in the morning?"

"Something like that." Kaine shrugs.

"Look," I start, knowing I do need to know when I'll be leaving. Even if it isn't right this minute, I just want to know when. "I appreciate you guys... saving me, but I really do need to get home. Rachel is going to be worried sick."

"Rachel is fine," Kaine adds.

"What?" I ask, shocked. "How do you know about Rachel? Is she hurt?"

"Hurt? No, of course not. She's home, happy as a clam." Kaine smirks. "We ran into her on our way here."

"And... she just let you take me?" That's a little odd, but not out of the realm of possibilities. Rachel would let me be saved by a couple of hot, tattooed guys in hopes I'd get some.

He shrugs again. "She was all for it. Egging you on actually. I recall some particular mouth gestures..."

Yep, that sounds like Rachel all right.

Okay, so they know her enough to know how she'd act... That information settles me a little more. I may not feel completely in danger here, but I'm definitely on edge. I'd feel better if I knew when I was going home and if I could just talk to Rachel, but after finding this out, I guess talking to her could wait a little longer.

I glance to Max who just blows out a breath, shaking his head.

"So, what do you say about dinner?"

I turn my attention back to Kaine.

"I guess I could eat."

"Perfect." He gets up from the bed. "I know just the thing."

# CHAPTER EIGHT

## BEXLEY

Thirty minutes later and we're seated at a table that could easily fit a hundred people.

Apparently, when he says he wants to eat, the servants get cooking right away. Yeah, *servants*. There's a bunch of those around here. I can't quite pinpoint what it is, but everyone that I've seen looks a little off. They don't hang around enough for me to get a real good look, but something about their features is funny. Though I've never been around servants before so maybe this is how they're supposed to act?

Kaine sits at the head of the table, leaning back in the tall armchair with his leg bent up, foot placed on the edge of the seat. He'd look like a spoiled rich kid if only his hair was clean-cut and he had on a sweater-vest instead of a black T-shirt.

He and Max have been doing nothing but shooting glares at one another, and it's the strangest thing. They really do look like they're talking to one another...

"Are you guys related?" I ask. "Brothers, cousins?"

Kaine barks out a laugh, as Maxen answers, "He wishes."

"You just seem very close."

"We've known each other a long time," Kaine says with a shrug.

It's silent again for a few moments and I wonder where the food is. Granted, it hasn't been all that long, but this is awkward as fuck. I've already looked around the room more times than I can count, but there is nothing to distract me.

Nothing hanging on the walls, no statues, nothing—outside of the lights, anyway. But those are just the same lanterns I've seen in every other room of this place.

"So, what are we—" I'm cut off as someone comes through a set of swinging doors at the opposite end of the room, carrying a tray. Following behind him are four more people. I try catching a glimpse of them, but I don't want them to catch me staring. They come over to the table and place plates with silver cloches over them in front of us. One puts down glasses and another pours what looks like wine from an oddly shaped glass decanter.

The last tray is placed on the table between us.

"As you requested, sir. Fruit from the Azenial tree," one of the servants says. His voice is deep and sounds almost robotic.

Fruit from... the what?

I glance at the tray as the man pulls the cover off.

Fruit that closely resembles grapes, aside from their color, are resting in an oblong bowl. They range from light pink to a deep purple. The smell wafts over to me and I inhale. It's sweet and reminds me of when my grandmother used to make strawberry pie. The scent eerily similar, but it settles me, and I'm reminded of how hungry I am. The fruit looks delicious, and I almost don't want to eat any of the food in front of me and fill up on those instead. Deciding I'll at least give it a try, I reach for it.

"Nuh-uh," Kaine tsks. "That is for after dinner."

"What are you? My father?" I ask, pulling my hand back and feeling like a child who was caught trying to steal a cookie.

"No, but I'm not opposed to you calling me daddy." His eyes darken and my cheeks burn. I'm far from embarrassed, it's just hot in here, I swear.

"In your dreams," I reply, sitting back in my chair with a huff.

"We'll see," he mumbles before pulling the lid off his plate, revealing a thick slab of steak that has my mouth watering.

It's too good to ignore, that much I know. I tear the cloche off mine and dig in, moaning around every single bite. The steak is so tender it melts in my mouth. The potatoes are so buttery I can't get enough. Even the vegetables that I normally hate, are seasoned so well they taste like candy. It's too good to be true. Who knew food could taste so good?

I try not to eat like a slob but I'm sure I look like a heathen, shoveling food into my mouth like I haven't eaten in weeks. Thankfully, neither of the guys notice as they're too busy with their own meals.

I finish before the both of them, clearing my plate completely. The glass of wine is still full in front of me, so I reach for it and take a small sip, wanting a taste. Wine isn't what I normally drink, but this is so good, so I take another.

"What kind of wine is this?" I ask, swirling it around in the glass.

Max raises his brow and looks to Kaine for an answer.

He wipes his mouth before telling me, "We make it ourselves."

"You make this?" I glance at the wine.

"Well, not *me*. The staff does."

"You have a vineyard?" I stop my jaw from dropping, trying to figure out who exactly these two guys are. They're hot and seemingly have a lot of money. Or Kaine does anyway, considering the size of his house, the number of servants, and the fact he makes his own damn wine.

Excuse me... *the staff*.

He huffs out a laugh. "Something like that."

I watch him closely as he leans back in his seat, leaving his food unfinished. I glance at mine again and feel a little self-conscious for eating so much, but I was starving. Oh well. Fuck them if they think I'm gross or something. Eating is normal.

A moment later, Maxen sits back in his own seat, and I'm happy to see his plate is just as clean as mine. He's been awfully quiet since showing back up, which is different than how he was when I first met him. When I first woke up and found them, he was very talkative, charming, and even flirty. Now he seems distracted, looking to Kaine for every answer like he doesn't know what to say. What caused him to change his attitude?

The same goes for Kaine, actually. He was like a raging ball of anger, then suddenly... not.

"You said I could use your phone?" I question, wanting to test the waters. If they continue to avoid my questions and not do as they say, that's going to be a problem. With what Kaine said, I know they've at least talked to Rachel, but I'd feel better if I spoke to her myself.

Kaine pulls his phone from his pocket and hands it over to me.

"Have a go."

I take it from him, noticing right away there is no unlock code or anything. I pull up the phone app that's on the main screen and dial Rachel's number. It switches to the dialing screen but then beeps a few seconds later and a "call failed" notification pops up, so I try one more time and the same thing happens.

I groan, handing it back to him with a huff. "Why have a phone if you don't have service?"

He shrugs, putting the phone on the table in front of him. "Games."

"No offense, but you don't seem like the kind of guy who likes to play games."

"Baby, games are my favorite thing in the world," he says in a low voice, and I clench my wine glass a little harder. His eyes roam over my face, then down to my chest for a quick second before he turns his attention back to the fruit in the middle of the table. I'd almost forgotten about it after finishing the full plate I had, but as I eye those small, colorful fruits again, I'm suddenly aware of that sweet smell that brings me back to my grandmother's house.

The one I was raised in with my mother that has all of the best and worst memories in it.

My father was in and out of jail often, so my mother and I lived with my grandmother. She did not approve of my mother's relationship with a person like him, but she helped my mother, nonetheless, being as supportive as she could with what she had. She stood by her beliefs though and made sure my mother knew she didn't approve and could do much better. Things I probably shouldn't have known as a child, but I was a nosy kid and eavesdropping was one of my favorite things to do.

For some reason, it never bothered me that Nana didn't like my dad. I almost understood it.

Despite their differences, we liked living with Nana and didn't have much of a choice as Mom could never afford an apartment in New York by herself. My father was happy that we were safe and taken care of. It was us three ladies for most of the time, and I loved it. As much as I could without my father, that is. I missed him every second he was gone, and some days were harder than others, but I managed, thanks to them.

No matter what happened, how long it was between visits from Dad, my mother always took him back. She loved him to a fault and would always tell me how important it was to never let go of love when you found it. She preached about how people make mistakes all the time and that it's okay. It's part of being human and knowing you're alive. It's part of life. Just because people make mistakes doesn't mean they didn't deserve love.

Everyone deserves love. It's the brightest light this world gives us, and when you're lost in the darkness, it's the only thing that can bring you back.

I take in a deep breath and push away the thoughts of my parents and my grandmother, none of who are alive anymore. I usually keep my thoughts away from them because it's too painful to think about. None of them left this world in a good way and I hate thinking of their last moments...

"Am I allowed dessert now, or will I be chastised again?"

"Do you want to be?" Kaine asks in that low voice of his, arching a brow.

By you? Abso-fucking-lutely. But I don't say that. Don't want to give him the satisfaction of knowing how attracted I am to him. Now that his anger is gone, he's turned into quite the cocky smart ass, and I don't like it.

I just roll my eyes and pick up a light pink grape thing and pop it into my mouth.

Flavor bursts across my taste buds as I bite down. Crunchy, but then soft and juicy—just like a grape.

"This is so good!" I say, reaching for more and taking a handful. "Do the different colors taste differently?" I look towards Maxen, who has a frown on his face.

"Taste? No. But perhaps you shouldn't eat so many..." he says.

"Shut it, Maxen. Let the girl enjoy her dessert." Kaine's eyes are on me, watching with interest. I look from him back to Maxen, swallowing the one I had in my mouth but wait to eat another.

"Why? Are they poisoned or something?"

He opens his mouth to answer, but Kaine beats him to it.

"Of course not. Let's just say they have rather interesting side effects."

Kaine reaches across the table and takes a handful of his own, popping two into his mouth at a time. He chews them thoughtfully, and I watch as his throat moves as he swallows, clenching my thighs as he draws his tongue along his bottom lip when he's done.

"Side effects?" I ask, feeling a tingling sensation in my lower belly.

Kaine winks and leans back into his chair, tossing a dark purple one into his mouth next.

"Fuck it," Maxen says, reaching for the fruit and picking out the rest of the dark purple ones.

He eats them quickly, then picks out a few dark pink ones.

"I thought you said they didn't taste different?"

Max meets me with a smile. "They don't. These are just stronger."

I open my mouth to ask what the hell that means when that tingling sensation moves from my belly to right between my legs. I flinch and shift in my seat.

What the hell...

It happens again, and I grip the sides of my chair and look down, trying not to be too obvious. The sensation between my legs feels like someone is touching me. I've had enough mouths between my legs to know what it feels like, and this is *that* feeling. That soft, almost tickling sensation.

"Well, that was faster than I thought," Kaine says, looking at me with a smirk.

My cheeks heat at the realization that he knows what I'm feeling. My head tells me I should be panicking, but my body... my body feels too damn good to be worried about anything. As each second passes, I become more relaxed, more calm, and more needy. I've never done ecstasy before but I know enough about it to guess this is what it feels like. I'm suddenly wishing I'd been a bit more daring because I could get used to this...

A grin splits my face as I look down at the berries in my hand, putting the pieces together.

They're not poisoned, but clearly they're laced with something.

Should I be worried? Absolutely.

Am I? Nope.

My instincts towards danger are broken, and as I look up at the two guys who are staring at me like I'm their next meal, I can't seem to care.

# CHAPTER NINE

## KAINE

She shifts in her seat a few times so I know the fruit is working.

It's something she's never had before, that I'm certain of. The only place the fruit can be found is here in Hell. It's one of the many indulgences I partake in every now and then.

Maxen hasn't had them in a long time because he tends to overdo it. It's in his nature to be a horny fuck; he's an incubus. He wants sex all the time and it makes him feel good. Better than it does for other demons or even humans, it's like a drug.

But mixed with the fruit? For him, it really is a drug, and it gets him into trouble because he will literally try to fuck anything that walks. A lot of demons enjoy sex, but not all of them do. And like humans, they don't like being forced into it. I mean, some do, don't get me wrong, but most like it to be consensual.

Bexley eats two more pieces of fruit, one light pink and one a few shades darker. The lighter the color, the less potent they are. It's why Maxen grabbed all the dark ones. He could eat a ton of the light pink ones and it wouldn't do a thing. For a human like Bexley, those light-colored ones will probably hit her the way the dark ones are about to hit Maxen... and I can't fucking wait.

I watch as she continues to squirm, her cheeks pinkening, and I instantly get hard. The thought of her getting turned on has me aching. Knowing she's feeling as if someone has their mouth all over her has me wild with need and a tinge of jealousy even though there is clearly no one between her legs. Humans have had orgasms from the fruit alone, and I wouldn't be surprised if she did...

The smell of arousal finally overtakes the scent of flowers that had my mind all out of whack. The fruit appeals to you by taking on the scent of one of your favorite things or memories. I much prefer the scent of Bexley's fluids than the scent of the old garden in the back of the castle—a place I was drawn to when I was younger.

Her cheeks flush darker and a grin spreads across her face. She eats another fruit and I smirk, moving my gaze to Maxen. He's focused on her, and I see the exact moment his pupils dilate. The exact moment he starts to fight the glow of his eyes. Us demons, once we tap into that instinctual piece of ourselves, our eyes glow bright as fuck. For me, it's when I'm in a pure rage. For him, it's when he's about to fuck like a damn rabbit and not a single thing can hold him back.

And I couldn't be any happier. It's been a while since he and I have had a good threesome, and it's only due after all the shit we went through last night to get Bexley here in the first place. To get her away from that goody-two-shoes angel.

I saw her first. She's mine.

And contrary to what she believes, she won't be going home.

Not today, not tomorrow, not ever.

She'll learn to love it here, and Maxen will have to accept it.

Sure, it'll cause some problems. August won't want to hear it, but I'll handle him.

I always do.

This girl, she isn't going anywhere. I laid eyes on her first, knew I needed to have her—even if at first it was for my friend—and so she belongs to me.

Well, *us*. Once Max gets over his bullshit, he's welcome to her whenever he wants.

Late nights, early mornings... on the bed, in the shower, in the damn hallway for all I care.

As an incubus, Maxen tends to think more rationally than me. When he's not hungry, of course. Though, that's true for most of us. No one thinks clearly when they're fiending for something.

Like the way Max is fiending for Bexley's pussy right now. Laid out on the table like a fucking feast, legs spread wide, and ready to be devoured. If her scent is any clue, she's going to taste fucking perfect. Just as I knew she would.

My cock grows impossibly harder as I watch the emotions roll through her eyes. She feels good but is slightly embarrassed, not sure what is going on, but going with it. I know this because it's what happens to humans when they ingest the fruit.

There are so many things going on in those bright green eyes of hers, so many things to be told, so many secrets... and I plan to find out every last one of them.

Not tonight though. No, tonight I have other plans that include my dick and her sweet cunt.

If I'd have told her what the fruit would do to her before she ate them, she wouldn't have eaten any.

And where is the fun in that?

Max's thoughts are going a mile a minute in my head. All of them dirty thoughts of what he wants to do to her. And when I know he's at the very edge, about to lose control, I speak.

"You see, Bexley," I start, and she turns towards me, panting slightly, fingers gripped onto the arms of her chair. "Fruit of the Azenial tree has special qualities. Think of ecstasy times ten, but without any of the negative effects. Just the pure need to *fuck*."

Her eyes widen at my words, but I keep going.

"You want us to fuck you now, don't you?" She doesn't respond, but I can feel her need. "Want the real thing sliding into your pussy? A nice, fat cock? Not just the sensation of my mouth sucking on that clit, no. You want it all, don't you?"

"Yes," she breathes out the word, looking frantically from me to Maxen who is holding back by just a thread.

I get to my feet and lean towards her, placing my palms flat on the table. Her mouth drops open and she sucks in a deep breath. "Beg for it," I say lowly. "Tell me how much you want this cock to fill you up." I reach down and grip my erection through my pants, giving it a little stroke. Her eyes dip downward and she bites onto her bottom lip. "Tell me how bad you want it, Bexley. *Beg.*"

"Fuck," she whimpers, her eyes falling shut. She takes in a deep breath before opening them again and looking at me with pure desperation. "Please, Kaine. Please... I need your cock."

"Mine?" I ask. "What about Maxen?" I nod towards him.

"Him too. Both of you," she says quickly, squirming in her seat once more.

"Well, I think we can manage that. Don't you, Max?" I glance at him from the corner of my eye.

He nods his head and gets to his feet, tearing off his shirt and dropping it to the floor. The silver barbells through his nipples glisten in the light from the chandelier that hangs above us. He is the epitome of sex. The bad boy all the girls love. All Lust demons are a fantasy come true. The pretty boy, the nerd, the bad boy, the rock star... they all have that perfect look about them. It's their weapon, there to lure people in, making it easier to feed when they need to.

Max keeps his gaze across the table and crooks a finger nice and slow at Bexley. She wastes no time getting to her feet and crawling onto the table, knocking everything in front of her to the floor. Her hips sway with each slide forward, and I have the urge to sink my teeth into her thick, fleshy ass.

I will too. Before this night is over, my mouth is going to be on that ass.

She crawls right over the fruit, careful not to destroy any of that, but when she reaches Max, she slides her arm across the table and swipes everything in front of him to the floor.

She sits back on her knees and grasps at his pants, fumbling with the button on his jeans as she tries to tear them down. He grips her wrists, yanking her hands away from him.

"Oh, no, no, no..." he says in a low whisper. He looks over at me, jerking his head the slightest. I move to his side, and Bexley glances from him to me. Her heart is thundering behind her chest, and her scent is rolling off of her in waves, the smell borderline intoxicating.

Maxen grips her hips and shifts her so she's sitting on her ass, and then leans her back with his fingers splayed out over her chest. She lies down, panting with a smirk on her lips and her arms up by her face. He pulls her pants off and tosses them to the side. I take in a deep breath, eyes glued to her body, her sweet scent filling my nostrils. Her panties are soaked, I can see them from here.

I move closer, running my fingers up the outside of her thighs and grip onto her panties, then slowly tug them down and drop them to the floor. My hands go to her ankles and spread her legs apart, then moving up, closer to her apex that is fucking sopping wet and needing my tongue.

It's rare for a girl to have me this wild with need. I can usually control myself when it comes to sex, but this girl... fuck, this girl is something else.

Maxen lets out a low growl on the side of me and my cock throbs as I take in the sight of her shaved pussy lips glistening in the light.

She mumbles something that I don't hear, so I cock my head and glance up at her. "What was that?"

"Please, make me come. Please..." She squirms again, not able to stay still.

I huff out a laugh and settle my hips between her thighs, then I lean forward, placing one hand on either side of her head. My cock presses against the table, and the pressure of it against the hard wood almost has a groan leaving me, but I hold it back.

"Oh, we plan on it," I tell her, dragging my nose along her jawline, her tiny body wriggling with need beneath me.

"We're going to make you come good and hard. And after that? We're going to do it again, and again, and again."

I find her center with my hand, running a finger through her folds; she's swollen and warm and so fucking wet.

With a hand to my back, Maxen moves to the side of me and I lift up, giving him room to enjoy her too. I slide my finger into her, curling it up, massaging her insides. Her eyes fall shut and she clenches around me. The low moan that leaves her lips goes straight to my cock and I'm a hairsbreadth away from slamming into her with a regret. Instead, I take in a deep breath and pull my finger out, add a second one, then slip them back into her with ease. I shift to the side more, caressing her thigh with my free hand, and Max lowers himself to bring his mouth right over her clit.

"Fuck!" she cries out, bucking her hips. "Fuck that feels so good," she groans. "So, so fucking good... ah!"

I fuck her nice and slow with my fingers while Maxen gives her clit all the attention it needs. Her hips thrust to get the rhythm just right and seconds later she's screaming out her release, squeezing my fingers tight. My cock aches to feel that squeeze but I know I need to wait my turn.

Max and I work together to let her come down from the orgasm, slowing our pace, letting her ride it out. She's in for a long fucking night and it's best to take it easy in the beginning.

We've done this once or twice and have a good idea how to work a woman through her orgasm.

We know how sensitive they get afterwards...

It's our favorite fucking thing after all.

# CHAPTER TEN

## MAXEN

It's been a long time since I've tasted the fruit of the Azenial tree and the moment the flavor spread into my mouth, I remembered why. A million memories of long nights and me losing control. I don't want to lose control with this girl... for some reason, I want to enjoy it. Enjoy *her*.

One taste of Bexley's pussy and I've turned into an animal, the urge to ravage her pussy is overwhelming, and I have the fruit to thank for that. Taking a breath, I tell myself I have to be patient and take my time. It makes it all the better later on.

She's panting and whimpering as I lazily drag my tongue around her engorged, post-orgasm clit. Her body trembles and shakes; she's sensitive and part of her will want to beg us to stop, while the other part needs us to keep going—all thanks to the fruit.

And this is what we fucking live for. What we feed off of.

I need the sex, Kaine needs the fear. And even though death by orgasm is the best way to go, it's still terrifying. I know the moment I press my forearm across her belly to stop her from moving, the fear strikes her. Kaine tenses, feeding off it like a drug. To make it all that much better, I don't wait another second before I'm back to sucking her clit into my mouth. She tries to buck me off, but I keep her down with ease. She's small and not much of a fighter, definitely no match for me, and really, this is what she wants. It'll be at least an hour before the effects of the fruit start to wear off.

I lick and suck and nibble on her. Her hands pull at my hair trying to tug me off, all the while bucking her hips into my mouth. She shouts and moans and whimpers and cries for us to stop but we don't.

Kaine keeps finger fucking her.

I keep sucking her clit.

And she fucking loves it.

She hates it, but fuck, does she love it.

It doesn't take long to force another orgasm out of her. Her cries resemble that of an animal in heat and I know it's all primal at this point. Her, him, and me.

It's the best kind of sex.

The kind that will keep me full for weeks but I'll want more in a few hours. It's why the fruit is so dangerous for Lust demons. It stops me from putting up that wall, the one that allows me to separate feeding from pleasure, necessity from indulgence... and damn, do I love to indulge in sweet pussy.

She's panting, eyes half-lidded as I back away and undo my pants, watching as Kaine buries a third finger inside of her, shoving them in as far as he can.

"You still want us to fuck you?" Kaine rumbles.

She murmurs a yes, nodding her head.

I know she does; she can't help it.

It's going to be a good night.

Best way to spend it since she'll be going home tomorrow. It isn't often we get humans to eat the fruit since we rarely smuggle them down here. It works on demon women, but differently. It isn't as potent and doesn't last as long. Basically, it's boring and useless. Though it sure does have serious effects on the demon men. Kaine is a lot more fun when he enjoys it. He can actually keep up with me for once.

"Haven't had enough yet?" Kaine asks, bringing his free hand down in a sharp slap right over her pussy.

She yelps, squirming around on the table but Kaine keeps her in place. He's wild tonight. I haven't seen him like this in a long time, which is probably because I can't remember the last time we did something like this. Something so... personal.

"You're going to take our cocks in every fucking hole of yours, do you understand?"

She doesn't answer him, probably because she can't think straight, so he slaps her again. Her body trembles and she jerks away, a wicked smile crossing her lips when Kaine firmly holds her in place, his fingers sliding in and out of her faster than before.

"Yes!" she shouts, her nails dragging along the table. "Yes. I want it all!"

Well, I guess it's going to be a really good fucking night.

Kaine turns to me. "Pussy or mouth?" he asks, fingers still sliding in and out of her, now more slowly. Enough to keep her wanting.

"Same rules?" I question, freeing my cock and gripping it with my hand. My fingers brush along the bottom, feeling each bump of jewelry beneath my skin.

Jacob's ladder. The women love it.

"Same rules," he confirms.

"Mouth."

Kaine and I have been doing this a long time and have developed a system since we both prefer actual fucking to blow jobs. The one who takes mouth first then gets to choose what they get next. Meaning they get first dibs on the ass, which I happen to fucking love. Not only is it tighter, but knowing they want me so much they'll go through discomfort for it drives me fucking wild.

"You ready for this cock, baby?" Kaine asks her.

"Yes, please," she groans.

Kaine removes his fingers and she instantly whimpers at the loss. He grips her hips and shifts her to her side so she's lying on the edge of the table with her ass at the end.

Kaine pulls her leg up, resting it on his shoulder as he quickly undoes his pants. He rubs the tip along her slit teasingly, and she jerks every time he brushes along her clit. I stroke myself slowly, nearing her mouth.

"Oh shit, is that—" I cut her off by rubbing my cock along her lips, and she darts her tongue out to run it around the head of my cock, closing her eyes and moaning in satisfaction.

"Sure is, sweetheart. Never seen one before?"

"N–no," she mumbles, still dragging her tongue around me. I take a step forward, urging her to open up wider, wanting to get deeper into her mouth. She responds so perfectly, swallowing as much of me as she can like the good girl she is. One hand goes to my hip and she pulls me forward, eager for more of my cock down her throat. The need for me pours energy into me, making me feel high as fuck. It's incredible.

I know the moment Kaine slides into her because she freezes, her teeth clamping down but not to the point of pain. I don't mind a little pain with my pleasure—I have a Jacob's ladder piercing and two dydoe piercings, so it's the least of my worries. As long as she doesn't bite it off, she can nibble all day long.

I slide my hand into the top of her shirt to cup her breast and squeeze as her jaw loosens and she opens wider for me to go deeper. She's barely got half in her mouth, but she's trying like crazy to take it all in. I know she won't be able to, but it doesn't even matter. It's all foreplay for when I stick it in her ass.

"Fuck, that feels so good," I tell her, running my fingers through her hair. "You are such a good fucking girl, you know that?"

She mumbles in agreement as I move my hips nice and slow.

"You're going to let me fuck that tight little asshole, aren't you?"

"Mhmm," she moans around me, and I feel the tiny vibrations all the way to my balls.

She pulls her hand from my hip, moving it to my shaft and stroking the part that won't fit in her mouth. One of the best things about being an incubus is having full control over my orgasms. I come when I want. I could fuck for hours or thirty seconds. It helps when needing to feed. This way I won't have to waste too much energy to refuel. I can get a quick fuck in and be good for a few hours.

It doesn't stop it from feeling any less good though. I can give into my urges if I want a more natural experience, which isn't usually the case for me because it isn't about the orgasms—not mine, anyway. Those are just my way of letting the girls know I'm done and ready to go home.

Yet, with this girl, it has nothing to do with feeding. I'm not even hungry anymore. When I left them earlier today, I was able to find some desperate Wrath demon to fuck behind a tree. It sounds sad, but the desperate ones usually fuck the best cause they let you do whatever you want. I'd feel bad knowing I'm about to be balls deep in Bexley's ass, but demons don't get STDs and we also don't do the relationship thing. Not usually, anyway, and certainly not Lust demons.

"You good over there?" I ask Kaine. One hand is digging into her calf while the other is squeezing her ass, holding her in place while he fucks her good and hard... just like he promised.

"So fucking good," he says, his gaze on his cock sliding in and out. He loves to watch. Whether it's him or someone else doing the fucking, he'll never pass up the opportunity to enjoy a live fuck show.

"I think it's time a get some of that ass then," I say, arching a brow. "What do you think, sweetheart? You want this cock inside of you?" She nods, looking up at me with tearstained eyes. Her mascara is a mess, running down her face, and she looks fucking beautiful. It's hot as fuck knowing it's because of my dick.

"Get on the table," I say to Kaine, pulling my cock free of her mouth. Without missing a beat, Kaine pulls out, hops onto the table, and lies down on his back, kicking off his shoes and pants all at the same time.

"Go ahead. Go sit on that dick, and ride him like it's going to save your fucking life."

As she gets up, she pulls her shirt off and drops it to the ground with the rest of the clothes. She swings her leg over Kaine's hip and wastes no time sinking onto him. Her ass is red, the imprint of Kaine's fingers left on her ass. I love the messy aftermath of sex.

She moans loudly, sitting in place for a moment and adjusting to the size of him in this position. I move between his legs, pressing my palm to her back and pushing her forward. She leans on her hands and starts to move. Her welted ass jiggles with each bounce and it's the most delicious-looking thing I've ever seen.

I squat down and run my tongue from Kaine's cock all the way to her tiny hole, getting her nice and wet. It's the best we have right now, so it'll have to do. I slide a finger into her asshole with ease and groan. Her head falls back and she moves faster on Kaine's cock.

Oh, she wants this so fucking bad.

"Such an eager little slut you are," I say, moving my finger in and out.

"Your slut," she responds.

"*Our* slut. Both of us, isn't that right?" Kaine adds.

"Fuck yes!" she shouts.

Not able to wait another second, I hop onto the table, spit in my hand, and rub it all over my aching dick. As I line up, I drop some more spit on her asshole and begin pushing in slowly.

"Just relax, and it'll feel so fucking good, I promise you."

# CHAPTER ELEVEN

## BEXLEY

I have no care in the world other than getting stuffed full of dicks.

Any way I can, in every hole I have. I'm in a craze, craving these men to the point of madness.

It's a primal need that I can't get enough of. I've come twice already and I just need more. I shout at them, telling them to stop, but I don't really want them to. I never want them to.

My body aches in the most delicious way, every muscle burning with use, but it feels so good, like nothing I've ever experienced before. It's exactly how I know I'm going to enjoy Maxen in my ass.

I've never experienced double penetration before— how could I with this being my first ever threesome? I've done anal before, though, I didn't actually want it. Not the way I want it now. Both other times, I was drunk and just didn't care. But now? Oh, I fucking *want it.*

I claw at Kaine's chest as I find my rhythm on top of him. He's big, and if I don't move the right way, it's slightly painful and I know it's only going to get worse once Maxen gets his cock in me too, but I need it. I need it so bad.

He lines up and tells me to relax, which I am. Trust me, I am.

With his hands on my hips, Maxen pushes forward and it burns just a little bit, but I relax even more. Kaine playing with my nipples is a good distraction, and I keep my focus on his hands roaming my body and how good they feel on my skin to help.

"Fuck, you really want my cock, don't you?" Maxen asks from behind me.

"Yes," I groan, grinding against Kaine. I slowed my movements on his cock to almost nothing to allow Max entry into my ass. Every part of me wants to move, wants to feel Kaine rubbing against my insides because I'm so close to coming again. So fucking close. But I wait, knowing it'll be so much better when there are two cocks in me instead of one.

Max pushes forward and I feel the first metal ring on the underside of his cock enter me. If I counted correctly when it was in my mouth, there are five total—along with two other piercings, one on each side of the crown—and he better fit them all. I need all of him, every last inch.

"This would be so much easier if we had lube," he mumbles, dropping some more spit directly from his mouth onto my ass.

I don't know what makes me do it, but I reach for the bottle of olive oil that somehow withstood my venture across the table, and hand it to Max. I glance over my shoulder, waiting for him to take it from me and he grins so hard and looks so fucking beautiful doing it.

"I love the way you think." He winks and takes it from me. It's cool to the touch when he rubs it around my asshole, but it feels just like lube, and fuck, when he starts to push into me again, it feels so good, and all concern of using a condiment to get fucked in the ass is lost.

Another bar pushes inside and I clench around Kaine, my entire body going tense. I can feel his heavy breaths from beneath me, his cock pulsing inside of me as he hardens even more.

I open my eyes, realizing they've been closed this whole time. I meet Kaine's bright blue eyes, his jaw clenched, nostrils flaring, dark hair messy. He winces as another barbell pushes in.

I lean down, taking his bottom lip between my teeth, and tug on it before letting it go.

"You like feeling his cock against yours?" I whisper.

He smirks. "You are so fucking naughty," he growls, thrusting up and hitting something that feels really fucking good. He raises a brow. "You like that?"

I nod. He does it again.

"Oh, fuck," I moan, my eyes fluttering shut again.

I can barely move as another barbell enters me and it doesn't hurt anymore. I only feel full and afraid to move. Max adds some more spit before shoving in the rest of the way. It doesn't work as good as the olive oil, but it's so much fucking hotter.

"Now that is more like it," he says from behind me.

A sharp pain against my ass cheek has me flinching and I realized he's slapped me. And hard.

Fuck, it felt good.

I look back at him over my shoulder, simultaneously turned on and wondering why the fuck he did it in the first place.

"All good girls deserve spankings," he says before pulling out of me just a little and settling back in. I wiggle, letting them know I want more.

"You ready to come again?" Kaine asks from below me and all I can do is nod. He thrusts upwards again, barely pulling out just grinding his hips into me, his pelvis rubbing against my clit, giving me the stimulation I need. Maxen pulls out and glides back in with ease. Slow at first, but quickly picks up the pace, and soon enough he's leading us, controlling the rhythm.

Kaine follows his rhythm. They work together perfectly, moving in and out at the same time and the feeling is almost overwhelming, almost enough to make me pass out—or maybe that's due to my panting and gasping for breath—but I refuse. I need to be here for this, I don't want to miss a second of it.

Kaine thrusts his hips up a little harder, his movements jerky and that's a telltale sign that he's nearing his end.

The thought of him coming has me rubbing against him, needing just a bit more friction before I'm thrust into another orgasm.

White spots burst behind my eyes, and my entire body goes warm as I vibrate with pleasure, my entire body vibrating.

With a deep grunt, Kaine stills and I'm filled with his warmth, his cock pulsing within me.

"Fuck, yes," Maxen says, fingers digging into my hips until he too pauses, his cock throbbing out his release deep into my ass. He pulls out almost immediately and moves to lie down beside us. I fall onto Kaine, resting my head on his chest. His fingers rub up and down my sides, causing goosebumps to litter my body, and I don't miss how he's still inside of me and still very much hard.

Even though I feel sated, I could go for more. Another orgasm would be great. What's one more?

"We should probably move this to the bedroom before the servants see and blab to your father," Maxen says, sitting up.

It takes a few seconds but the words hit me.

"Father?" I ask, pushing myself up. Kaine thrusts into me and I fight the urge to react but I can't help it, my pussy clenches around him again and he grins.

"You thought I lived here alone?"

"I don't know," I snap.

A warm arm wraps around my waist and I'm hoisted into the air, cum seeping out of both holes. I'm put onto my feet gently and handed a cloth napkin and T-shirt from Maxen. Immediately, I realize the T-shirt is his, and I assume he means for me to wear it. I take them both, and tug on the shirt before wiping myself up as best I can. When I'm done, they're both back in their jeans and look sinfully delicious. There is something about guys in tight, low-slung jeans and no shirts. Especially guys with narrow hips, chiseled abs, and covered in tattoos like these two.

My pussy is pulsing all over again, needing more.

"Let's go," Maxen says, gathering the clothes into a pile. He walks to the door the servants came out of and pops his head in. "Hey, get this shit cleaned up!"

If I wasn't in a post-orgasmic bliss, his way of speaking to the servants would bother me, but luckily for him, I'm three orgasms deep and needing more, so we head upstairs.

# CHAPTER TWELVE

## BEXLEY

We reach Kaine's bedroom, and I'm immediately swept up into Maxen's arms. He's in such a good mood now, practically glowing, which is much different than the brooding guy he was during dinner. I giggle as we move towards one of the doors to the left, my entire body feeling better than it ever has before. I swear I could be glowing too.

"Before we fuck again, because trust me, I will be fucking that perfect pussy of yours before the night is through, a shower is in order."

We enter into a bathroom that's bigger than my kitchen back at home. The floor is dark gray, while the walls are black brick-styled tile. My favorite part is the grout, which is a deep red that matches the rest of this place. I've noticed a theme throughout this entire house—dark.

He puts me on my feet and the first thing I notice is how warm the tiles are under my feet. Now I'm certain these guys are rich. Who the hell has heated floors in their bathrooms? Rich people!

Maxen turns the shower on as I continue to marvel at how lavish this bathroom is. He then slides the glass door open and his T-shirt over my head just as Kaine walks into the bathroom, eyes finding my hardened nipples.

I'm helped into the shower by Maxen, who guides me in and under the hot spray. It's only from inside that I realize how big this shower is. You could fit an entire football team in here, if they tried hard enough.

There are five nozzles, all of which are spraying out water—one above me, one on the opposite wall, and then three along the wall to my right. I take in everything around me, amazed at how some people live. Kaine enters and moves across from us without saying a word. It seems he's back to his grumpy self, but as I rake my eyes over every inch of him that is now dripping with water, I can't find it in me to care.

I just want to fuck him.

His cock is still half hard, and even though he lacks the piercings like Max, he feels just as good. His arms tense as he runs his hands through his dark hair, thoroughly wetting it, and I love the way his muscles bulge in his arms.

I find myself aching all over again, practically drooling just at the sight of him.

I glance up to his face, the slightest bit of stubble is along his strong jaw. He has perfect lips and skin, with a straight nose that some may say is slightly too big, but I think it suits him.

He opens his eyes, his gaze directly on me and my breath catches in my throat. He doesn't say a thing, doesn't make a sound, we just stare at each other until I'm spun around to face the wall as Maxen stands behind me. His large hands roam over my shoulders, down my back, up my ribs, and then over my breasts. He pays special attention to them, giving my nipples a little squeeze before moving down and running his hand over my still swollen pussy. He's careful when he washes me, almost as if he's done this a million times before. I don't like the thought of him having his hands on other women. Not one bit. When he's done washing me, he moves to stand in front of me and I look up to meet his bright silver eyes. His features are softer than Kaine's, friendlier.

Kaine exudes darkness, the monster you'd meet in your nightmares, but crave nonetheless; whereas Maxen is the one you'd dream about, willing to commit every sin possible for just a moment of his time.

He may give off a different type of energy, but he's no less intimidating. They're equally beautiful, both in the same way and not. From afar, you see how much they look alike, but up close like this, you see it's not really true.

They have the same body type, lean and muscled. They're just about the same height, at least six-foot-two is my guess. Both have matching midnight hair and piercing eyes. Yet I have the feeling the more I get to know them, the more I'll realize they're barely alike at all.

They both radiate power and dominance. I can tell Kaine has his walls up and he'd rather die than let someone in. Maxen is more vulnerable because he doesn't give a fuck what anyone thinks.

I barely know these guys, but something about their eyes tells me all I need to know. There is something about someone's eyes that gives them away. It's my go-to in trying to figure someone out. My secret weapon when trying to read someone.

I'm almost positive they're telling me the truth about saving me, and even if this place is weird as hell, I can't find it in me to care as I enjoy my time away from my tiny ass apartment and busy city streets.

Kaine finishes washing before we do and makes his way out. I watch through the frosted glass as he pulls a towel from the rack and wipes himself down. Maxen washes my hair for me in a way that's almost sweet, but I feel his hesitance. Like he's trying to be nice but not fall in love. His walls are up.

Love is for the weak. It only gets you hurt and killed, either mentally or physically. Sometimes both.

I watched my mother suffer for years over the stress my father, the love of her life, caused her, and then, in the end, it ultimately caused her physical death too. I guess in a way he did the same to me, except I'm still living, still here with this gaping hole in my heart caused by the one man who should never hurt me.

Yeah, I'm all set with love and all that comes with it.

I snap out of the thoughts I allowed myself to get lost in and face the reality of my life.

"What's the plan for tomorrow?" I look over my shoulder, catching Maxen's eyes.

"And here I was thinking you were fantasizing about my cock." He smirks and I roll my eyes but don't miss the pulse of my clit as he runs his fingers through my hair one last time.

"Shower sex isn't fun," I add, turning back to face the glass door, realizing Kaine is gone.

"You're right," Max whispers in my ear, pressing his front to my back and wrapping his strong arms around my waist, tugging me to his warm, wet body. "Which is exactly why I'm going to carry you into the bedroom and fuck you right into that mattress."

If his hands hadn't been around me, I'd have fallen.

Damn, my pussy is a needy little bitch today.

"I don't think your friend is up for another round." That's not true. Kaine hasn't done a damn thing to show that, but I'm interested to see what Maxen has to say about it.

"Oh, don't worry about him. He'll be just fine watching."

And that's all I needed to know.

I never knew I would be into someone watching me get fucked, but apparently, I am.

Because as Maxen feasts on my pussy, building me up to the fourth orgasm of the night, I find myself reaching that peak quickly at the feel of Kaine's eyes on us from the other end of the bed.

His cock is rock-hard, I can see the outline in his sweatpants, but he doesn't acknowledge it. He only stares, watching us without making a sound. In fact, the only thing that gives away he likes what he sees—outside of his erection—is the constant tick of his jaw, as if he's holding himself back from doing something he really wants to do.

I can't tell if Maxen is putting on a show or if he's this good with his tongue normally. Is he always this attentive to girls he's with or is it just me?

Now that thought, on top of the one I had in the shower, has jealousy rising up. Though I have no reason nor right to be. Why am I thinking of them with other women and why do I care?

Maxen adds two fingers inside of me, stroking my G-spot and I'm a goner. The orgasm hits hard and quick, my entire body tensing, lungs aching for air as I cry out, unable to catch my breath.

"Bend over," he growls, and I quickly turn over, resting on my forearms and sticking my ass straight into the air. I'm eager to feel him, along with all of his jewelry inside of me.

I've never been with someone with dick piercings before. I felt them sliding into my ass, but I wonder if it'll make a difference in my pussy too.

Maxen lines himself up, prodding at my entrance in a teasing way before sliding in slowly. A smile comes to my face when I feel each and every one of those barbells slide into me. When he goes hard, I don't feel the piercings, but when he slows down, getting the angle just right... fuck, it's so good. I'm lost to the sensations, my hands gripping the black bedsheets as I'm fucked into oblivion.

# CHAPTER THIRTEEN

## KAINE

My cock is as hard as diamonds but I refuse to touch myself. It's a little game I like to play, to practice self-control. See how long I can ache for a pussy around my dick before I give in. Before tonight, I thought I was doing good. It was easy for me to ignore a boner, but with Bexley, it's so hard to hold back that my hands are trembling.

I'm almost certain I'll come in my pants without so much as a stroke of my hand.

She's ass up, not even five feet from me, and every inch of me wants to be inside of her in some way or another.

Something tells me she'd like a good fucking even without help from the fruit and I'm eager to find out. Just another reason she'll have to stay, I guess.

My cock aches and I have to shut my eyes for a moment and just breathe. When I open them again, Bexley's bright green ones are on me. Her lips are parted, and a tiny whimper escapes her each time Maxen slams into her. He could keep this all night—fuck her till she's raw and bleeding—but what's the fun in that? It'll only stop us from fucking her more tomorrow. Unless Marionette returns and I can convince her to give us a balm. Doubt it, since I'm sure her guard will share with her every choice word that came out of my mouth when I realized she was busy drinking fucking tea topside, like she can't do that shit down here.

I bring my attention back to Bexley. Her bottom lip is pulled between her teeth and her eyes keep going unfocused. I've spent uncountable nights sharing girls with Maxen and he's good at what he does. More than good because he was made to fucking do it. He's like a perfectly designed-by-woman-for-woman machine. I bet that girl is on cloud nine right now.

"Play with that clit for me, sweetheart. Come again so I can fill you up."

Maxen has the filthiest mouth. I admit, his words even have me wanting to jump in and fuck her again, but I won't. Not tonight. Not until that fruit wears off and I see how she reacts to me for real.

It's all about control, about power. And something about her... she makes me want to lose it and that is not okay. Nothing but chaos happens when I lose control. Bad fucking things.

I follow Bexley's hand as she slides it between her legs, watch her eyes flutter shut as she does what she's told.

She listens so well.

It's almost annoying.

It has to be the fruit making her so submissive. She has a sassy mouth and doesn't take any shit. I know that much from talking to her at the coffee shop. She's feisty. It's exactly why I had to force her here in the first place. I really hope she isn't too attached to her life up there because I don't plan on bringing her back. Ever. I don't care what it takes. I'll kill August if I have to, she's staying and she'll have to deal with it.

I do find it a little strange she doesn't remember anything about what happened up there. It's normal for humans to have memory loss when traveling here since their bodies aren't made for it and their brains can't process it, but hers is stronger than most I've seen. Normally, they only forget a few minutes prior to travel. She forgot a lot more than that. At least a half-hour, maybe more.

"That's it," Maxen coaches. "Just a little more. You're almost there, aren't you?"

His eyes flash bright silver, a sign that he's about to let go. He always loses control of himself for just a second before he gives himself over to the pleasure and allows the orgasm to consume him.

"I'm coming," Bexley groans, her face scrunching up in pleasure. "Holy fuck, I'm coming!"

"Fuck yeah, you are," Maxen says.

With one more thrust, he stills, grinding against her. My hands shake so fucking hard they ache. The need to reach down and touch myself is fucking overwhelming. I'm so hard it hurts and I'll no doubt end up with a case of fucking blue balls for this, but hopefully, this fifth orgasm will put her to sleep and I can just go into the bathroom and rub one out.

Bexley collapses on the bed, panting, and Max pulls out, heading into the bathroom and returning a moment later with a wet towel.

He's only being nice because he knows she's staying here. Part of him probably feels bad too, knowing she didn't choose to come here. He still has a conscience, unlike me.

Max doesn't agree with the shit I do, but he knows I need it, knows I have to do it. Just like him with sex. He does what he needs to feed, and so do I. He just got lucky that sex is normal and my way of gaining energy is less accepted, even in Hell.

He rolls Bexley onto her back and cleans her up gently before going to one of my drawers and takes out one of my T-shirts to give her. He even helps her put it on, the kiss ass.

She does look as if she needs the help though. Her body looks boneless and she's barely moving, probably half asleep. Hours of sex will do that to you, especially when you're forced through five orgasms. She's limber, clearly exhausted. Once the shirt is on, he slides her up the bed and gets her under the blankets. She rolls to her side, black hair spilling behind her, and she's sleeping in seconds, her soft snores filling the otherwise silent room.

The urge to reach out to her and run my fingers through her soft hair, bring it to my nose and smell it just so I can remember it for days to come has me getting out of bed.

I can't be doing shit like that.

This isn't about feelings and memories, it's about my need as a demon and claiming what is mine. Which is exactly what she is.

Mine.

Max pulls on a pair of shorts and climbs onto the bed just as I go into the bathroom.

I'm still hard as a rock and won't be sleeping until I take care of it, so I do.

Pulling down my sweats just enough to free myself, I wrap my hand around my cock, resting my back against the cool tile and stroke. It's seconds before I feel the need to come, and I don't stop like I normally would. I don't want to drag this out, I just want to avoid blue balls and fucking Bexley again tonight.

I give into the feeling and come with a grunt, thick ropes of cum shooting out and dropping all over the floor. My heart is pounding, chest heaving as I rest my head back and try to control my breathing. After a moment, I finally feel like I can breathe normally and push off the wall. I grab a towel and wipe up the floor before going back into the bedroom.

"Why do you do that shit?" Max asks, leaning against the headboard. "You could've just fucked her. She was more than willing."

"You don't have to be in my head all the time," I respond. "Maybe I'd like to jerk off alone."

"Where is the fun in that?" He grins and I roll my eyes as I get into bed.

"I take it you're sleeping here tonight?" Sharing a bed with Maxen is somewhat normal. He has his own room here, but most nights we crash here together. The bed is big enough that it doesn't get annoying.

"Already in bed, aren't I? Besides, it would be nice to have a good morning fuck before we bring her back."

"You really think she's going to want to fuck you without the fruit?"

"Do you know who you're talking to?"

"You are so full of yourself." I shake my head and reach for the switch by my bed to turn the lights off. It'll be daylight soon, but I'd like to get some sleep in before then.

I settle down, trying to get comfortable but I can't seem to sleep, even though I really want to. I shift around from my stomach to my side until finally resting on my back. It's no use. My mind won't stop. I don't know what makes me say it, maybe because I'd rather forewarn him than spring it on him tomorrow... Or maybe it's because I'm grumpy due to not being able to sleep and I want him just as annoyed as I am. Either way, there's no taking it back after the words leave my mouth.

"I'm not letting her go home tomorrow." My words are simple, holding no amount of emotion.

"What?!" He's... Well, he's pissed. As I expected him to be.

"She's mine."

"You're out of your mind. Do you have any idea what'll happen if we don't return her and make sure August knows she's back?"

"Fuck that angel," I spit out, turning to meet his hard gaze. "He can kiss my demon ass."

"This isn't smart." He shakes his head, running his hand through his hair.

"I know," I agree. And I do know that. I know how stupid it is, how many problems it'll cause, but I can't even think of letting her go and never seeing her again.

And to think, we found her for Maxen, yet I'm the one who is addicted.

"You're gonna owe me," Maxen says, shifting to lie down. "You are going to fucking owe me so hard for this shit, Kaine."

"I'll suck your dick, how's that?"

He barks out a laugh. "Definitely not good enough. Maybe if you did it every day for a month?"

"Fuck off. Not happening."

"Fine, but you're paying me back for this. If I end up in the Pit because of you, I swear I'll chop your dick off myself. And then I'll make you eat it with a side of mashed balls. And to be clear, they're your balls."

Avoiding the Pit over this is going to be the biggest obstacle.

Along with convincing August to drop this. Actually, I'm not sure which of those will be the hardest. Then I have to worry about hiding her from my father and anyone who has a Wandering Tablet. Each kingdom has one but not everyone uses them consistently. Seeing a human on the map won't be that big of a deal as humans do come down here, but if someone is watching and sees it's a constant thing, it may raise suspicion. I'll have to talk to Marionette at some point to see if there is a way to hide Bexley from popping up on it.

When I was a kid, I thought that thing was pretty cool. Being able to see every demon in Hell as a little dot, wandering around. Now? I'm wishing I'd have broken it that first time Marionette showed it to me and I almost dropped it cause it was too heavy for my scrawny thirteen-year-old ass to hold properly. No way would we be able to get another. Not unless someone was killed over it, which I doubt my father would do for something he couldn't care less about.

One of the good things is I'm pretty sure ninety-nine percent of these servants are more loyal to me than my father, since they see me more frequently. Though, he is the king so I could be wrong. Then again, they see what I keep in the dungeons, so...

I guess that could go either way, but I don't foresee them being a problem.

Bexley, however, may not take it well at first. Especially once she finds out where she is.

I glance over and watch as her shoulders move up and down ever so slowly as she sleeps, and I know it won't matter because I always get what I want.

She'll have two options. She can stay willingly, or I'll make her. Everyone else can be dealt with. It's that simple.

# CHAPTER FOURTEEN

## BEXLEY

I stir in my sleep, feeling as if it's time to wake up but my bed is so comfortable and warm and my head is throbbing. I don't want to move, don't want to get up. I shift and hug my pillow tighter, noticing every muscle in my body is sore as fuck. They ache as if I worked out for hours on end yesterday, but I haven't been to the gym in years. Tried that shit once and never again.

So what the hell then...

I peel my eyes open, expecting to see the familiar surroundings of my depression-inducing room: my messy desk that has books piled a mile high all over it, white walls that are covered in band posters because the paint beneath them is peeling and cracking, and the rack of clothes in the corner that is overfilled and falling apart, the bar curved and ready to snap because my shitty room doesn't have a closet and that one was the only one I could afford.

Yet, I see none of that. Instead, I see a wide-open space. A very clean and bare room that's dimly lit by a few lanterns on the walls. The furniture is all black, as are the walls, ceiling, and floor.

Where the hell am I?

A snore from behind me catches my attention and I freeze, my blood turning to ice.

Damnit. Who did I go home with now?

It's been a while since I got so drunk that I ended up having a one-night stand. The mornings are always so fucking awkward, and I usually try to leave at night, no matter how fucked up I am. Guess I was pretty wasted last night if I didn't remember to follow my own rules. As if I didn't already know that from the state of my body.

I just hope I remembered to use protection. I do not have the time nor the funds to make another clinic trip...

Knowing I have the worst case of beer goggles whenever I drink, I'm terrified to turn over and see who I'm in bed with, but I need to. I need to just get it over with, rip it off like a Band-Aid. Then I need to get out of here and go home, take a shower and let Rachel know I'm okay. Though if I got that fucked up, she probably knew all about it. I wouldn't be surprised if she's the reason I'm here right now. Even less surprised if she was in another room with another guy.

I count to three and turn over. I'm met with a head full of dark hair. Well, at least it looks clean and not oily. That's a good sign.

The rest of his body is tucked under the blankets, so I can't see anything, but judging from this angle, he has broad shoulders, so I guess that's another good sign.

Maybe I scored a hottie this time.

Carefully, I scoot myself up, trying to get into a sitting position. I'm met with a wave of nausea and have to close my eyes before I throw up. I take deep breaths, hoping to settle my stomach. After a few moments, it goes away and I open my eyes, but then I'm met with a sharp sting to both of them as the light hits me just right.

I curse under my breath as I squeeze them shut again and shift myself down a bit.

Today is going to be a shit day.

Fuck, I hate days like today. I wish there was some kind of magic cure for hangovers.

I fight the pain, knowing I need to get a glance at this guy. He hasn't woken up yet, even through all of my moving, gagging, and groaning so maybe he drank as much as I did.

Taking another breath, I open my eyes slowly and fight the gasp as I notice not one, but two men in this giant bed. And as I blink, trying to clear my vision and get a good look, I'm flooded with memories of last night.

Sex.

Lots of it.

All over the table.

Double penetration.

Oh my god, I let that guy put it in my ass.

With olive oil!!

What the fuck is wrong with me?

I run a hand down my face, my cheeks warming with embarrassment.

"That's a whole new level of depravity, Bex," I say to myself, shaking my head.

I remember having like half a glass of wine. That's it. No way hal—

Then it hits me.

Oh fuck. They roofied me.

It's the only thing that makes sense.

I glance at them from the corner of my eye. Toned bodies, nice hair, tattoos... yeah, they're total fucking roofiers... or whatever someone who roofies people would be called.

And if they drugged me, they probably have been lying to me about why I'm here.

Holy shit, what did I get myself into?

I hold back the groan, cursing myself internally at how stupid I've been. I've done some very questionable things, made a lot of stupid decisions, but this takes the cake. Easily.

God, I am so stupid!

I glance around, grabbing the only thing I can—a pillow.

I pick that sucker up, rear it back, and slam it down so hard on the head of the guy closest to me.

"What the fuck!" he shouts, jerking up to a sitting position, and blocking his face with his thick forearm. I untangle myself from the sheets in a rush and get to my feet, pillow in hand, ignoring the thrum of my head.

"You fucking drugged me!" I shout, looking around for something else to throw, something that'll do more damage than a pillow, but I see nothing.

"I did not," he says, looking at me like I've lost my damn mind.

Maxen, that's Maxen. Yep, I remember that much.

"Then he did!" I point to the other one—Kaine, I think—who is just waking up. Rubbing one eye as he sits up, glancing at the other guy. "You roofied me," I accuse.

Another flash of them fucking me strikes and I have to push the thought away because I'm supposed to be angry with them.

Kaine's eyes narrow on me. "People who are roofied rarely remember a damn thing." His gaze darkens and he smirks, which is all too damn sexy. "And from the look on your face, you remember last night all too well."

My cheeks warm.

"You should probably ask what you're eating before you eat it," he says as if it's a great piece of advice. As if that is going to help my situation at all.

"That's a real asshole thing to say," I respond, crossing my arms over my chest and holding onto that pillow for dear life. It's all I've got, even if it'll do next to no damage. With each second that passes, my head feels a little better, and I will forever be grateful for that.

"Never claimed to be nice."

I grit my jaw, filling with anger as more of the night pieces together. It's nice to know his cocky facade is back in place. Long gone is the fucker that was talkative and nice, now that he got what he wanted. Which was clearly just to get laid.

"Bring me home. I want to go home. Now," I demand, stomping my foot for effect.

"No," Kaine grunts, throwing his feet over the side of the bed, giving me his back, and running his hand through his hair. I try to ignore how sexy his back is but fail miserably as I ogle him shamelessly. But only for a minute, because I soon remember that I'm mad, at him specifically.

"You said you would bring me home today." I'm not backing down from this. I want to go home.

"Later."

I glance at Maxen, noticing the asshole is asleep again! Sitting up, leaning against the headboard... just sleeping. Well, that just *really* pisses me off. So I step forward and whack him with the pillow again, right in his face.

He jerks away again. "Wha–what the fuck. Stop doing that!"

"Stop sleeping!"

"It's sleep time!" he shouts back.

"No, it fucking isn't!" I scream back at him even louder. I'm not mad he's yelling at me, but if he thinks he's going to win this he's lost his damn mind.

"You two need to shut the fuck up," Kaine growls getting to his feet. "My head is pounding."

"Shouldn't have eaten so much of that fruit," Maxen says, once again with his eyes closed.

Fruit? What fruit? Oh, these slimey douchebags.

"That fruit! What was it?" I shout, throwing the pillow onto the bed out of nothing more than frustration. Maxen glances at it, grateful it's out of my hands, I'm sure. "Did you put the drugs in them?" I look from Maxen to Kaine who is rounding the bed. He walks past me, completely ignoring my question as if I'm not even here. He disappears into the bathroom so I do the only rational thing possible... I stomp after him.

He stops in front of the toilet, obviously ready to pee, but I grab onto his arm, yanking him away.

"Are you fucking crazy!" He shakes me off and turns back to the toilet. "I need to piss."

"And I need to go home."

He ignores me, so this time I place my hands on his bicep and push, but he barely moves.

"Fuck off," he warns. "Don't mess with a man who needs to have a morning piss!"

He does his business, and I stand there the whole time, watching and waiting, ready to throw a fist at his face if I'm being honest.

When he's done, he stalks towards me with dark eyes, and I back up until I'm hitting something cool—the wall. He leans forward, pressing both hands on either side of my head, boxing me in.

"If you don't calm the fuck down, you can take your own ass home, and trust me, you don't want that," he threatens. His jaw is tense, eyes set on me with a look that could kill and for some reason, sparks go off between my legs and I have this overwhelming urge to drop to my knees and suck his dick.

I don't though. I fight the urge as my instincts kick in.

"If you think walking the streets of New York City scares me, then you are sadly mistaken." I jut my chin in challenge, and his eyes flicker with something dark.

"You are so…" His voice is low and husky, his words trailing off. His body is warm against mine, hard and firm, and his scent? Fuck, it's intoxicating. I take a greedy breath, wanting more, even though I know I shouldn't.

"What?" I ask, my voice just above a whisper.

His gaze flicks to my lips, lingering for just a second before they dart back up to meet my eyes. I hate that I want him to kiss me right now. That I wish he would spin me around and fuck me so hard it hurts. But he doesn't. Instead, he pushes off the wall and storms out of the room, leaving me panting and wondering what the hell just happened.

# CHAPTER FIFTEEN

## BEXLEY

Maxen walks in moments later carrying a pile of clothes.

"Here." I glance from them back to his face in question. "They're yours and they're clean." He holds them out and I snatch them, holding them close to my chest. "Get dressed so we can go get some breakfast."

I keep my gaze on him when he doesn't move, hoping he'll take the hint and get the fuck out.

He arches a brow. "Seriously? You're getting shy now?"

I give a cocky smile. "People tend to be a little different when they aren't high off their ass."

He chuckles, taking a step closer. "Don't act like you didn't love every fucking second of it, sweetheart." His words are just as dirty, but the playfulness from last night is gone. Now he sounds annoyed. Which could be from my hitting him with a pillow and not allowing him to sleep... or it could be because he's an ass. I'll go with him being an ass because it seems more fitting.

I bite my tongue to stop myself from reacting to him. He doesn't deserve it.

These guys are dangerous. I may blame what I did on the drugs—or the fruit, whatever the fuck it is—but hell... I'd probably have done it anyway.

They don't need to know that, though.

When he realizes I'm not going to play into his little game, he takes a step back and leaves the room with a huff, mumbling under his breath about how he's going to kick Kaine's ass.

I'd pay to see that. A lot of freaking money... if I had it.

I get dressed quickly, knowing the sooner I finish, the sooner I can eat, and the sooner I can eat, the sooner I can get home.

Once I'm dressed, I look inside the cabinet above the sink, grateful when I find a bottle of mouthwash. I take a mouthful, swishing it around before spitting it out. It'll have to do since I don't have a toothbrush. Looking in the mirror, I try to tame my hair. It's a wild freaking mess from not doing anything with it after the shower... the shower where Maxen washed my body from head to toe.

*Stop it, Bexley. Stop!* I close my eyes and take a deep breath before opening them again and focusing on what I need to do.

Not finding a brush anywhere, I finger-comb my hair. It'll have to do. Besides, I don't really care what I look like. I'm not trying to impress anyone. In fact, I should probably have left my breath stinky and hair a mess to make them regret last night. Maybe I should take a giant shit in his toilet and not flush. Stink up the place nice and good. Too bad I don't have to go right now because I'd do it.

Maxen is waiting by the door when I enter the bedroom. He's looking at his phone, and I think of asking if I can use it, but something tells me he's just going to say he doesn't have service. Doesn't really matter anyway, when breakfast is done, I'm leaving. Whether they help me or not, I'm out of this place.

Maxen jerks his head towards the hallway, pushing off the wall, and I follow after him, not caring where Kaine is or what he's doing. He doesn't lead me back to the elevator—wherever that is because this place is a damn maze—instead, we take the stairs. Definitely what I *don't* want to do while fighting a hangover.

I've never been a fan of heights, so as we walk down, I stay as far away from the railing as I can, trying to avoid having to look over the edge. The thought of being so high up and knowing I could fall over the edge with as much as a small shove from Maxen has me fighting nausea again.

Maxen doesn't say a word as we walk, just stays a few steps in front of me as we make our way down, but we don't go to the very bottom—thank fuck. Last night when we had dinner, and uh... other things, we were definitely on the first floor. Now, we go down about three flights before he turns off a platform to the left and heads down—you guessed it, another hallway.

As we walk, I consider making small talk, if only for the sake of annoying him, but decide I don't want to talk to him. There is no point. I just want to eat and leave.

I shouldn't be surprised when we step into another dining room but I am. With the size of this place, it's not shocking that there is more than one—and I wouldn't be surprised if I was told there are ten more—but it's not something I'm used to. Not after living in a tiny two-bedroom apartment that I pay out the ass for. One that has a bathroom so small you can barely turn around and a kitchen that only has enough space to store food for a week. It doesn't even have a full-sized refrigerator or stove.

I hate that being here is making me hate my life back home...

The dining room we enter is empty, not surprising. Kaine probably skipped breakfast for the sole purpose of avoiding me. He just seems like that kind of person. In fact, he's probably pissed off and moping around this big ass castle on the verge of a tantrum.

"Sit," Maxen snaps, pointing to a chair. Grumpy ass. I want to say no, tell him to fuck off, but I know that'll only prolong breakfast and I don't want that.

He presses a button on the wall before taking his own seat, and a few moments later, people are bringing food out to us. There are three people who come out; two are carrying a tray and the other has glasses and a decanter of what looks like orange juice—but could be some weird liquid that makes you grow a second head, for all I know.

A plate is placed down in front of me, and the waiter pulls the cover off for me, taking it with him when he goes.

The scent of scrambled eggs, bacon, and French toast has my mouth watering and me biting back a moan. My stomach rumbles and I pick up my fork and scoop up a big heaping of eggs but pause before putting it into my mouth. I put my fork down and look up at Maxen who is happily eating his food, not paying me any mind.

"How do I know this isn't going to drug me like that other stuff?"

The last waiter, who is standing way too close for comfort, places down a glass of that juice—that smells like orange juice, but I don't know if I trust it—by my plate. He then disappears through the doors like the others.

Maxen pauses, putting down his fork and picking up his napkin to wipe his mouth. He looks at me with a bored and almost annoyed expression.

"It's just breakfast. But if you'd like more of the fruit, I could ask them to bring some." He smirks.

I narrow my eyes at him. "No thanks," I grit out.

"Very well then."

He picks up his fork and starts eating again. I stare down at my food, my stomach feeling so empty that I'm hit with a wave of dizziness. Knowing I need to take my chances if I want to get out of here, I decide I'll take the risk.

I'm starving and my head is pounding. I'm on the verge of throwing up or passing out—maybe both.

I dig in without giving it another thought.

The eggs are light and fluffy, and the French toast has the perfect amount of vanilla and cinnamon. It's the most delicious breakfast I've ever had... which I also hate. I don't want to like anything here. I don't want to like this place, the food, or these stupid guys.

I just want to go home.

After eating half of the food on my plate, I go for the juice.

It's sweet, tart, and definitely freshly squeezed.

Of fucking course it is.

I've only ever had fresh orange juice once before, but I'll never forget the taste of it. It's so different than the stuff you buy at the store.

I work on finishing my breakfast and can't stop thinking about how these guys are exactly the type of people who would steal a poor girl from the city and keep her hidden away in their giant mansion.

Fucking rich boys thinking rules don't apply to them. I'm just grateful they aren't torturing me or threatening to wear my skin...

So why did they take me at all? What is the point?

I'm still on the fence about the whole thing but am trying not to think about it because in the end, I want to go home, no matter what. I'm going to find my way out of here and make my way home to Rachel. Kaine isn't around, and it should be easy enough to slip away from Maxen. He looks hungover as fuck, also annoyed that he's on babysitting duty.

I take the last bite of my French toast, wishing I had a large mug of coffee and a gallon of water, but I don't plan on opening my mouth and asking for it. I'm feeling some type of way after all that went down yesterday. Uneasy, maybe? I'm not angry about it, not really embarrassed either, just... uptight. Something like that, anyway. I'll process it all when I'm safe in my own bed and not on the verge of dying from dehydration.

"Is there a bathroom around here?" I ask.

"Out the door, to the left," Maxen answers without even looking up. He just continues to eat his food and stare at his phone.

I don't bother thanking him, I just get up and go.

Getting down here wasn't as difficult as getting to their bedroom. It shouldn't be too hard to make my way back to the staircase and from there I just have to go to the bottom and out the front door. I saw the staircase when I first walked into this place, so it should be easy. Then I'll just have to go right out the front door and figure out where I am and which way is home. Nothing outside looked familiar to me but if I make it to a road, maybe I can find someone to give me a ride or even just directions. I have no problem walking. I try not to worry about it right now, knowing I'm usually pretty good with winging it. One thing at a time, that's what I need to focus on. Right now, I just need to find the stairs.

As I leave the room, I glance back at Maxen whose back is to me. He still doesn't bother to pay attention to me, and I wish I could be around when Kaine realizes Maxen lost me...

Knowing I'm good to go, I turn right instead of left. I quickly backtrack and find my way to the stairs. As I go down, I once again stick close to the wall and scurry down as fast as I can. Every time I reach a landing, I slow down and pop my head around the corner to make sure I'm not caught by anyone. Though I've noticed this place is like a damn ghost town, which adds to the creepy factor.

I pass by the last landing and excitement fills me as I see the bottom floor. Moving down the steps quicker than before, I make it down in no time. Only problem is, this room is nothing like I remember. There is no large set of doors to leave from and I don't even see where the elevator is...

*Damnit.*

I knew I would end up lost in this damn place. I'm surprised they don't need a map just to get around.

Staying close to the wall, I look around, thinking maybe it looks different because I'm looking at it from a different angle. But as I move around, I realize that is not the case at all.

I have no idea where the fuck I am.

# CHAPTER SIXTEEN

## MAXEN

"You're late," I grumble, eyes glued to my phone. I've been browsing the chat board for a while now, wondering if anyone has made comment about an unauthorized human entering Hell. It doesn't always happen, but sometimes things get leaked and are posted on here. Normally, I'm not into the drama and gossip of Hell, but I'm also no stranger to these chat boards and am satisfied when I see nothing about a human.

I don't bother glancing at Kaine as he enters. I know it's him because his thoughts are loud as fuck.

All demons have the mind link, but most keep it quiet. Kaine and I always keep ours open to the other. It's a pact we made long ago, in case either of us needed help. Something that hasn't come up in quite a few years, but you never know what's going to happen.

It's rare for demons to be as close as he and I are. Not the sharing girls or the hanging out in general, but the bond we have. I'd bet there are no other demons in Hell who care about one another the way he and I do. Demons are selfish by nature, and I have no idea why things are so different with him, but they are.

"I had things to tend to," he says, taking the seat beside me and giving a quick look around. "Where is she?" he snaps.

"Don't get your panties in a twist." I look up at him. "She went to the bathroom. You just missed her."

He doesn't respond and I don't expect him to. After all the sex yesterday, I figured he'd be in a good mood today, but the hangover from that damn Azenial fruit is enough to put even me in a foul mood, which is not common. Now I remember why I hate that shit and I swear I won't let the fucker convince me to do it again.

I drop my phone to the table and turn towards him.

"Please tell me you have a plan."

He lifts his head, eyebrow arched, and meets my gaze.

"I will."

"Damnit, Kaine," I grit out. "This is not going to work."

"I will take care of it," he says through clenched teeth.

"What is the big deal anyway? Why can't you just bring her home? Those humans are a dime a dozen."

He looks at me for a long moment and I can see he's trying to decide what he wants to tell me. Even though we have that mind link, we can keep thoughts to ourselves, which we do often. We just don't stop the other from sending thoughts to us.

"Do you not feel it?" he asks me.

I frown.

He runs a hand down his face and leans back in his chair.

"There is just... something about her."

"You sure it's not just because you want to piss off August? Or the fact she has a beautiful pussy?" I smirk.

He huffs out a humorless laugh.

"Part of it, yeah, but there's something else... something I can't explain."

"You mean like... feelings?"

I'll give it to him, the girl is different than any other I've been with. I don't know why but I'm not making a big deal out of it like he is. Shit happens. Sometimes you meet someone and you just click.

Kaine and I. Case and point.

But that doesn't mean you kidnap them and take them to your home. Is she worth a war? That is what this could lead to. The kingdoms are already at each other's throats, all we need is to give them more fuel. And that will only infuriate King Tzalli, Kaine's father. If we are the reason he has to fight in a war to save his kingdom, he won't think twice about sending me and his son to the Pit for the rest of our lives.

Is she worth getting sent to the Pit for? Hell fucking no. There is pussy everywhere.

He sighs. "I don't know what the fuck I mean. I'm tired and hung-the-fuck-over."

"You're telling me. I feel like ass."

We stay quiet for a few moments, and I'm about to open my mouth to ask if he's going to eat when it hits me.

Bexley has been gone for a long time. Longer than it would take to get to and use the bathroom.

Kaine and I glance at each other at the same time, and I curse as I get to my feet, slamming my hands on the table in annoyance. We both rush out of the room and straight to the bathroom. He bursts through the door, finding it unlocked and empty.

Kaine turns and glares at me, his eyes flashing bright blue.

"If my father finds her, she's dead." He slaps his hand against the marble wall and stomps off. I go after him.

"I didn't think she would try to leave. What was I supposed to do, fucking babysit her while she takes a piss? Maybe you should have told me that was my duty before you left the bedroom in a fit," I call after him.

We rush down the hallway, me only a step or two behind him, and reach the stairs in no time.

"I'm going down, you go up. Tell me immediately if you find her."

I nod and make my way up the stairs, heading back towards his room. It's the only place she knows of outside of the two dining halls we've been in and if her plan wasn't to escape, then I assume she'd want to go back to bed. It's exactly what I'd love to do right now.

Unless she's just stupid and thought it was a good idea to roam the castle and try to leave...

Which is the worst idea she could possibly have. Especially if she plans on going outside.

I race up the stairs in record time, jogging down the hallway and barging into the bedroom. I'm not at all surprised when it's empty. Annoyed, but not surprised. I check every place I can think of. The bathroom, shower, closet, even under the bed.

Empty, empty, empty, and empty.

"Damnit," I groan aloud, clenching my fists.

This castle is huge, and it'll take days to search each and every room for her. Especially if she's purposely hiding from us.

When Kaine and I were little, hide-and-go-seek in this place was the best. We had so many rules in place, otherwise, we'd never find one another. We kept it to certain hallways on certain floors. We laid out exactly which rooms were good to use, and if you went out of bounds, you automatically lost.

We could go round and round for days looking for this girl, missing each other by just a hallway or even a room.

Leaving his bedroom, I pop right into the lounge room around the corner. I check every space big enough for her to fit and even spaces that she wouldn't fit, just in case. When that comes up with nothing, I make my way down the hall, walking into every room I pass, even the ones that are full of dust from not being used in hundreds of years.

I want to be mad at her, I really do, but all I can think about is how I can get even with Kaine for this. It's his fault. He fucked up. If he could just get his temper in check, none of this would be happening.

# CHAPTER SEVENTEEN

## BEXLEY

After searching this bottom floor and finding nothing except another freaking hallway, I decide I must be misremembering where I came in from. I'm certain it was the bottom floor. The way this staircase is, there is no possible way for me to go down more. It's the same circle room, same circle staircase...

And this is definitely the bottom floor... I think.

Maybe we did walk through a hallway first? This place is like a damn maze. I take one last quick walk around the room before I make the decision to go the only way I can—down the damn hallway. I am not going back up. That is not an option, not at all. It has zero chances of leading me anywhere other than back into Kaine's labyrinth. No thanks.

The corridor is dark and the deeper I go, the darker it gets. There is not a single window down here, though that doesn't seem all that strange. I'd gone by a few areas while walking around that had no windows. Again, it just adds to the creep factor.

There are lanterns on the walls, giving off a small amount of light that lingers by the walls, leaving what looks like a carpet of black centered down the hall—an eerie trail for me to follow. The light is just enough for me to know I'm not walking into anything and still have a long way to go. Not that I know where I'm going, but I need to get to the end. And if I get there and it's nothing, then I know the only option I have is to go back up and... I don't know? Tell Maxen I got lost because I wanted to explore? Maybe he'd believe it.

Hopefully, it won't come to that, and I won't have to worry about it.

The more I walk, the more this area reminds me of the place I was in when I first woke up. That dark and damp prison. Only down here is scarier. Maybe it's because I'm on a time limit and it's possible there are people looking for me.

When I was in that other place, I didn't know a damn thing about what was going on and for some reason wasn't thinking it was anything bad. How fucking naive am I? That place was also a little brighter and had a lot of rooms.

This is one long and dark hallway, completely made of cement bricks. My shadow has scared me more times than I'd like to admit. My entire body is on edge, senses on overload, and all the hairs on my body are standing straight up. Even though I know I'd hear someone down here with me, I can't help but worry someone is following me. Like a secret ninja who is silent on his feet. Though I'm moving so quickly my own footsteps are echoing around me so maybe I wouldn't hear another set...

*Chill out, Bex, you're going to be fine.*

I keep telling myself that because I have to. I need to find a way out of here. Stopping is not an option, I need to keep going.

After what feels like forever, I take a break and press my back to the wall. I look to my right and can't see the opening to that main room anymore, so I've gone a decent distance. I look left and have to close my eyes and take a deep breath so I don't freak out. There is nothing on either side of me, nothing but a four-foot-wide hallway basked in a blackness. At this point, I know for sure this is not how I came into the castle. There is no way I'd forget something like this. And not only am I worried about that, but I'm also starting to worry about where I'll end up. It's turning out to be a mile-long tunnel that I'm pretty sure is underground. Why? Where does this lead to? Part of me wants to believe it'll lead me outside. Like one of those drainage pipes you see in movies?

Deep down I think I know that's not the case, but all I have at this point is hope.

I push off the wall and keep going, knowing if I stay here for too long, someone will probably find me. Kaine and Maxen are a lot of things—annoying, arrogant, cocky... hot—but they aren't stupid. It only makes sense that I would go down and try to leave, meaning it's only a matter of time before someone finds me.

I move quicker this time, knowing there has to be an end in sight. This can't go on forever, can it? No. It absolutely cannot. There has to be an end. Just as the thought hits me, I slow my steps and tilt my head, trying to get a better glimpse through the dark.

Is that a... wall? I think that's a wall. I try not to lose hope, assuming there must be a turnoff and it's not a complete dead end. Why in the world would there be a long ass hallway that goes nowhere? Now that makes no fucking sense at all. So I pick up my pace and keep going, both grateful and nervous when I see there is, in fact, a turnoff to the left. I take it, the sounds of my hurried footsteps still echoing around me. Before I know it, there is another turn and I fight off the thoughts of me being lost. This has to lead somewhere, it just has to. I can't turn back, not now. So I keep going forward. My legs ache as I push them to keep up at a jog's pace, and I fight off the throbbing in my head that's returning. I should have drank some water before I left... who knows how long it'll take me to get home. I have no money and my cell phone is lost... depending on how far from the city I am, I could be walking for days...

*Don't think like that,* I tell myself. *You'll be fine. You've survived worse.*

And I have.

The foster system. It's worse than being homeless, that much I can tell you. If I can get through years of that and make it out alive, I can get out of this.

So with my hands sweaty and my heart beating rapidly in my chest, I keep moving.

The deeper I go, the higher my anxiety gets but I have to do this.

My heavy breathing and footsteps are the only sounds I can hear, which I'm grateful for. If I heard any other kind of noise, I'd probably be shitting my pants.

I turn my fourth corner, getting a glimpse of light and convinced I'll be popping back out at the stairs, but the room I walk into has me halting, a gasp leaving my mouth.

# CHAPTER EIGHTEEN

## Bexley

My heart is thundering in my chest, blood pumping so loudly I can hear it in my ears. My mouth is dry, and my body feels like it's going to give up on me and crumble right here, in this room... this dungeon. It's dimly lit by a couple of lanterns and there are no windows. None.

Three cells with nothing but beds topped with blankets and buckets line the wall to my right, while the one to my left has a long line of cabinets, with one larger cell on the end. Only, that one looks different. The bars are spread further apart and there is no door, only a large opening... I guess it isn't really a cell at all, so what is it?

I step farther in, curiosity getting the best of me and I find an exam table against the back wall, but nothing else.

"What the fuck," I say under my breath, a million thoughts going through my head at this point. I can barely process what I'm thinking, can't even imagine what this place is used for. I step farther in, needing to know if there is a door or another turn off, anywhere to go other than back. I brace myself to see dead bodies, or limbs, or jars with organs in them, but I don't. It's just a wide-open space... with no doors.

The only way out of here is to go back the way I came. I look over my shoulder and fight off the tears that are threatening to spill over. This was all for nothing. I have no idea how long I've been running through these tunnels, and in the end, it got me nowhere. Maybe I missed something? Maybe there was a hidden door or a smaller turn off that I didn't see because of the dark? There has to be a way to get outside from here.

I take slow steps deeper into the room, scared out of my mind, but needing to be absolutely sure that there is nothing here.

I curse under my breath when I find nothing, not even a small window, and throw a little tantrum by slamming my fists on my thighs, trying to stay as quiet as possible.

"It's okay, Bexley," I whisper to myself. "Everything is going to be okay. Just go back down the hall and—"

I stop in my tracks when from the corner of my eye I see one of the blankets atop the bed move. I don't move, don't breathe, I don't even think. I keep my eyes glued to that spot. Did I make that up or did it really move? Either I'm seeing things or there's got to be rats roaming around down here. The thought doesn't bother me so much as I'm not overly terrified of small vermin. I'd be more concerned if there were people down here...

"Hello?" I call out, my voice shaky. I turn my body to face the cell head-on, needing to see more clearly. I have no other choice but to be brave, so that's what I do. Or try to do. I let out a sigh of relief when I hear nothing and don't see any other movement. With my hand on my chest, I take a moment to breathe and calm my nerves.

I really need to get the fuck out of here, and there is only one way to do that. I have to go back.

I let out a deep breath and move back towards the hall without thinking about it too much. Just as I reach the doorway, preparing to make my way back, I hear it.

A low, raspy, ghost-like sound.

A voice.

"Hello."

My eyes widen, and once again I'm frozen in fear. With my hands clenched, I turn around, hoping to find nothing but emptiness. I'm not so lucky. There, in one of the cells, are two dark, dead eyes staring straight at me.

Those beds aren't piled with blankets, it's people under there...

I stare, unsure of what else to do. If there are people down here, this deep down in the asshole of the castle then they must be dangerous, right? Prisoners? Murderers? Rapists?

"Did he send you here?" That same voice sounds again, only this time there is a tinge of fear in it, and I realize there is another option. Maybe they aren't here because they're dangerous, maybe they're here because someone is keeping them here for their own sick and twisted pleasure?

"Who?" I respond, taking my chances with speaking to them. I take a good glance at the cell bars. The doors are chained and padlocked, and not even a child could fit through those bars, so talking can't hurt, right? Maybe they know a way out of here...

"Master."

I take a look down the hallway and when I'm certain I hear nothing coming from that way, I decide talking to this person is my best bet. Keeping a few feet from the cells, I move back towards the middle of the room, closer to the voice. I can't trust these people, I don't know a damn thing about them. This person could be a murderer or they could be an innocent like me.

That thought is terrifying. The worst I've had so far. Because if they are here against their will, then this is most likely what's in store for me if I don't get the fuck out of here.

Those guys, Kaine and Maxen, what if they're serial killers? What if this is what they do? Kidnap people and bring them here to keep. And when they don't do as they're told, like me, then they get put down here where no one will ever find them.

A lump forms in my throat and my mouth becomes even more dry. It's hard to swallow, but I try.

"You need to calm down or he's going to find you," that same voice says softly.

"What? What do you mean?" I ask, glancing around, feeling all sorts of eyes on me now. I look closer and see eyes peeking from under the blankets on all of the beds.

"Even I can smell your fear. It's certain he will."

Smell my fear?

Maybe this isn't part of Kaine's house... maybe I somehow ended up in a secret insane asylum or something. I was walking for a long time, I could have entered another building. In fact, it's most likely I did because Kaine's castle isn't so big that I'd still be in it, right?

I fight back tears as I try to keep my thoughts clear. Nothing makes sense to me, and I don't know what to do. I'm stuck, with not a clue how to help myself.

There is movement from the middle cell, where the voice has been coming from. The blankets are slowly removed and the person sits up. It's a man, maybe in his late twenties? He's shirtless, dirty, and scarred. His hair is shaggy, oily, and matted. He takes a deep whiff of the air, closing his eyes and when he opens them again, he looks right at me, his eyes wide and full of worry.

"You're human," he whispers.

A gasp comes from one of the other cells.

"What?" I ask.

Of course, I'm fucking human. I'm not a horse.

He gets up quickly, reaching the bars in seconds and I step back even farther. He places his face between two of the bars, resting his face in the opening. Each hand grasps the bars above his head as he speaks.

"Did he bring you here?"

"Who is he?" I demand, this time not being so quiet. My fear is getting the better of me and I can't control my emotions. I'm worried I'm going to completely lose it and get myself in deeper shit than I'm already in. The only way I have a chance of getting home is by keeping a level head, but this entire situation is not helping me.

"Master," he repeats.

"I don't know who that is," I snap.

"Oh, but I think you do." He smiles, showing a mouth full of teeth that look much cleaner than the rest of him. "You have no idea where you are, do you?" He huffs out a laugh, his expression changing, turning a little darker...

"Knock it off, Aver, or you'll get us all into trouble," someone hisses from another cell. This one also sounds male.

I take a step closer, but not close enough that he can reach me—or so I thought. I open my mouth to speak, to once again ask him what the hell he's talking about, but when he reaches his arm out, I don't move fast enough and he has me by the shirt, pulling me forward. I let out a scream and he pulls me close, knocking me into the cold metal bars. I grip onto them, using my hands and feet to try to get away, but he's got me with both hands now, pressing so close against the bars I can feel his body heat. Never in a million years would I have expected someone who looks like him to have this much strength.

"Let me go!" I shout, pushing against his body but it's no use. I slap and punch, but none of it bothers him. He's got me in a grip I can't get out of. The bars stop me from being able to get a good hit or kick in, but I try my hardest. Finally, he whispers in my ear and his voice makes me want to throw up. "You're in Hell, little girl. And in Hell, you will spend the rest of your days. You—"

"Enough!" someone roars, and I'm let go just as I go for another swing. My hand connects with the metal bar, and I cry out in pain as I fall back, landing on my ass, groaning as I hit the cold stone of the ground. Looking to where the voice came from, I see Kaine standing in the doorway, his eyes full of rage. I'm struck with fear, knowing this very well could be the last minutes I'm alive.

The man who had me against the bar scrambles back to bed, getting under the blankets and tucking himself back underneath. The rest of them do the same. I see no more sad and blank eyes staring at me, they look like nothing more than a pile of old blankets.

I'm panting again. Head foggy with confusion. The only thing I know for certain is that I'm terrified. Fucking scared out of my wits of where I am, and of the man who is currently making his way towards me.

When he reaches me, he offers out his hand to me. I glance at it, not sure if I should take it or not.

Do I go along with him or fight him?

Even though my entire body is shaking with fear, there is something about Kaine, something about those bright blue eyes of his that tells me he'll make all my worries go away, and I think that's the most terrifying thought of all.

# CHAPTER NINETEEN

## KAINE

The closer I get to the bottom of the stairs, the stronger her scent becomes.

Not the scent of her, the way her skin smells like fresh rain, or how her arousal smells as sweet as strawberries. No, not any of those intoxicating scents. It's the smell of her fear. The most decadent one of all.

Fear.

It's what feeds me, what fuels me, what keeps me going.

I need it to survive.

And as I make my way down to the bottom floor, her scent only growing, I know I'm about to have the most delicious feast of my life.

As I expected—why I told Maxen to go up while I came this way—she thought coming down these stairs would lead her to the main foyer we entered when I first brought her here. Only this staircase is the one that leads to the dungeons. To my own personal work space.

Upon first glance, when entering the castle, it looks as if there is one grand staircase swirling around to bring you up all the floors. It was designed well, by a very smart man, but you see, it's not actually one staircase, it's two. And they will not bring you to the same place. Ever. Each staircase brings you to a separate part of the castle.

The servants know it well, as does Maxen, and everyone else who lives here. But for someone like Bexley, who has never been here, she'd have no idea to expect something so complex in one's home.

Which only heightened her fear.

The deeper I get down the hallway, the harder my heart beats, the bigger my cock grows.

Feeding on fear is not always a sexual thing. In fact, it never is—not intentionally. If it happens, then it's great. Two birds, one stone. But for some reason, with Bexley, the smell of her fear turns me on like nothing I've ever encountered before.

The attraction is astounding, indescribable, and I know she feels it too. She just doesn't know how to handle it yet.

It's why I can't let her go. Why I won't. No matter what the fuck I have to do to keep her here, she is staying.

Maxen will see it. He has to accept it because he's a part of this Bexley situation too.

Why? I have no fucking idea, but something about being together with the both of them filled some sort of fucking hole I've had in my heart for a long time. A long fucking time.

Maxen and I already have a bond like no other, something demons just don't get, but for some reason, we're different. And it's not like we run through the roads of Hell shouting about it, so I have no answer for it. Maybe it's more common than we know, but no one talks about it because you know, demons. We're proud creatures and have reputations to uphold. We don't go around talking about feelings.

But whatever the reason is, it has to be the same for her because I can't explain it otherwise.

She hasn't been here long, just over a day, and most of that time was spent fucking. I think we did that more than we slept. That's normal for Max. He doesn't bond with people through sex, it isn't intimate for him, he doesn't do it for love or because he craves the feeling of someone, it's almost like a chore sometimes. It's his way to survive. And maybe his excitement over last night was because of the Azenial fruit, but I'm telling myself it's something else.

Whatever that something else is that's brought us three together. That's what I'm choosing to believe.

Normally, I have sex to let off steam and stay levelheaded, to party, to have a good time, and because Maxen enjoys threesomes. It's rare for me to fuck someone without him, honestly.

Except for her. The need to be inside of her last night, even outside of the fruit because I didn't have all that much, was overwhelming. Same as this morning and every time I look at her. This need to have her, claim her, make her fucking mine is going to drive me to insanity if I don't find a way to handle it.

Maxen will see it. I'll make him see it. He needs to know she is worth whatever shit I go through to keep her. And if I get sent to the Pit, I'll find a way out and go topside, go rogue if I have to, just to get her back. Once he spends more time with her, he'll feel it too. He just needs more than sex, more than the normal shit he deals with on the day to day. He needs something else from her, and I'm confident whatever it is, she'll give it to him.

Him being a part of this is just as important as her staying here. He's a staple in my life; always has been and always will be.

My footsteps are quick down the hall, and I hear the voices before I even reach the last turn. I'm careful on my feet, wanting to know who it is that's speaking to her. They'll be punished for it. It'll be nice to have something to punish them over for once. They've been trained so well that they barely set a foot out of line anymore, and I'm pretty sure it's time for a new set. It gets boring when they start to listen. The best part is the training; the fear they have when they realize what's going to happen if they don't listen. At this point, their fear is just about gone. They've accepted their fate, lost all the hope they had of ever getting out of this place.

I'll let them go, though, and I won't kill them.

And I do this for two reasons.

One, if I ever need a quick fix, I know just where to find them. Setting eyes on me will give me the instant fix I need because no doubt the thought of being thrown back into a cage is terrifying. It's the only thing they'll ever associate me with until their dying breath.

And two, because I fucking can.

There are laws down here. Rules we have to follow just like topside and like Heaven too. And maybe I bend those rules a little...

None of these morons will rat me out because they know who my father is.

King Tzalli, Ruler of Wrath.

No one in their right mind would dare say a negative thing about his only son.

Never.

I'm more than halfway down the hall when that little shit, Aver, grabs Bexley and my blood boils. I can't hear what it is he's saying, but if he doesn't get his foul mouth and grubby hands off of her, he'll lose his head. I'll saw it off with a dinner knife, just to make him suffer. Hold his head to the ground with my boot, and force that knife right through to his esophagus. Maybe cut his vocal cords first, pull them out and shove them down his throat, just to be a dick.

"Enough!" I shout and he lets her go instantly. She falls back, hitting the floor hard and the little shit rushes back into his bed, hiding under the blanket he's lucky I even allow him to have.

Oh, he is definitely going to pay for that later.

I roll my neck, trying to calm my anger and also the energy that is overcoming me. The amount of fear in this room is so much it almost brings a smile to my face, but I fight it off, not wanting anyone to see the thrill I feel while being here.

So many different flavors and scents, but there is only one I care about.

Hers.

The amount that pours from Bexley as she looks at me is so thick, I can almost see it. Like thick smoke surrounding her, wisping towards me... feeding my desires.

I move to her side and offer out my hand, sure she won't take it.

But she does.

This brave girl does and I know she feels it too. She has to.

She's not dumb, I know this much. The only explanation for her taking my hand and my help is that she feels it too. Whatever this is between us. At least I know I'm not crazy. I haven't lost my mind. This is all real.

Along with my anger, and the fucking hard-on that's straining against my jeans.

As I pull her to her feet, her eyes meet mine and something clicks in her brain.

"You," she whispers. "You're..." She glances towards the cells, and I wonder what kind of bullshit they said to her before I made it here. "Are you the reason they're here?"

"Yes," I answer without hesitation.

"Why?" she asks, looking back at me. She isn't scared, doesn't seem worried, though her fear is still present. She only looks curious. I admit I love seeing how feisty she can be. Her tiny hands trying to push me around in the bathroom was entertaining, and maybe part of me wants to fuck with her just to see how far she'll go.

"I need them."

Her eyes flicker with something but I'm not sure what.

"For what?"

I don't answer her question, just take a step forward so we're only inches apart. I look down at her and she tilts her head back to meet my gaze. Her eyes are the brightest green, but darker around the center. They're mesmerizing.

"What did he say to you?" I ask instead.

"He said..." She chews on her bottom lip, searching for words. "He said I'm in Hell."

"And what do you think of that?" I try to hide the humor I feel at her bravery.

"I think he's crazy."

"So you don't believe him then?"

She raises a brow, cocking her head to the side just a bit. "Literally or figuratively?"

I huff out a laugh and move my hand up to run my knuckles along her cheek. Her skin is so soft. The softest I've ever felt and all I want to do is run my hands along every inch of her body. Along her stomach, her thighs, her ass, slide right into her pussy and feel how wet she is.

"Both," I whisper back, challenging her. I've always loved a good challenge. I can be quite the competitor, stubborn than most. I hate losing.

"I... I don't know." She gives a little shrug of her shoulder, eyes still on mine.

I slide my arm around her waist, pressing my palm against her lower back and pulling her against me. She groans and grinds against my erection when she feels it. Sliding my hand up, I tangle it in her hair and pull. She yelps as her head is yanked backwards, but she doesn't fight. She doesn't try to run, and those eyes stay glued on me.

"I should punish you for running away," I growl out, looking from her eyes to her lips, wanting to nibble on them, run my tongue along them, suck them into my mouth.

She darts her tongue out to lick that perfectly plump lip, and I hold back the groan that wants to escape me.

"Do it," she says, jutting out her chin.

Oh, this girl...

# CHAPTER TWENTY

## BEXLEY

I always knew there were bad parts of me. Dark pieces that I ignored because I know normal people wouldn't understand. Those parts are the parts I got from my father. I mean, how could I not? It's only fair I get pieces from him too. I'm just glad what I got from my mother was stronger and I'm able to hide the other stuff. I saw how my father lived his life, and I didn't want that for myself, so I pushed down every part of me that was a reminder of him.

As I stand here, in the bowels of this castle, in a dungeon with prisoners that I'm sure did nothing to belong here, I'm now certain it's the dark parts of me that calls to Kaine.

Nothing else makes sense.

No part of me that I've ever allowed out before would be okay with this or anything else going on around me. Yet, for some reason, standing here with him so close to me, I can't help but be sucked in by his presence. His overwhelming energy that is both terrifying and thrilling at the same time.

I should be scared. I know that.

Yet, I can't.

And that's why I say it.

"Do it."

He moves closer without missing a beat. His warm, firm body presses against me, and his heartbeat is pounding away behind his chest... or maybe that's mine.

Kaine's jaw ticks and he looks as if he's going to say something but decides against it.

Waves of energy are vibrating off him and I want it, need it. Everything about this makes me just want more of him.

"Fuck it," he growls just before his hand tightens in my hair.

He moves us so quickly I almost fall again, but he holds me upright until my back is pressed up against the dirty stone wall. His hand on my head softens the blow as I hit the wall hard, but my back scrapes against it, my shirt snagging on a jagged piece. He isn't nice about any of this, pressing his body against mine so harshly that I know I'll have scrapes and bruises tomorrow.

Yet I can't find it in me to care.

I want them.

I want the reminder of this, of letting go, of giving in to whatever part of me I just let out.

I like the fact he isn't taking it easy, isn't treating me like a delicate little flower.

His mouth is on mine, and it's a clash of teeth and tongue but he tastes so delicious that I can't get enough.

He pulls back, raking his teeth along my jaw, nipping as he moves down my neck, his hot tongue leaving a trail of warmth. He tears my shirt off my shoulder, the rip of fabric almost drowning out my pounding heart. His mouth latches onto my skin, that perfect spot where my neck and shoulder meet and he's sucking.

Sucking so good.

So hard, so violently that I know there will be a mark for weeks.

I moan. My nails digging into him wherever I can reach—back, sides, arms—hopefully causing blood, and he doesn't even flinch, doesn't even seem to care. It's as if he's so caught up in me that he can't feel the pain.

I like that too. Like that he's lost in me.

He spins me around, pressing my front to the wall. The stone is cool on my exposed skin, and my cheek scrapes against the rough surface. He pushes against my back with his forearm, holding me in place while rubbing his erection against my lower back.

He wants to be inside of me, and I wonder if it's as much as I need him to be.

I push my ass out, grinding against him without shame, not giving a shit what he thinks about it. If his quiet chuckle is any indication, then I think he likes it too, so I keep going.

"You play with fire, you get burned," he whispers in my ear. "That's how it works." He nibbles on the shell of my ear and my head falls back the slightest, a soft moan leaving my parted lips. The pressure of his body only gets heavier as I fight for breath. "You will not move."

He eases off of me and I suck in a breath, allowing my lungs the air they need to breathe. But it's all I do. I don't step back, don't move my hands to brush away the hair from my face, and I certainly don't rub at myself like I want to. My pussy is aching to be touched, but I don't do it.

I listen.

Something I can do well, but usually choose not to because I don't like being told what to do.

But with him, everything is different.

Footsteps tell me he's moving away but he hasn't gone far. There is a small squeaking sound, then a little bit of shuffling before he returns.

He snaps his fingers once. I have no idea what it means but the anticipation of finding out has me clenching my thighs.

He's behind me again before I know it. I expect him to press his body against me, use his mouth more, maybe even spin me around, or have me get on all fours, but he doesn't.

His hands go to my pants and he shoves them down to my knees, then uses his boot to get them down to my ankles.

I gasp at the surprise of it. The sudden chilled air on my skin has goosebumps covering every inch of my exposed skin.

The memory of people in the cells not too far from us hits me and a thrill shoots through me.

They were in their beds, he made sure of it, so I don't think they can see. Clearly, they're terrified of him, and I wonder what he's done to make it that way.

The cool air is on my calves, thighs, and ass for long moments. My skin prickles with awareness as I wait for whatever it is he has in store.

He said punishment and punishment is what I expect. I don't want him to go easy on me, though I've never been punished before so I don't even—

"Ah!" I shriek when a sharp sting spreads across my right ass cheek. My fingers scrape at the wall beside me, and I press my head against the harsh stone, but I don't move otherwise.

"One," he counts in a firm but husky voice.

I have no idea what he will be counting to. Hell, he could go to a hundred for all I know. I don't find myself upset though, not even with my ass stinging something fierce. Instead, I'm craving more.

So much fucking more.

And more is what I get.

Another sharp sting, only to the other side.

"Two," he says, and I hear the humor in his voice. He likes this, and that only makes it so much hotter.

I want to ask what he's counting to and for what, but I keep my mouth shut, squeezing my eyes closed. They're watering and tears want to spill. It hurts, hurts so fucking good.

I flinch when something soft brushes over my stinging ass—his fingers. He dances them along my skin, barely touching me at all, but it's there. Traveling along like a whisper, soothing the ache he caused.

Over my ass, down the outside of my thigh, all the way down my leg until he's at my ankle.

He lifts it, pulling off my shoe and removing my pants. Then he repeats it for the other side before I lose his touch entirely.

"You listen so well." His words startle me even though they're whisper-soft. "Can I trust you to keep that up or will I need the shackles?"

I give a quick jerk of my head.

"Words, Bexley. I want your words." His fingers trail along my lower back and the goosebumps are back.

"I won't move," I say softly. "But..." I stop myself, figuring it's probably best not to question him.

"But what?" he asks in a tone that makes me think he actually cares about what I have to say.

"The... the prisoners. What if they see?"

He chuckles again, deep and raspy, fingers trailing up my back, raking into my hair from underneath before he grabs and turns my head towards the other cells, pressing his cheek to mine.

"Darling, they're already watching."

And he's right. Five sets of dark eyes stare on and all I can do is smile.

# CHAPTER TWENTY-ONE

## BEXLEY

Standing at the front of their cells, five men stare at us. At me without pants, getting spanked.

It's... confusing as fuck, is what it is.

I shouldn't be liking this, shouldn't enjoy being watched.

So why do I?

Why does it turn me on knowing they're watching this happen to me?

Why does it make me soaked thinking of them watching while he teases me, fucks me?

"You see," Kaine begins, his voice low and husky, "I've trained them well."

I'm entirely aware of what is going on around me, of this entire situation. I'm not afraid anymore. My body wants this, all of it. My brain, the logical one, knows it's dangerous. So I go back and forth with being blindsided by overwhelming panic that is then quickly washed out by the need for him to dominate me.

"Why?" The word barely comes out above a whisper, my bottom lip trembling. He ignored me the last time I tried to get this answer from him, and I'm not sure he'll give me one this time either.

He huffs out a laugh. "Because I can."

He steps back, then kicks my legs apart and puts a knee between my thighs. The bottom of my foot scrapes along the rough floor and I hold back the cry of pain. Surely I lost some skin.

I'm pulling in air but I still feel as if I can't breathe. I run my tongue along my bottom lip, tasting nothing but salt and the dirt from the wall that my face is still pressed against. My fingers tremble, needing something to grab onto but there is nothing other than the stone wall. My body is on sensory overload and even though there are five people standing not too far from me, I don't really see them. I'm too focused on Kaine behind me to pay attention to anyone else, but I want to grin when I think of what's going through their minds.

Do they like watching? Are they afraid?

Does he do this to them too? Or to others and make them watch?

"Do—"

He cuts off the rest of my words with a hand around my mouth.

"No, no. We are done talking. Understand?" I move my eyes to the side, unable to move my head but I can't see him, I can only feel him against me, hear his voice in my ear. So I nod.

"Good girl," he coos. "You're going to want to listen real well from this point on so you don't get hurt."

A chill rolls up my spine and my eyes widen.

So I don't get hurt? What does that mean?

Will he actually hurt me? Leave me here in those cages with the others?

He can't do that. He wouldn't.

What would those men in the cells do to me? Nothing I want, I know that much.

Kaine removes his hand before dragging it across my shoulder, down my side, and rests it on my hip.

Something cold runs up the inside of my left thigh, and I flinch at the surprise of it. It isn't very big, but it certainly isn't a sex toy. It doesn't feel round, soft, or even made of plastic. It's cold, hard, and flat.

Goosebumps erupt over my skin again, and I'm reminded of the spankings on my ass as they irritate the welts that will surely still be there tomorrow.

Whatever he's running across my skin, continues slowly up the inside of my thigh, but stops just before my apex. I want to cry out in frustration. I just want some relief; want him to touch me and make me come. Just once for now to take the edge off, because I know it won't be the only one.

"I hope you're wet," he says, "or else this is going to hurt."

All of the air leaves my lungs as I try to figure out what the fuck he has in his hand. What is he going to put inside of me? Fear shoots through me, but I push it away. He wouldn't do anything to really hurt me. I don't know why I believe that, but I do. He doesn't want to cause me pain, he wants something else from me.

My submission? To dominate me? To have me at his every will and demand?

I have nothing to worry about, though, because I'm dripping. Sopping wet. It's running down my thighs and it wouldn't matter what he has in his hands—it'll go in with ease. At this point, I don't even care what it is, I just want to come.

A cool, hard object slides up and then back down between my ass cheeks before settling right over my pussy hole. He moves it back and forth a few times, but not far enough to reach my clit. Not enough to give me what I need. I swear, if he just touched me, I'd shatter into a million pieces. Be putty in his fucking hands.

He pushes the mystery item inside of me and I stick my ass out, making it easier for him to get it in. Whatever it is, it feels good in there.

It's hard and rectangular but with soft edges.

Maybe it's some sort of tool he uses to torture the prisoners with? I don't have experience with that sort of thing, so who knows.

Toys and restraints are not my forte. I don't know a damn thing about any of it—other than I'm going to need to learn some stuff. Up until lately, my sex life has been pretty straightforward. I wouldn't say vanilla because I've done anal, have used some toys, and one guy even choked me a little bit. This is quite a few levels up from that.

My body is trembling, sweat gathering on my brow, and it's getting hotter in here by the second.

He pulls the object out of me before sliding it all the way back in.

He groans as he fucks me with whatever he has, and he seems to be liking it. I rock against him, and I'm so fucking turned on, so swollen that just the littlest movement is giving me the friction I need.

My hands slide up the wall, pressing my palms into the rough surface above my head as I clench around his toy, the orgasm blinding me, sending wave after wave of pleasure through me so fiercely I swear I black out for a second. It's quick but a fucking force to be reckoned with. And just as I suspected, I want more. So much more.

He pulls the thing out of me, chuckling as he grasps my hip, spinning me to face him.

I'm panting, trying to catch my breath, as I rest my back against the wall, hands tense by my side.

I peel my eyes open and meet Kaine's bright blue ones. They're wild and heated. His jaw is clenched tight, and I can tell he's fighting with something in his head. Trying to hold on to his control maybe?

He lifts his hand to his mouth, and with the slightest smirk, he runs his tongue along the butt of a knife.

The fucking "toy" I just came all over.

Before I have a second to react, a second to even process what the hell just happened, he's moving closer.

He drags the dull side of the blade across my collarbone and my eyes fall shut, fear gripping every inch of me now.

He really could kill me. Shove that knife right through my throat, into my heart, a lung, anything.

And he just might do that.

With his free hand, he grips the rest of my shirt and with one swift slice, cuts it down the middle with ease. Next, he slides the knife sideways under my bra before flipping it and cutting it right between my breasts. It snaps open and my breasts fall free, heavy and full, nipples hardened peaks.

I'm afraid to meet his eyes but take the chance and look up anyway. His gaze isn't on me like I thought it would be. He's following the trail of the knife that is moving closer and closer to my nipple.

Kaine runs the sharp end side to side, causing me to gasp, and my nipple hardens even further. So much so that it aches.

"Is this too much for you?" he asks, trailing the sharp end of the knife down the center of my chest before sliding it over my left breast, skimming the blade right across my nipple.

He flicks his gaze up at me and I'm met with the most stunning blue eyes I've ever seen. They're so blue they're almost glowing. Practically neon in color.

I shake my head just the slightest and he smirks, continuing to move the knife and pausing at the hollow of my throat. He glances down at the knife for a second before straightening it. The tip digs into my skin and I can't fucking breathe. I feel like I'm going to throw up. My head is dizzy and foggy. This is it for me. He could end my life right now, push this blade into my throat and I'd be dead.

Forever.

There is no coming back from death. It's the end. The final chapter.

So why don't I do anything about it? Why don't I fight him off? Why don't I *try*?

Because I'm enjoying having zero ounce of control. I am loving how Kaine takes charge and is pushing every limit, every boundary, I thought I had.

"How about now?" he asks slowly, those bright blues eyes glancing back up at me, testing me, challenging me, all the while my pussy is still dripping, craving more of him.

"No."

# CHAPTER TWENTY-TWO

## KAINE

This darling girl is brave. More so than I thought she would be. I will be full for weeks with the amount of fear rolling off her. I want more. Need more. And I don't think I'll ever get enough.

The threats gave me the sweetest taste.

The spankings added just a bit more.

Fucking her with a random object did just about nothing, which is a little surprising.

She also didn't seem to care when she realized people were watching us. In fact, I think she likes it.

But the amount of fear that rolled off her when she saw this knife, was enough to bring me to my knees. The fear, that even now with this knife at her throat, threatening her life, is slowly dissipating.

I'm going to have to do more. Push the limits. Give her my best.

Go full fucking crazy with this girl because I can't get enough, and she just keeps pushing back.

There is something about it, about her fear that I crave.

Like that stupid fruit Maxen doesn't fuck around with because he can't control himself. That's how I feel with her. Like I can't control myself and I certainly don't want to.

I want more and I'm going to get it.

She tells me this isn't too much for her and I believe it.

I'd know if she were lying because I'd get that fear. Wrath demons are like human lie detectors. Most humans give off just a bit of fear when they're lying, afraid they're going to be caught. It's how I always know when I'm being lied to. Unfortunately, it doesn't work on demons the same way because they couldn't care less if someone finds out they're lying.

Still, as the seconds tick by, her sweet fear fills the air less and less.

So I do the only rational thing, of course.

I push the knife forward.

She gasps as it pierces her skin, her nails gripping into the stone wall behind her. They're going to be a mess after this, and I'll have to find her something to fix them. I don't think she'll want to deal with ragged, broken nails.

Her eyes squeeze shut, and her heart is pounding so hard I'm sure it'll explode. But she doesn't move otherwise. Doesn't tell me to stop and doesn't try to stop me.

I'm hit with a wave of fear and suck it all in like it's the best tasting dessert I've ever had and revel in it for just a moment.

It's delicious, but it's just not enough.

Blood beads at the tip of the knife; the smallest amount that then drips down her chest, trailing down between her full and supple breasts. Without removing the knife, I lean down and drag my tongue between her tits, catching the end of the trail and licking it up to the blade. When I pull back, I meet her gaze and run my bloody tongue over my bloody lip, smearing the metallic taste all over. Her eyes widen, and her breath hitches, and I know I need to go a step further.

So I fucking do.

Because I need more.

I pull the knife away and she sucks in a sharp breath but still, she stays. She doesn't run, doesn't try to get away. She stands here with her whole body on display for all the prisoners to see because they won't move until I tell them to.

They know better.

They'll sit there and watch and long for pussy. They'll only hope they can get someone a quarter as beautiful as Bexley. They never will though. I'd bet my life on it.

With my free hand, I slide it between her legs, running my middle finger over her clit and she relaxes into the wall as her thighs start to tremble.

I lean forward again and lick up the rest of the blood along her chest, sucking at the tiny wound once I reach it. Groaning in satisfaction over the sweetness of her blood mixed in with her fear, I allow my eyes to fall shut for just a moment. This is what I fucking live for.

She grinds against my hand, her hips moving faster and faster, chasing another orgasm that'll surely happen any second now.

*This can't be real...* it's all I keep thinking. *How can this girl be real?*

I have a moment of weakness where I open my mouth to ask but shut it in just enough time.

I can't get all emotional right now. I haven't even come yet.

And I will, fucking trust me, I will.

Just as I'm sure she's close, I pull away and she growls, eyes darting open and full of anger, directed right at me. I smirk and raise a brow in challenge, but she says nothing, only bites down on the inside of her cheek.

I bring my hand back to her center, rubbing over her swollen clit, and again, just as she gets close, I pull away. Only this time, she catches me around the wrist and my eyes dart to where she's holding me. I could easily pull away from her, but I want to see what she's up to. She urges my hand back to her needy little clit, but I don't allow her, which is why she goes for the knife in my other hand instead.

Shamefully, I admit she gets it from me too. I let my guard down. Forgot all about it, if I'm being honest. I'm too caught up in her beauty, her bravery, the fucking whimpers that leave her lips as she gets close...

Too caught up in her showing me what the fuck she wants.

She doesn't know I have healing powers because she doesn't know I'm a demon. Not that I think she'd stab me, but she'll have a hell of time processing that when I don't die.

I am met with a slight annoyance at her disobeying me. I told her not to move and she did.

So I reach for the knife, but she twists and I grab it around the blade.

We both freeze. Her eyes slide up to meet mine slowly, they're wide and terrified.

She knows she fucked up now.

I grip it tighter, the blade cutting through my skin. She flinches, her fingers trembling and I think she's going to drop it.

Don't fucking drop it, I think. Don't do it.

We stand there for a long moment, just staring into each other's eyes, a silent battle to see who will give up first. I hold back the smile when I realize she isn't going to.

Good.

I didn't want her to.

"Do it," I challenge.

I know what she's thinking, what she wants to do. Exactly what instinct tells you to do.

She doesn't hesitate after hearing my words. She grits her teeth, and pulls the knife away, slicing open my hand.

It burns in the best way possible.

My healing isn't automatic, and right now, I want to bleed.

I bring my sliced hand around her throat and squeeze, cutting off her air supply. The blood trickles down her chest, pooling between her breasts and the knife clatters to the floor. Her mouth is open, fear back in those pretty green eyes.

I drag my tongue along her jaw before stopping right over her lips.

"You are..." I don't finish my sentence, only pull in a deep breath, inhaling her scent before I slide my hand down her chest, painting it with my blood.

Her breasts, her stomach, every part of her body have traces of me; the bright red stains of my blood.

The fear that hits is overwhelming this time. I place my good hand on the wall by her head just to hold myself upright, but it probably looks to her like I'm getting ready to fuck her, not that I'm trying to steady myself because she's too fucking much. No one has ever been too much before, and I have a feeling Bexley will be the only one.

I don't miss how she spreads her legs just the slightest as my hand moves back between them, effectively mixing my blood with her delicious arousal, spreading it all over her pussy, her thighs, and when I shove three fingers inside of her, I know it's there too.

I am there. I am fucking everywhere as I paint her with my blood. Marking her all over with parts of me no one else has ever had.

Then I drop to my knees, dig my fingers into her thighs, and lick her clean until she's coming, gushing all over my face with an orgasm that hits so hard the only thing keeping her on her feet is me.

And when she's done, when her body is limp, eyes half-lidded, heart pounding, I spin her around and fuck her from behind until I reach my own orgasm.

I lay my head on her back when I'm done to catch my breath.

The fucking was quick. I couldn't hold back and I didn't want to. This wasn't just about me fucking to come, this was about what she does to me, what she makes me do, and how much I can control myself. This was a test to see how far things can go, and I now know they can go all the way.

I pick up Bexley wedding style, her body almost lifeless in my arms, but I know she's only exhausted and possibly sleeping. As I walk past the other cells, I glance at the prisoners who are still standing in place, staring, watching as we go.

I don't miss the tents in their pants either.

Fucking slobs.

"You've met your purpose. You'll all be free to go home tomorrow morning," I call to them as I enter the hallway, fully prepared to carry her all the way to my room, wash her, and put her to bed.

Then I need to find Maxen and figure out what the fuck we're going to do to appease that piece of shit angel.

Because if I thought I wasn't letting her go before, no way in fuck am I doing it now.

# CHAPTER TWENTY-THREE

## KAINE

With Bexley fresh out of the shower—which she was pretty alert for—and sleeping soundly in my bed, I head out in search of Maxen and easily find him in the lounge room around the corner.

"The fuck?" he calls out as I walk in.

I respond with a shrug, not having the words to explain what the fuck I've been doing for so long.

Being reborn?

That's way too fucking deep, but it's exactly what it feels like. I feel like a whole new person. Like that sex unlocked a whole new me. No, it wasn't just the sex. It was her. Bexley.

It makes no fucking sense, so I haven't bothered trying to make sense of it. I just have to go with it. And if I can't make sense of it, no way in hell am I going to explain it to him.

The one who almost never takes anything seriously.

"Well?" he says when I still haven't said a word.

"She's fine. In my bed asleep." He narrows his eyes at me as I tuck my hands inside my front jean pockets.

"And?"

"And what?" I ask.

He blows out a breath. "Kaine, whatever the fuck you're thinking, the answer is no. She needs to go back." He glances at his phone. "August probably ratted us out by now."

"About that..."

He lifts his head and stares blankly at me, slowly blinking.

"I'm going to go have a chat with him and I need you to keep an eye on her."

"Kaine—" I know he's going to try to reason with me, but I cut him off. I'm too far gone to see reason so it's pointless, I can admit that and I don't want to waste his or my time.

"Doesn't matter, Maxen, don't waste your breath. I've made up my mind."

"You're going to get us both thrown into the Pit," he argues.

"I'm not," I say sternly. No way in fuck will I allow that to happen. I won't let another day be wasted in that fucking place. "I would never let that happen to you."

He squeezes the bridge of his nose and gets to his feet, dropping his hands to his side. When he reaches me, he grabs onto my shoulders, staring directly into my eyes.

"I seriously hope you know what the fuck you're doing."

And with a shake of his head, he walks away.

"Don't wake her up!" I call over my shoulder, a grin forming on my lips. "She's fucking exhausted," I say under my breath.

Trips topside used to be fun. I used to love everything about coming up here. Now, they're just a way to waste time and make the days go by quicker. There is literally nothing for Maxen and me to do in Hell that's worth our time. Thanks to my father, I don't have to work or do any bullshit while I'm down there. I strictly get to live my days fucking around.

Sort of. I mean, those days are dwindling away. I am supposed to take the throne when he dies. He's been trying to prepare me for it and is getting increasingly annoyed with the fact that I keep brushing it off.

Hell runs similarly to how it does up here.

There are demons at different levels, and not everyone who goes to Hell after death becomes a demon. Some are literally little hellions who run around without a purpose. Like the prisoners I keep in my dungeons. The ones no one will ever miss.

People still need to work to make a living. People who fuck up and don't do what they're told get sent to the Pit as punishment. A place you really don't want to go. A place made of literal nightmares and torture of the worst kind, specific to just you. Day in and day out you relive the most terrible things you can imagine. And not just visions. No, you actually live them out.

Terrified of being eaten alive by rats? Well, you better enjoy the next six hundred years of your life while that happens over and over and over again. Little teeth gnawing through your skin, lapping at your blood, chomping on your veins.

Scared of boats? Welcome aboard and live through it sinking in the middle of the ocean during a storm with hundred-foot waves, taking you down with it to drown. Over and over and over...

It's fucking Hell. Worse than the actual Hell, and we all, even the assholes, do everything we can to avoid it, yet it still stays quite busy.

Thanks to my constant need to disobey my father and get away with whatever I can because I can, I know the streets of New York like the back of my hand. The hustle and bustle about it has always been interesting to me. There are so many shitheads up here it's quite entertaining if I'm honest. Plus the bars are fun. I also know exactly where that sad ass angel and all his butt buddies hang out on a daily basis.

They, unlike us, spend a lot of time here, but as protectors.

We have demons who roam the earth, doing, you know... demon things; possessing people, murdering, keeping the balance. Which is why the angels are allowed to live amongst the humans to "protect" them. Though, if we're being honest, they do a pretty shit job of it most of the time, considering how high the crime rate is and the fact that there are still serial killers and cannibals out here getting away with it. But I digress.

I make my way down Canal Street and then turn towards Columbus Park once I reach the right street.

The bar they hang out at is a hole in the wall, but apparently, they make the best dumplings. Cause a bunch of guys hanging out together and eating dumplings is where the party is at, for sure. Definitely how I want to spend my Friday night.

I still have no idea what August was doing by the café that night. I've never run into him in that area of town before. I usually don't see any of the angels hanging around those bars at night because the most you see are college kids fighting. None of the big time crime that takes place deeper in the city.

I turn into the alleyway and head down the steps, pushing through the door that has a little bell above it that dings to let everyone know someone is coming in, though it can barely be heard over the chatter of patrons and the frying foods—which smells amazing and if this were under different circumstances I would stay to eat, but it isn't. I have one task and that's it. Just one—getting back to Bexley.

I spot August the moment I walk in. Sitting straight in his seat with his perfect hair and snobby fucking outfit. No one wears sweater-vests and khakis anymore... doesn't he know this?

Wasting no time, I head towards him. I don't want to be up here any longer than I have to. I'd rather be back home with Bexley.

My father sent word that he would be returning today and that is a potential issue.

I can't hide a human in his castle forever. We don't speak often but he's bound to find out between his roaming, lack of knocking, and hearing the servants talk, because even if they won't purposely rat me out, they need gossip like they need air to breathe. Oh, and there's also Marionette who has full control over the Wandering Tablet and could rat me out at any moment to save her own ass.

He spots me before I reach the table, but he doesn't get up, just allows me to walk towards him and his group of angel friends. There are six of them total and they all look like the biggest douches. Like the golden boys who grow up to play golf on the weekends and cheat on their wives with the fucking secretary, then when the wife finds out, he just buys her a new car and sends her on a vacation to Cabo to shut her up. Then all is good in home life again.

Demons may be assholes but when we link with someone, it's for life. Like Maxen and me. More than friends, less than mates. It's too complicated to talk about, so we just let it be. I don't think "linking" is an official term or anything, just what I refer to it as.

But that's how demons are when it comes to love and feelings. It isn't often we feel something close to love, because I'm not sure that's really what it is or if we are even capable of that, but there is definitely a sentimental attachment that is formed and it's rare for a demon to break any bond like that. No matter the reasoning behind it.

"Gentlemen," I greet with a smile as I reach the table.

"What a lovely surprise," Dawson says with a gleam in his eyes. His smile is as fake as his tan.

"I bet it is." I smirk and glance at August, not wanting to chitchat with any of these morons. "We have things to discuss," I say to him before looking back at the others. "Privately."

"As you wish," August says with no amount of emotion. "Excuse me, won't you?" he then says to the other guys around the table who all give their versions of approval with head nods and hand gestures. August gets up and I turn to head outside so we can talk without being interrupted. Sure, the streets are full of people, but no one is going to stop and listen to what two random guys are talking about in an alleyway.

I walk up the steps and turn down the alley, leaning up against the building as I wait for August to catch up. I pull out a cigarette and light it.

"Disgusting habit," he says as he reaches me, though his words hold no disdain, he's merely stating an opinion. August shoves his hands into his front pockets, adding to his laid back demeanor.

"Demon," I respond as way of explanation.

"What do you want?" he asks, and I cock my head to the side in confusion.

"Did you not threaten my balls if I didn't return the girl today?"

"First of all, I said no such thing. Second of all, there is nothing I can do about the girl."

I narrow my eyes and take a drag from my cigarette before taking a step closer and releasing the smoke from my lungs. "Did you report me?" I ask in a low tone.

He looks me over for a moment before a smile grows on his lips.

"You don't know who she is."

I rear back at that.

"Excuse me?"

He barks out a laugh. "You know, I've never liked you or your kind, but I always assumed you were smart."

"What are you talking about?" I ask, or demand, I guess.

He considers me for a moment, eyes searching my face. "I'd love to tell you but watching this unfold is going to be so much more fun."

"Isn't it written in your fucking DNA to be nice or something?"

"You know as well as I do that angels aren't required to do anything other than our duty, which does not include being kind to anyone, only to protect humans from the likes of you."

I grunt, taking another drag.

What in the world would make him not be able to do anything about taking Bexley from me? And why doesn't he want to tell me? What could be so fun about watching this?

I could make him tell me, threaten him, stab him, whatever it takes, but I don't want to give him the satisfaction... I also don't want to get into trouble.

"Fine." I toss my butt to the ground and crush it with my shoe. "But tell me where the friend is so I can relay a message."

He doesn't give it up right away, being the royal pain in my ass that he is, but eventually, he rattles off the address and we part ways. Luckily for him, he still has all of his limbs and organs intact.

Taking the subway back to Washington Heights, I get off as close to her street as possible and only have to walk four blocks to find it.

It's a brownstone that resembles all the others on the street and has barred windows and doors that probably have seven damn locks, which are certainly needed in a building like this that rents to mostly college students.

Jogging up the steps, I find the buzzer I need and ring it.

"Who is it?" she calls happily, as if she enjoys people showing up at random.

"Kaine," I respond.

"Who?" she asks.

I groan. "The guy from the café."

It's silent for a moment before she says, "The good one or the asshole who kidnapped Bexley?"

"Are you fucking for real right now?" I mumble to myself, shaking my head. "I just wanted to let you know she's fine and has decided to stay with me for a few days."

"That's exactly what a serial killer would say! How do I know you aren't lying? Why hasn't she called me?"

I look around me, not able to believe I am standing here having a conversation with a girl through an intercom about kidnapping and serial killers. Though this is New York, so I shouldn't be worried. Two kids walk by, both with headphones and backpacks on, probably on their way to class.

"I don't live around here, and I don't have good service."

I wait and don't get an answer. At least a minute goes by, maybe two, and still nothing. I consider leaving. I did my due diligence, more than I even needed to, honestly. Bexley didn't ask me to come here, didn't even know I'd be in the area. I just thought it would be a nice thing to do.

If this girl calls the cops when I'm doing something selfless for the first time in my life, so help—

The front door opens up and there she is.

The best friend.

I take a step back, half expecting her to pull a gun or throw a punch. She does neither. Just tosses a backpack over her shoulder and looks up at me. "Prove it."

"Excuse me?" I step back, still unsure what she's going to do. This one seems feistier than Bexley, which is hard to believe but I'm trusting my gut on this one.

"Take me with you. I want to see her."

"No," I say, standing firmly in place. There is no way I'm risking getting caught over taking this human to Hell. She isn't anything to me. Though, it would make Bexley happy...

"You will take me with you or—"

"Or what?" I ask as I take a step closer, looking down at her. She looks up and blinks, smiling sarcastically. Before I know what's happening, she's lifting her knee, catching me right in the balls.

"Fuck," I groan, reaching for them and falling into the wall. My stomach aches and I feel like I'm going to be sick. My eyes water and I bite my tongue to stop myself from fucking killing this girl right on the spot.

"Or else next time, I'll fucking chop them off," she whispers in my ear, then pats me on the back and trots down the stairs.

What the fuck did I get myself into?

# CHAPTER TWENTY-FOUR

## BEXLEY

I wake up groggy and sore—a normal occurrence nowadays. My skin is soft, and my hair is damp from the shower, so I know I mustn't have been sleeping too long.

The sun is shining in through the window when I roll over and realize I'm in bed alone. It looks much bigger when it's just me in it, and I can't decide if I like that or not. I push myself up, running a hand down my face as I look around. The light is on in the bathroom, and I wonder if that's where Kaine is.

I find out a moment later when the light goes off and out walks Maxen in a pair of jeans and no shirt. Quickly averting my eyes, I focus on the ground instead.

"You're awake." He seems surprised.

"And you're not blind," I respond, leaning against the headboard.

"I've always had boners for smart mouths," he retorts with a smirk.

"Who in their right mind still uses that word?" I scoff. *Boner?* That's something a thirteen-year-old would say.

He looks slightly offended but just laughs it off.

"Where is Kaine?" I ask, looking around the room as if that will make him appear.

"Had some running around to do. He asked me to watch you."

My mouth drops open. "Watch me? Like I'm a fucking toddler?"

He takes a seat on the bed, right by my feet, and turns his body to face me. I ignore his perfect abs and sculpted chest.

"Well, I do recall you asking to use the bathroom and then just disappearing." He sounds annoyed and it makes me happy because that's exactly how he makes me feel—annoyed.

"I was... exploring."

"Okay, Dora. Sure, let's go with that." He rolls his eyes.

"How old are you?" I ask as a way of an insult and not because I really want to know.

"None of your business," he snaps back.

"Well, it's kind of creepy when a man has a body like that, but a mind like a fucking five-year-old. Boner and Dora? Are you serious?" I cross my arms over my chest.

He just shakes his head.

"What's wrong, sweetheart? Did Kaine not live up to your sexual fantasies? Is that why you're grumpy?" He trails his fingers along my leg, and even though the blanket is between us, my skin still pricks with electricity. "Need me to take care of it?"

I pull away from him. "Fuck you." I meet his gaze as I say it, hoping it'll drive the point home.

He huffs out a laugh. "You wish."

"Actually, I already did, and it wasn't that great." I jut out my chin in challenge.

He gets to his feet and says, "Well, I hope the memory is burned into your brain because it won't be happening again." He turns to leave.

"Good!" I shout, grabbing a pillow and whipping it at him. It hits him in the back of the head and falls to the floor with a plop.

He turns around, eyebrows furrowed. "Why do you have to keep throwing shit at me?" he growls out.

"Because you're infuriating!"

"I'm infur—I'm sorry, I'm the infuriating one?" He places his forefinger on his chest, ducking his head in confusion. He walks to the side of the bed after a moment of me not answering him. "Do you not listen to yourself speak?"

I do the only thing I can think of next.

I stick my tongue out at him.

He grins, crossing his arms over his chest. "Who's the child now?"

"Figured I was doing you a favor by speaking to you on your own level."

"That smart mouth is going to get you into trouble."

I smirk. "Good. Maybe Kaine will punish me again then."

"Ha!" He leans forward, placing both palms flat on the bed beside my thighs. He stops only an inch from my face. "Baby, you don't know what punishment is until you've gotten it from me."

My eyes dart from his brilliant silver eyes to his mouth. Those beautiful pouty lips that are just begging to be nibbled on. I think of doing it. I'm just about to lean in and take his plump bottom lip between my teeth, but I don't get the chance because he pulls away and stands up straight.

"Like I said though, you won't be getting any more of this."

I open my mouth to say something smart back, but the thought is lost when someone starts shouting down the hall and Maxen goes stock-still beside me.

"Shit," he mumbles under his breath, looking to me with a wrinkled brow. "You need to get up. Now."

He grabs me by the arm and yanks me out of bed, practically pulling my arm from its socket. I yelp in pain, my body still sore from all the sex I've had over the last twenty-four hours. Maxen drags me to the closet, shoves me in, threatens my life if I make a sound, and then shuts the door softly.

The stubborn part of me wants to tell him to fuck off, but the part of me that is sometimes smart, well, it tells me to shut the fuck up. So I do. I sit there and pout by myself.

"Where is that infernal son of mine?"

I don't recognize the voice, but I listen anyway, knowing it must be Kaine's dad. Like I said, I've always been a nosy bitch.

It's pitch-black in here, and I'm pretty sure this is how you know someone is rich. Most houses have those little non-perfect things about them that you learn to love. The little inconsistencies that just make the house your home. The notch in the wood, the fact the banister on the stairs isn't straight, or the warped boards on the floors that you know to avoid because they squeak when you step on them. All the little things I remember about my Nana's house.

But here, everything is so pristine, so perfect, not a thing out of place. The closet door lines up so well that not even a stream of light can make it inside. I didn't even know that was possible. I've never in my life seen such a straight door before.

"I'm not sure," Maxen says, his voice pulling me from my ridiculous thoughts.

"Lies," the other man growls. "I don't even know why I ask, you won't rat him out. Surely he's up to something if you aren't together."

"I have no idea what you're talking about," Maxen responds. His words scream sarcasm, but his tone is pretty serious. Is that fear or respect?

The other man mumbles something under his breath but I'm not sure what it is.

"How was your trip?" Maxen asks, trying to sound light-hearted but really he just sounds like a kiss ass.

"Lousy. Those fucking lazy pricks should be forced to move their asses once in a while. How can it be that every quarterly meeting is there? The farthest away from here, of course."

"I agree. It's only fair."

"When Kaine returns, tell him to find me immediately. We have things to discuss."

"Will do, sir. Welcome home!"

After a long moment, Maxen pulls the doors open and drags me out by the arm.

"What's wrong? Not allowed to have girls over? Didn't want to get punished and lose TV time? Worried you'll miss Barney?"

"I just want you to know that if you were a man, I'd sock you."

"Good to know you're at least chivalrous." I roll my eyes and yank out of his grip to head into the bathroom, needing to pee. "So, Daddy-o can't know I'm here?" I call to him as I sit on the toilet.

Maxen stands in the doorway, leaning against the frame, arms crossed. I try not to ogle their perfection, but it's hard...

"Correct."

"Why not?"

Maxen studies me for a moment, but not in the creepy *he's trying to watch me pee* kind of way, more like he's trying to figure me out. I'm not shy. People pee. It's part of nature. If he wants to watch, he can.

I wipe, get up, fix my pants, and flush. Then move to wash my hands.

"I'll let Kaine explain that to you."

I pump the soap and purple foam shoots out. I lather it into my hands before rinsing.

"And when shall we be expecting him?"

"Fucking soon, I hope." He sighs and I shut off the water, drying my hands on the towel. I glance over at the shower, getting an idea.

"Is there a bathtub around this place?"

I'm not dirty, but my muscles would love the hell out of soaking in a tub right now.

Maxen raises a brow and a smirk crosses his lips.

"I've got something even better."

# CHAPTER TWENTY-FIVE

## BEXLEY

"Holy shit!" I shriek as we enter into a room that I can only describe as an in-home spa.

There are three massage tables lined against one wall. On the side of them is a row of shelves with all kinds of oils and lotions. To the left, on the far wall, is a glass door that leads to a sauna.

But the best thing about it, the only thing I care about in this room, is the in-ground hot tub. The one that could easily seat ten people.

"How infuriating am I now?" he asks as my mouth drops open. He walks over to turn it on by pressing some buttons on a panel on the wall. It's already filled with water, but it's completely still.

"Hmmm, ten," I say, walking towards the hot tub just as he presses the button to turn on the jets.

"Ten? Isn't that what the scale goes to?"

"Yep. You were at a twelve, so be grateful." I squat down and dip my hand into the water. It isn't freezing, but it's not what you would expect from a hot tub.

He rolls his eyes, still fiddling with the buttons.

"The water is always warm, but I turned the temperature up. It'll take a few minutes to get hot, but it'll do for now." He nods towards the water. "Get in."

He didn't need to tell me, I was going to anyway.

And I have no modesty in this moment because I strip every ounce of clothing off my body. He's already seen me naked, so what does it matter? Hell, he's seen parts of me even I haven't.

I leave the clothes in a messy pile in the cubbies by the tub and waste no time stepping down into the water. It's already starting to get hot, and I groan in satisfaction as I step farther into it. The water just covers my breasts at the deepest part, right in the center. I find a seat and settle in.

He presses another button and the lights in the room go off and I'm shrouded in darkness. I gasp, thinking something is wrong, but a second later the hot tub is lit up in a bright neon pink that isn't too overwhelming. My eyes widen as I look around and find a grinning Maxen watching me. "You're welcome," he says in a cocky tone.

"Thank you," I say cautiously, and he rears his head back, clearly not expecting that. "Don't get used to it," I say.

"I'll keep that in mind." He turns and walks towards the door.

"You're not coming in?" I call after him. He freezes.

"Wasn't planning on it," he calls over his shoulder.

"Oh." I run my hands along the top of the water, leaning back against a jet that is pulsing into my lower back, kneading against a muscle I didn't even know needed it. I look away, bringing my attention to the bubbles in the water.

He sighs and I hear his footsteps getting louder, alerting me that he's decided to come back.

He stops at the side of the tub to my left and I glance up at him. He pulls his shirt off and tosses it to the ground. "I'm telling you right now," he says, pulling down his pants and briefs in one go. The jewelry at the tip of his dick glistens off the pink lights from the tub. "You're not getting any of this."

I scoff. "Don't flatter yourself."

I rest my head back against the soft cushion and close my eyes. The water heats around me, soothing my muscles, and the jets help too.

It's been a few moments, so even though I didn't hear Maxen get into the tub, he must be in by now.

My thoughts are confirmed when I feel something grabbing at my foot. My hands instinctively go beside me, thinking he's going to pull me under, but he only lifts it as he ducks into the water and starts to rub the tired muscles. He works his thumbs deep into the balls of my feet, to the point of it almost hurting but it feels so good. I finally settle back and let him do his thing, even though I have no idea why he's suddenly being nice. He uses just the right amount of pressure and eventually makes his way to my ankle and then my calf. When he reaches my knee, he stops, picking up the other one and repeating the motions.

I'm basically in heaven right now.

The only thing that would make this better would be a bouquet of chocolate covered fruit and a cool, tropical drink.

Heaven, though...

It's something that's been going through my head since that prisoner spoke to me. He said I was in Hell, and Kaine didn't deny it. We all have a different idea of Hell, and I could see why he would think that. He's locked up and for no reason, according to Kaine. This isn't a prison, it's Kaine's home. Putting that fact together with him having a cabinet of torture tools, I can only come to one conclusion.

They're there for his pleasure.

He asked what I thought about what that prisoner told me, asked me if I believed him.

Why would he ask that unless it was a possibility?

Hell, though? Can I be in Hell?

From the get-go I knew I wasn't in New York, I just didn't want to admit it to myself. I know I am somewhere far from home. Everything around here is different from what I'm used to. Outside is weird. Hell, even the servants walking around are weird.

These two guys—Kaine and Maxen—it would make sense that they aren't... human.

They're too perfect.

If they're demons...

I'm no stranger to bad guys. I'm born from one. Maybe my father wasn't an actual demon from Hell, but he was certainly one walking on Earth. He did a lot of bad things to a lot of good people. I'm a dangerous mix of him and my mother. A dark part deep down that I've only just let out, paired with the carefree and ever-forgiving parts of my mother.

The dark things don't bother me, and I allow them to happen, forgiving those who do them.

I know why those prisoners are there. I know it's against their will, and I know it's for nothing other than whatever sick shit Kaine gains from it.

Yet, I can't find it in me to care. Instead, I find myself justifying his actions, and recalling my mother's words.

*Everyone deserves love, Bexley, even the bad people. Because without love, who really are you?*

I can practically smell the inside of Nana's house, as if the memory was from just moments ago and not years.

Did my mother have a bad part of her too?

No. I don't think she did. She was never okay with the things my father did. She never helped him or approved of it, she just looked past it. She chose to forgive him. Each and every time he messed up, she forgave him.

So if Heaven and Hell are real, and I'm sitting in a hot tub in Hell with a demon who is massaging my feet, well, I'll take it for what it is. What else is there to do?

I moan as Maxen reaches a spot in my calf that is more sensitive than the rest of my legs. He spends a few extra moments working out the knot until it feels better and then he moves on. Only this time, he doesn't stop when he reaches my knee, he continues up. Pressing his fingers into the muscles of my left thigh. I spread my legs and the hot water hits my clit, causing me to flinch. It takes a second to get used to that feeling, but soon enough I'm focusing on his hands on me again.

He doesn't move to the other thigh when he reaches my center, instead he brushes his fingers along the outside of my pussy in a teasing way.

"I thought we weren't doing this," I say without opening my eyes.

He leans forward, his hot chest rubbing against my hardened nipples as he finds my ear. Waves of heat flow off of his body from the water warming his skin. "You didn't say I couldn't touch you," he whispers.

And he's right. I didn't.

How I'll be able to endure another orgasm, let alone have one at all, I have no idea, but I am not going to stop him from trying.

"And if I did?" I ask, opening my eyes and finding his only a few inches from mine.

"I wouldn't listen."

His fingers find my clit and he pinches. My mouth falls open in a silent gasp, and I reach out for his waist, fingers digging in to help relieve the pressure I'm feeling between my legs. It doesn't work though.

He lets go, wrapping his hands around my sides and lifting me up, setting me on the edge of the hot tub and spreading my legs. His tongue feels cool on my pussy, thanks to the temperature of the water heating everything else. I lean back on my forearms, allowing my head to fall back as he ravages me, sucking and licking, using his tongue like he was born to eat a girl out.

He knows exactly what the fuck he is doing. And even though jealousy swirls in my gut over the thought, knowing he must have a *lot* of experience, I like that he isn't awful at it. I've wasted too many moments on guys who can't even find my clit, never mind make me orgasm. I thoroughly enjoy reaping the benefits of Maxen being a whore.

His body count is higher than a high school stoner, I'd bet my life on it.

He inserts what has to be at least two fingers inside of me. Parts of me are sore, I swear some are even numb from all of the sex I've been having, but I still feel him in me as he crooks those fingers upwards, rubbing along my inner walls, making me clench and want to come all over his face.

He circles my clit with the tip of his tongue before sucking gently. I cry out, bucking my hips.

The orgasm is right there, right out of reach. My belly swirls with anticipation, and I'm amazed I'm going to come this quickly. He's teasing me, though, and doing it on purpose. His mouth feels so good, and I don't want this to ever end, but hanging on the brink is maddening. It's torturous and I just want to explode.

"Make me come, make me come," I beg, lifting my head to watch him feast on me.

He pulls back those perfect lips glistening with my wetness.

"Say please."

"Please, make me come," I say, not breaking eye contact, and not giving one shit that I'm begging.

He leans in, placing a kiss to my clit and my leg jerks. I swear under my breath, panting.

"Say my name." He moves his fingers in and out of me slowly. Keeping me right on the edge but I'll never come like this.

"Maxen," I breathe out, "please make me come."

He winks at me, and I'm not sure if it's that, or the way he laps at my pussy the moment his tongue touches me once more, but I'm a goner.

My back arches, and the orgasm is so powerful, the pleasure so strong, my entire body tenses up, my vision goes black, and it's possible for a moment my heart stopped beating. I may have just died for a moment, but it was worth it. So fucking worth it.

When I come down from the high of an all-consuming orgasm, I open my eyes and sit up, still trying to catch my breath.

Maxen places his hands on my hips and helps me back into the water, carefully since my body is basically jelly.

"Still a ten?" he asks with a raised eyebrow.

I smile. "Nine and a half."

# CHAPTER TWENTY-SIX

## MAXEN

I can admit I like Bexley. She's not a horrible person and she's certainly good in bed, but I still don't think she's worth all this trouble Kaine is going to get into for hiding a human away in this castle. Not only will his father have a fit, but the entire Wrath community will if word gets out. And when word travels, the rest of Hell will know all about her too. Then his father is going to get even more angry over everyone finding out and Kaine making him look like an idiot.

This entire situation screams the Pit and I'm just not into that. Not one fucking bit. You only eat enough down there to survive. And I don't mean food, I mean the other stuff. The sex I need to survive? It's barely sex at all. They shackle me up and have someone suck me off. Yeah, it feeds me, but just barely, and it's boring as fuck. I don't like getting off on having my dick sucked and I certainly don't like being restrained. I like doing the restraining...

Yeah, I'm not sure anything in this world, or another, is worth that shit, even if I can't stop thinking about Bexley's pussy.

And it has nothing to do with being hungry, because I'll be energized for weeks after the sex we had yesterday. There's something about her that I crave. Her flavor, the sweetness of her pussy on my tongue. The way her thighs clench around my ears when she's coming so hard she's seeing stars.

I've always loved a woman having an orgasm. It feeds my fucking soul, or lack thereof, I suppose, but her? It's more.

And that smart fucking mouth of hers. I think that's my favorite thing. The way she just doesn't care and speaks her mind, no matter the consequences.

Still not worth this mess, though.

She's asleep in Kaine's bed now. Has been for the last hour. After I ate her out so good she saw Jesus, we spent another hour in the hot tub. Neither of us saying a word, just relaxing. It's been a long time since I spent time in a hot tub, and I can't remember why I ever stopped. I feel great, better than I have in a long time and don't want to admit that it may be because of her...

I've been sitting in Kaine's room, basked in darkness in the high-back chair that sits in the corner of his room, spending half my time zoning out and the other half watching her sleep. I keep wondering when that moron is going to make his way back here. It's been long enough. Traveling from here to there takes minutes. The only issue I can imagine him having is not being able to find August, but he and his friends are almost always hanging out at that sissy dumpling place. Though, August could be pissed over whatever excuse Kaine tried to give him. He also could have ratted him out already and Kaine could be detained... I doubt that though. Surely I'd have heard about it by now. His father would have and then he'd no doubt scream at me about it, like he normally does.

He's kind of like a second father to me, but not in that loving way, just in the way he treats me the same way he treats Kaine. Like we're pains in the asses who do nothing right.

Still, it's better than my biological father who is so fucked in the head he tries to have sex with me just for the fuck of it. The man has a problem. A serious problem. He does too many drugs it's turned his brain to mush. He lives to fuck, and the old man can barely control his orgasms anymore, which is a sad, sad life for an incubus. But it's the main reason I spend all of my time here.

Though I do go back and check on him every now and then to make sure his body isn't rotting in our house, being eaten by maggots. Because that would be a bitch to clean up and it's not something I want to spend my time doing.

I can't remember the last time I saw my mother, but she's roaming around Hell somewhere, I'm sure.

It's not uncommon for demon women to pop out baby boys and leave them with their dads. Demons don't tend to have strong bonds with people, especially those who come from Lust. Our need for sex makes it hard to really connect with anyone. Which is another reason why I hang around with Kaine so much. He's one of the only people I care about, let alone can stand to be in a room with for more than five minutes. Don't get me wrong, when I'm hungry, I'm the most charismatic fucker you'll ever meet. I could talk the panties off a parrot.

Not that I'd want to. There's no where to stick my dick and I'm not into bestiality anyway. Tried it once with a Hellhound... and yikes, I learned my lesson real quick.

The things a lonely and hungry incubus will do... I'm just glad I walked away with my dick and balls still attached and the knowledge to never, ever attempt that again, no matter how persuading they can be.

My eyes start to grow heavy, and I rest my head back against the soft cushion of the chair. It's been a long and boring day, so I'm not surprised when I find myself dozing off.

The next thing I know, there's a sharp pain in my shin, pulling me from sleep.

"Ouch!" I hiss, opening my eyes to find a glaring Kaine. "The fuck is your problem?" I keep my voice quiet but don't hide the annoyance I have. I glance towards the bed, thankful to see Bexley undisturbed and still snoring away.

"Why are you sleeping?"

"Hmm, I don't know? Because it's fucking nighttime." I point towards the window. He ignores me and heads into the bathroom, stripping his clothes for a shower.

I stand and stretch, my back popping in a few places and aching in others. I should not have fallen asleep on that lousy chair. I follow after Kaine, stopping to lean against the wall and watch through the frosty glass as he washes his hair.

"Your father is back," I say.

"I know."

"Have you talked to him yet?"

"Nope, and I plan to keep it that way for as long as I can."

I roll my eyes. "The longer you hide from him the more pissed he will be."

"I'm hoping he'll just forget about me altogether."

"You'd only be so lucky."

I walk over to the mirror and check my reflection. I look better than I have in years. Being this full hasn't happened in as long as I can remember. My skin is clear and smooth, not a spot on it nor a patch of dry skin and no oiliness either. My hair is its usually shaggy self, only it's shiny and smooth when I run my fingers through it. My eyes are bright, no bags underneath. I feel good. Amazing, actually. I could get used to this.

The shower turns off and Kaine steps out, grabbing a towel and wrapping it around his waist. I turn towards him with a glare. "Is it really that big of an issue?"

"I am not taking over this kingdom. It's not happening. I want nothing to do with it, he can find someone else." He reaches for another towel and dries his hair, shoulders, and arms before walking over to the sink. I move out of the way and rest against the wall once more, crossing my arms. He pulls out his toothbrush from the cabinet above the sink and starts to brush his teeth.

We really should get one of those for Bexley.

One of the demons cleared for travel must be making a run topside at some point. That's usually how we get all the good amenities. Back in the day, when everyone hated everyone beyond comprehension, no one was allowed outside of their own "worlds," nor did they want to set foot onto another. Humans don't willingly come here or to Heaven, but angels and demons travel to the human world and even have duties up there. I'm not really sure why that is but I also don't care. It's just how the world we live in worked out its issues.

Demons have jobs and some of those require them to be topside. One job in particular is a carrier, and they get sent up there to get us the good stuff like toothbrushes. For thousands of years, demons went without because they were too proud to make some sort of treaty to set foot up there. We don't have the resources down here to make things the way they do up there. We've tried, and it doesn't work. It's truly like this world just wants us to suffer.

"Why the hell are you going on about toothbrushes?" he asks as he rinses his and puts it away before wiping his mouth with a hand towel.

"Stop changing the subject."

He turns to stare at me, resting his hip against the porcelain sink. He crosses his arms, mimicking my stance.

"I do not want to be the King of Wrath. I don't want to be anything but me. I don't want the responsibility, I don't want *shit*."

"You sound like a spoiled brat, you know that?"

"Then so be it. I've said it before and I'll say it again. I don't care."

"You're such a child."

"If you want it so bad, then you take it."

I bark out a laugh. "A Lust demon holding the throne in Wrath? Are you asking for my head to be on a stake?"

I follow as he turns and leaves the room. He opens a drawer on his tall bureau and pulls out a pair of sweatpants, dropping his towel and pulls them on. He runs his hand through his hair before picking up the towel and tossing it back into the bathroom. He meets my eyes and glares for no reason other than he's Kaine and he enjoys annoying me.

"You going to tell me what happened or what?" I finally ask, following him out of the room and into the sitting room directly outside of his room.

This isn't the one we usually hang out in because the couches are uncomfortable as fuck, but he has the same idea

I do and doesn't want to leave Bexley here alone. Especially not now when daddy is home. We probably should just have the servants switch the furniture around.

"Nothing happened." He drops onto the couch and picks up the remote. We don't get cable down here, but we have good old DVDs and a player that holds up to a hundred at a time. He scrolls through the list, trying to find something to put on.

"You were up there for hours and nothing happened?"

I don't believe him.

He continues to stare at the TV, acting like he doesn't care about this conversation, but I can tell there's something he wants to say.

"There is no way August is just going to let this go. Not only is he not that kind of angel, but it's part of his duty or something."

Kaine sighs and leans back, fiddling with the remote. "He knows something," he finally says.

"Okay..." I say slowly, moving and taking a seat on the opposite side of the couch.

"He basically told me it didn't matter what happened because it's out of his hands. He then made that stupid face he makes, and made it seem like Bexley is someone important and then told me he can't wait to see how this whole thing plays out."

That can't be all that's bothering him. There has to be more.

"And..." he starts, looking back towards the TV.

I fucking knew it.

"I may not have come back alone."

I shut my eyes for a moment and pull in a breath. "What?" I ask as calmly as I can, though I feel anything but. "Kaine," I say his name softly, "we have enough issues with Bexley right now. Who the fuck else could you have brought here?"

He turns towards me with his lips pursed before huffing out a breath.

"Her friend."

# CHAPTER TWENTY-SEVEN

## BEXLEY

I wake up and it's dark.

I swear when I get home, if that ever happens, it's going to take days to get back to a normal sleeping schedule. Though I guess it won't matter since I'll no longer have a job to go back to. What's the point in keeping normal sleeping hours if there is nowhere to go?

I sit up and scrub my face. I'm still tired, exhausted, but my muscles aren't as sore, thanks to the hot tub... and maybe in part to Maxen, but he doesn't need to know that.

Turning onto my side, I slide back down to lie down, facing the large, empty space of the bed, and hug the pillow tighter.

Am I ever going to go home? Is Rachel okay?

I hate admitting that I feel comfortable here, almost like I belong. It makes no sense. But it's as if I could make a new life here and never look back without a care. Other than Rachel, of course. I'll need to know she's okay. She's the only thing I care about, the only person I have in my life.

I let out a sigh and close my eyes, willing myself back to sleep. It does nothing. I'm tired, but the sleep just keeps evading me. Knowing it's no use, I groan and get out of bed. After what I found the last time I tried to leave, on top of being hidden away from Kaine's father, I know better than to try to leave this room. I know nothing about this place or how dangerous it is. I've already come across a secret dungeon with unlawfully prisoned people inside, who knows what else I'll find? I shiver at the thought... If what that man said was right, if my suspicions are correct and I am in... I swallow hard.

If I'm in Hell... I don't even know what that means, never mind what I would find, or worse, what would find me. The thought of coming across mangled bodies or grotesque demons upsets my stomach but doesn't illicit fear in me like it should. I'm starting to grow concerned with how in touch with this dark side I'm getting.

A sharp pain zaps through the front of my head and everything around me fades to black.

*I open my eyes and it's still dark, so I know it's not time to wake up, but what woke me then?*

*Maybe it was a bad dream. Pulling the blankets up higher and tucking myself in as best as I can, I close my eyes and try to go back to sleep. That's when I hear it.*

*Daddy's voice...*

*He's home!*

*My eyes fly open, and I throw the covers off, jumping out of bed and racing out of my room in search of him. It's been over a year since I've seen him this time. Mommy said it would be a long time until I saw him again, but I didn't think it would be this long. My feet scurry down the hall, my footsteps loud but I don't care.*

*Normally it doesn't take me long to reach Mommy's room but tonight it feels like forever, like the hallway is never-ending and I'll never get there, but I finally do. I skid to a halt, grabbing onto the doorframe to help stop me.*

*"Daddy!"*

*He whips around, greeting me with a smile so big his whole face scrunches up. "Bee!" He kneels down and holds out his arms and I run to him, leaping into his arms and throwing mine around his neck, holding on tight.*

*I bury my face in his neck and breathe him in. No matter how long he's gone for, he always smells the same when he comes back. Always.*

*"I missed you," I whisper to him.*

"I missed you, too, Bee." He squeezes me even tighter, to the point I almost can't breathe, but then he lets go and I step back, my face hurting from the smile. "It's late, why are you awake?" he asks, trying to tame my wild hair. It's no use, even Mommy says so.

"You woke me up."

"Did I?" He laughs. "I'm sorry, Bee, I didn't mean to."

I turn to my mother who is standing off to the side, dressed in her pajamas, her eyes a little red. He must have woke her up too.

She already knows what I'm going to ask and speaks before I can get the words out. "If I'd have known, I'd have told you. I'm going downstairs to get some water, spend a few more minutes with Daddy but then it's back to bed, okay? School tomorrow."

I groan. "Do I have to?"

"Of course." It's my dad who answers and I turn to him as my mother leaves the room. "School is important, Bee. Don't ever let anything get in the way of your education, no matter what."

"Okay, Daddy."

He stands to his full height, and I have to crane my head back to see him. He's very tall, like the tallest man I've ever seen. He holds his arms towards me, and I jump into them again, wrapping my legs around his waist and he walks out of the room and back towards mine.

He places me in my bed and tucks me in good and tight, just the way I like it, and sits on the edge of my bed.

"Do you have to leave again?" I ask.

"Not for a few days."

I smile and take his hand. "Good." It's always good when he can stay.

"I'm sorry it's like this, Bee. I wish things were different, but..." He sighs. "One day you'll understand."

"Why not now?"

"Well, there are just some things that you will understand better when you're older."

"*After going to school?*" *I ask.*

"*Exactly.*" *He leans forward and presses a kiss to my forehead.* "*I love you, Bee. I always will, nothing will ever change that, okay?*"

*I nod. He smiles once more before getting up and leaving my room, closing the door behind him.*

*He hasn't been here in a long time, so he doesn't know that I don't close the door anymore because it scares me, but it's okay. With him home I can be brave. He won't let any of the scary monsters get me.*

*I close my eyes with a smile still on my face and try to go back to sleep.*

"*Is she sleeping?*" *my mom asks in a quiet voice from outside my door.*

"*Not yet,*" *he answers.*

"*She let you close the door?*" *He doesn't say anything, but I guess he answered her in another way because she asks something else.* "*What are you going to tell them?*"

"*I'm not going to tell them anything. They'll need to get over it.*"

"*You know it doesn't work like that.*"

"*I don't care. I don't want to leave you or Bexley again. I'm staying this time.*"

"*You know that's dangerous.*"

"*That's why we're going to leave.*"

"Bexley?" The voice sounds worried, and I open my eyes expecting to see my father's face, but it's not. I'm confused for a moment before I remember who I am and who is standing in front of me. "Are you okay?" Maxen asks, sitting on the side of the bed... the same way my father was in the dream I just had. Or the memory, really, because that's what it was. A memory I lost for a long time but I'm glad to have it back. It was the last time I saw him.

"Yeah," I answer, sitting up and running a hand down my face. "Just a bad dream."

I look around and notice it's light out and the other side of the bed is still made. "Did you sleep?"

He shakes his head and I narrow my eyes in question. He doesn't look tired.

"I don't need a lot of sleep," he says before getting up and then quickly changing the subject. "Get up and get dressed. Kaine has a surprise for you."

"He's back?" I jerk up straighter.

Maxen nods before heading towards the door. "I'll be back in ten minutes to bring you to the breakfast room," he tells me over his shoulder, and I waste no time getting out of bed and getting dressed, all the while not being able to shrug off the feeling that dream left me with.

I always thought when my parents talked that they were talking about the people my dad hung out with, the people who got him into trouble and he did bad things for... but why do I now think that may not be the truth? That maybe there is more to it than my dad being a common day criminal?

# CHAPTER TWENTY-EIGHT

## BEXLEY

Maxen returns ten minutes later, just as he said he would, and now he's escorting me down to the breakfast room. The same one we were in yesterday that I effectively escaped from.

"Kaine is already down here."

"And you were ordered to fetch me like a servant?" I ask with a smirk, turning my head just the slightest to look up at him. He ignores me completely, keeping his chin up and his gaze straight. I roll my eyes. "You'd think after getting laid so much you'd both be in good spirits," I say to myself, but loud enough for him to hear. Still, he doesn't respond. Nothing. Not a smirk, not an eye roll, nothing. I'm wondering if he's suddenly gone deaf, but I doubt it. He's just stubborn as hell.

And annoying.

We reach the room and walk in together. Kaine is sitting at the table and there is a girl sitting beside him. My stomach turns, remembering the girl from the other day, the one who I thought was his girlfriend but now I'm sure she was just a fuck buddy and clearly not one he cares about since she hasn't been back. This girl isn't her though. This girl has dark hair and very closely resembles...

"Rachel!" I shriek. She turns around in her chair, her smile instant. I run to her just as she gets up and we hug, squeezing each other tightly. "What are you doing here?"

"What do you mean?" She pulls back. "Obviously, I needed to make sure you were okay and not chopped into tiny pieces or turned into a lampshade."

I smile and shake my head. "You are ridiculous." I hold up my arm to inspect it. "Though, I do think I'd make a rather nice lampshade, if I do say so myself."

Maxen scoffs and takes the seat Rachel was just in. I take her hand and walk to the other side of the table and we both sit down, across from Kaine and Maxen. "Have you eaten yet?" I ask her.

"No. Mr. Bossypants over there told me we couldn't eat until you got here. I've been starving for hours." She shoots him a glare even though he ignores her.

"Hours?" I look to Kaine, then back to her. "How long have you been here?"

"Since last night."

My eyebrows raise.

"Surprise," Kaine says with a grin, finally looking up. The servants carrying the food come out, so I don't bother to argue with him or ask him why the hell he didn't tell me this sooner. He knew I was worried about her. I asked about her, and even if I wasn't, she's my bestie so of course I'd want to see her.

Rachel and I each get a plate placed down in front of us and she wastes no time pulling the top off and digging in. I take a sip of my juice before picking at my food, not feeling all that hungry.

"You guys have any coffee around here?" Rachel asks, taking a bite of her toast. She looks up at Kaine who nods, and she goes back to eating. I keep my eye on him though and he meets my gaze. Without even a word, one of the servants walks out with a tray topped with a carafe, sugar bowl, milk or cream, and four mugs. It's placed in the middle of the table and Rachel moans in delight as she reaches for it.

I narrow my eyes at Kaine in question, but all he does is smirk, and bring his attention back to the food in front of him.

It's possible the servant heard her ask and they're told to just do things like that, but I'm not so sure that's the case.

I think there is something more at play here. The idea of being in Hell is starting to make a lot more sense and so is them not being human.

"Did Kaine tell you where we are?"

Rachel looks up at me from across the hot tub. After breakfast, I convinced the guys to let us have some girl time... meaning alone time. They were wary because of Kaine's father, but finally agreed, though they said one of them will be waiting outside of the room. It took a lot of going back and forth but it's finally what we agreed on.

"Yeah, why?"

I cock my head to the side just the slightest. "What did he say?"

"That we're in Detroit."

I hold back my laugh, remembering that's exactly what I was told when I asked the first time, and I wonder if there is more to that than just a joke. Because I know for certain we are not in Detroit.

"And you believe that?"

"Oh, not for a second." She smiles and rests her head back on the cushion behind her. "But I really don't care, I'm just glad to see you."

I'm wondering how long he's going to let her stay. I'm also wondering when we're going to have an actual conversation about what's going on around here. I doubt either of them will just open up about it, so I'll probably have to ask. Or demand it, more likely. Which I am absolutely fine with doing.

I lift myself up and push off the floor with my feet and float over to sit beside Rachel. I look down at the water, skimming my hand across the top, trying to figure out how I want to word what I have to say. "Where do you think we are?" I ask quietly not wanting either of them to hear. They're just outside the room, or at least one of them is, but who knows if they're eavesdropping or not. I wouldn't put it past them.

"I have no freaking clue. I don't even remember getting here. Kaine said I fell asleep but that didn't seem right." Her voice is low too, and I wonder if she's worried because she knows something.

"Are you afraid of them?" She turns her head to look at me. "Being next to them. Does it scare you? Do you get bad vibes?"

"I feel like I should, but no."

I let out a breath, not sure if that should be a relief or not.

"Neither do I," I say slowly.

"Why does that sound like it's a bad thing?"

I fight with myself, wondering if I should tell her or not. She wouldn't judge me if I told her what I thought, but I don't want her to freak out. Rachel is a tough girl but if I'm right about this, I don't know what she would do. I don't want her trying to stay here. I'm on edge enough knowing I don't belong, I can't put her in that position too. Honestly, the best thing to do would be to go home, but I don't want to leave the guys behind. And I know that sounds crazy since I just met them but being here just feels right.

"I don't know." I rest my head back and close my eyes. She doesn't ask any more questions and neither do I, we just sit in the hot tub and relax for another hour or so before Maxen comes in to get us.

# CHAPTER TWENTY-NINE

## KAINE

I head down to the third floor which is where all of the servants live. The castle is way too big for my father and I so it made sense to give all the help their own space. I turn onto the landing and then down the hallway to the left, knowing exactly where I need to go. Not just because it's my house, but because I've come this way many times. There are plenty of places in this castle I'm not all that familiar with, but this isn't one of them.

I reach the door I'm looking for and knock before opening it. Eskrin is lying on his bed, nose in a book. He lowers it as I walk in.

"The men downstairs need to be let go before the night is over."

He nods. "And will I be gathering others?" he asks.

"Not right now." He raises a brow but says nothing more. He's young and only here because he's the child of one of the other servants. He's seventeen but great at following directions and very loyal. He helps me whenever I need it, does all the dirty work so I can keep my own hands clean.

His species of demon are called Zexha and were born of Hell. Meaning they've never been human or have anyone in their ancestry that was. No one really knows where they came from, they were just here, as if the world was giving us something to help us along. It's why they look human but not enough to pass as one. Their eyes are slightly bigger, necks a little longer and their face shape is a little off. At a quick glance, you wouldn't know the difference, but the longer you look at them, the more you realize they aren't human at all.

The Seven Kingdoms each have a ruler who was somehow related to the original demons—Lucifer, Mammon, Asmodeus, Leviathan, Beelzebub, Satan, and Belphegor. They're all long dead but have left just as vile demons in their place. So yeah, my family originated from Satan. I was born in Hell, was never a human, but my mother was... wherever she is.

The rest of the demons down here are the humans who committed too many sins to be let into Heaven. Some people don't go anywhere but stay on earth as ghosts. Those who come down here get classed into one of the kingdoms and after so long, they forget their human life entirely. In fact, it doesn't take long at all. Sometimes it's as quick as a day, but not usually longer than a couple of weeks. Maxen was born down here, meaning he wasn't ever a human either, but his mother was before she ended up here. I think it's why he has a conscious still sometimes. He can't help it.

"Send word when it's done." I don't wait for a response, just turn and head out of his room. Eskrin will do as asked; he always does. Now I need to find the next person on my list.

Marionette.

The witch has returned from her little vacation topside. A trip that was supposed to be for just tea but turned into a four-day affair. If I'd have known how long she would be gone when I first went looking for her, I'd have made sure someone went and got her, and returned her immediately.

Turning off onto the first floor, I head down the hallway and knock on her door.

"Come in!"

I open the door and enter into the studio-type apartment that the witch calls home.

There aren't many witches in Hell, it's a power only a few get. Sort of like how it is on Earth, too, I guess. Wrath houses one of them, there are four living in Greed—surprise,

surprise—one in Sloth, who is most unhelpful, two in Pride, and then another who roams around.

Marionette doesn't need to live in the castle, but it was the safest option. The demons who live in this kingdom here aren't the nicest.

"Welcome back," I say kindly.

She lifts her head from the newspaper she is looking over and pulls off her bright-green-framed glasses and pushes them atop her head.

"Wasn't expecting to see you at my door," she says.

"That's disappointing."

She rolls her eyes and folds the paper before placing it down on the table in front of her. She takes trips topside often—witches get free passes up there to come and go as they please—and always comes back with stacks of newspapers. I have no idea what she finds so fascinating about what goes on up there, but whatever.

"What do you want?"

Moving farther into the room, I take a seat in the armchair across from her.

"Your help." I pick at the small threads of fabric that are popping out of the arm.

She raises a brow. "What did you do?"

"Nothing." I hold my hands up innocently, and her brow goes up higher. "Promise," I say with a grin.

"Then with what?"

"What I am about to tell you does not get repeated, understood?"

"I think I know the drill by now, Kaine. This is nothing new."

She's not wrong.

"I brought someone down here with me a few nights ago. Sh—"

"A few nights ago?" she questions, her brow furrowing in confusion.

"That's what I said."

She narrows her eyes at me. "There was no alert of human entry from a few nights ago. Just the one from last night. I assumed this was what you needed help with?"

That's... interesting.

"It's not. That will be taken care of shortly. I have one more task to attend to after you, then I'll be returning the human to her home." She nods. "But back to what you said... is there any chance the system is broken?"

She shrugs. "I suppose it could be. It's old. I'm not sure when it was serviced last..."

I get to my feet. "Find out for me?" I walk towards the door.

"Is that all? You're ordering me to do something one of your servants can do?"

I stop and turn. "I trust you to be discreet."

"I have better things to do."

"You could add finding a new place to live to that list?" Her mouth drops open. "That's what I thought. Get back to me by tomorrow evening."

My father's office, the area he spends most of his time in, is at the complete opposite end of where I spend most of my time. And that is not an accident.

The door is open, so I knock before entering. He's sitting behind his desk, looking over files. I still have no idea what he spends most of his day doing and I plan to keep it that way.

"Nice of you to finally show your face," he says without looking up.

"My face is always around." I sit in the high-back leather chair across from his desk, fold my hands, resting them on my thighs, and lean back. After a moment, he looks up at me, dropping the file to the table. There is a bunch of writing on it, but I can't see what it says, nor do I care. "You wanted to see me?"

"I did." He clears his throat. "The Kings want to see you at the next meeting."

"For what?"

"You know for what."

I let out a huff. "We've talked about this."

"You're right, we have. Which is why I don't know why you continue to play stupid. This is your duty as son of a king. You have no choice."

"Bullshit."

His eyebrows fly up into his hairline. My father is... difficult. He isn't cruel, but he's stern and strict. He believes in duty and responsibility, though he instilled that upon me a little too late. I don't know why he allowed me to do whatever the fuck I wanted my whole life, until springing this idea of me taking over the kingdom a few years ago, like I'd have any interest in doing it.

I don't. Not at all. Not in the fucking least.

I want nothing to do with this kingdom, let alone run it.

"Kaine—"

I get to my feet. "If all you are going to do is tell me what my duty is, I don't need to hear it. Tell the others it's time they figure they're shit out because once you're done, this kingdom will be left without a ruler. I'm not doing it."

I turn and head out of the room, and even though we didn't argue about it as expected, I'm still vibrating with anger over the whole situation because I know it isn't going away.

This is what I'm expected to do and unless I find someone else to do it for me or figure out a way to get them to change their minds, I'm fucked.

# CHAPTER THIRTY

## BEXLEY

"How long are you going to let her stay for?"

It was hard to get those words out, submitting to him willingly, admitting I know he's in charge and that it is up to him to make that decision. Ultimately, it is, I know that, but my being stubborn doesn't like admitting those sorts of things.

Kaine looks up at me from the couch in the small lounge room by his bedroom. Maxen is getting Rachel settled to take a shower. Yeah, I'll admit the thought makes my stomach a little sour. I don't like knowing Maxen is alone with *any* other girl. Yes, even my best friend who I know would never do anything, even with someone as hot as Max because if she would, she wouldn't be my best friend. Rachel isn't that type of girl.

"She needs to go home tonight. Soon, actually."

I nod and move to sit beside him. There is no point arguing with him. If I did, he'd probably just make her leave now. Kaine looks upset but I don't ask him why. I haven't known him long, but I know enough to guess he won't tell me anything, not unless he wants to, and even if he did, he'd probably still keep his mouth shut. Kaine isn't the talking type.

"Are we going to talk about what happened downstairs?" He won't talk about himself, but hopefully he'll talk about us.

"What's wrong? Regrets setting in?"

I purse my lips, thinking of how I want to respond. My instinct is to be a smart-ass, but that isn't the best option here. So I stay as calm as possible.

"Actually, I meant about what I learned. Where I am?"

He nods and chews on his bottom lip.

"What is there to talk about?"

"There's a lot to talk about, like how am I here? How are you here? And what does it all mean?"

"Why would it mean anything?"

"Are you serious?" I stare at him and wait for an answer, but he doesn't give one, only returns me with a blank stare of his own. "Learning that Hell is a real place answers so many questions." I huff out a laugh. "Yet, it obviously creates so many more." I look away from him and take in everything around the room.

Everything looks normal here, just as it would at home. There are houses, beds, and running water. There is grass outside and trees too. Even though they looked a little creepy, it still seemed the same. They have electricity and a sun and moon. Or what looks like a sun and moon, anyway, because I don't even know how this works geographically, but I'm assuming the moon I'm looking at through the window is not the same one I've been looking at for the last twenty-seven years of my life.

"I can see this is going to be a long conversation. One I'm not really in the mood for," he says tiredly, bringing his attention back to the TV.

"Oh okay, well I'll just let you be then," I snap, and move to stand. He snatches my wrist and yanks me down onto his lap. He grinds up into me, and I feel his hardness against my ass. His free hand snakes up my side and rests around my throat. He doesn't squeeze but the threat is there. My hands fist in his shirt, right below his rib cage.

"That attitude of yours does nothing but make my cock hard, so if that's your intention, by all means, keep it up. But if you're not trying to get fucked five ways to Sunday, I suggest you keep your mouth shut."

My heart is pounding fiercely behind my ribs and my pussy is throbbing. I open my mouth to tell him to fuck off, hoping it'll rile him up enough to flip me over and fuck me right here on this couch, in this room, where anyone could walk into.

"Kaine."

My attention is brought to Maxen, who is standing in the doorway, hands in his pockets. "She's all good and ready to go."

I know he's talking about Rachel. Kaine is going to take her back home soon, and I have no idea when I'll see her again. I shift, trying to stand up, but Kaine grips me harder so I freeze in place.

"I sure hope that pussy of yours is ready for me because when I return, you're going to get fucked by something much more interesting than a knife."

I gasp as he stands, taking me with him and propping me up on my feet. He makes sure I'm steady before dropping his hands from me and leaving the room.

I run my hands through my hair and try to calm myself before heading to see Rachel. As I pass Maxen, he gives me a knowing smirk and I wonder if he heard what Kaine said to me. Not that it matters. Him joining or not, I know it's still going to be good.

Rachel greets me with a smile as I enter the room. Her hair is still wet from the shower and as I hug her, her skin is still warm.

"I'm sorry you can't stay longer," I say quietly.

"I'm just glad you're okay." She pulls away but keeps her hands on me. "Do you know when you're coming back?"

I chew on my bottom lip and shrug.

She smiles. "You know I am your number one supporter no matter what. And as weird as this whole situation seems to be, as long as you're safe, do you, girl. Live it up. You just better check in with me, okay?"

"Am I being crazy? Staying here with these guys I don't know, in... well, wherever this is?"

"Maybe? But does it matter?" She leans in closer and lowers her voice. "Those guys are hot as fuck, and if the sex stays as good as you say it is, then fuck New York. I'd much rather spend time with these two hotties then Fucking Derrick."

I laugh at that and pull her in for another hug. I wish I could explain what it is that is making me want to stay here, what's making feel that this is the right thing to do, but I can't. Rachel is the only person in this world I've been able to open up to. The only person who knows my feelings about my parents and my life growing up. The only person I've ever been able to go to for literally anything. So I don't know why it's so hard to put into words what I'm feeling now...

What is it about these guys?

Why do I want to stay here?

And why does this feel like home?

# CHAPTER THIRTY-ONE

## BEXLEY

Maxen and I are sitting on the couch in the lounge room watching Pineapple Express. He had one of the servants bring us up some popcorn and the large bowl is placed on the couch between us like we're two middle school kids who are afraid to get too close. As if he hasn't had his entire eight-inch dick inside of me already.

The movie is just about finished when Kaine shows back up, his trip much quicker than it was the last time.

"Did she get home okay?" I ask.

He nods.

"You're sure? You made sure she went inside? The door was locked?"

"I've been going to that city longer than you've been alive, so you don't need to talk to me like I'm an idiot. Besides, that girl can take care of herself."

I smile, despite being thrown off over his first comment. I've already assumed he's not human, but I hadn't thought of him being any older than he looks. I'll save that conversation for another day because he looks even more tired than he did when he left. I am, however, happy he thinks Rachel can take care of herself. She can. I know that. It takes a certain type of person to live in NYC and be okay with it, that's for sure.

I frown as he walks over and stops directly in front of me.

"You make a better door than a window," I say, shifting to the side to see the rest of the movie.

He leans down, and I expect him to give me some threatening comment, but instead, he lifts me up and throws me over his shoulder, spilling the bowl of popcorn everywhere. Granted, there wasn't much left, but you don't just waste popcorn!

"What are you doing?" I growl, slamming my fists into his ass as he starts to walk. I look up and see Maxen laughing as he leaves the mess and follows us. Kaine turns and heads into his bedroom, where he tosses me onto the bed, and crawls over me.

The door clicks shut, and I hear the flick of the lock.

My heart speeds up as I look up into the bright blue eyes of Kaine.

"Did you forget what I said to you before I left?" he asks in a low voice. I shake my head. "Good."

His fingers slide under my shirt and lift it before he brings his mouth down, his hot tongue running along my skin, circling my belly button.

It tickles, but fuck if it doesn't feel so good to have his mouth on me again.

"The only question now is..." He pulls his mouth away and looks up to Maxen. "Do we make her come before or after we show her?"

Show me? Show me what?

I look to Maxen, finding that sinful smirk of his resting on his lips.

"Definitely now," he says, tugging his shirt off over his head. My, how quickly his attitude changes when he's about to get sex. What happened to me not getting his dick?

Kaine sits back on his knees and tugs down the sweatpants I'm wearing, revealing me without any panties. He growls, running his thumb between my slit and bringing it to his mouth. He drags his wet thumb along his tongue, his eyes closing and lips wrapping around it before he pulls it out. He slowly blinks his eyes open and they're even brighter than they were before, almost glowing, actually.

He gets my pants off the rest of the way and tosses them somewhere behind him. He lowers himself down, hooking his arms around my legs and spreading them. Dragging his nose along my thigh, he breathes in deeply, a satisfied sound leaving his throat as he gets closer to my pussy. The anticipation builds in me, the need for him to touch me is agonizing. I both hate and love how much I want him.

His lips wrap around my clit and he sucks gently. My eyes fall shut, and my hands find his hair, slipping through the silky strands before digging into his scalp and gripping it tightly. Kaine moves his tongue around slowly, enjoying the taste of me, taking his time to give me the orgasm he's promised.

"Open your eyes." It's Maxen, and his voice is less carefree, more serious, and it sends a shiver up my spine. Maxen is like two completely different people. A fun, carefree person day to day, but when it comes to sex, he's like an animal who craves it, needs it to survive.

I could say something similar about Kaine. He, too, is like two different people, only in a different way. He's grumpy and then not so grumpy, but he's intense all the time, no matter what.

I open my eyes and find Maxen in nothing but a tight pair of black briefs that are tugged down just enough for his cock to be free, his hand wrapped around it. "Watch me," he says. "Watch me pleasure myself as Kaine licks that sweet pussy of yours."

I fight to keep my eyes open as the orgasm gets closer and closer. Kaine is in no rush, taking his time with perfect strokes of his tongue, but it's doing the trick. I keep my eyes on Maxen though. Outside of his demand of it, I want to watch.

There is something so sexy about watching a man jerk off. The way he moves his hand, how the muscles in his forearm and bicep twitch and bulge. The way his body makes the tiniest, jerky movements, the way he brings his bottom lip between his teeth. Most of all, I love how his eyes are dark and settled right on me as I watch him, eyes roaming over every inch of his body. He loves it too. I just know it. He likes me watching him.

Of course there are no feelings here, so there is no need for jealousy. It's sex and it's fun, so why wouldn't he like sharing a girl with his friend? That's what guys do. It's all about sex for them, that primal instinct to fuck. And damn, are they good at it.

The piercings around the crown of Maxen's dick glisten with each stroke, hitting the light pouring in from the window just right. Kaine shifts and a moment later he's filling me with his fingers and sucking my clit into his mouth.

I'm a fucking goner. My eyes flicker shut as wave after wave of bliss fills my body. My muscles clench, my fingers tighten in Kaine's hair, and I allow the moans to escape, my cries of pleasure fill the room as Kaine works me through my orgasm nice and slow. And a smile spreads across my face as I come down from it.

I'm still panting as Maxen lifts me up from the bed, standing me on my feet. He tugs my shirt off over my head and drops it to the floor. Rachel was smart enough to bring me a change of clothes. It's not a lot, but it's enough. I can't expect her to have packed my entire bedroom, but she at least thought I'd want to change into something comfortable, and she was right. Even though it seems most of my time spent here has been naked.

Maxen rakes his fingers through my hair before dragging them down the front of my neck and then along the top of my breasts. My nipples harden and I bite onto my lip to hold back the sounds of pleasure wanting to escape. He takes a step back, his cock so hard and I try not to stare but it's not easy to pull my gaze away. Even after an orgasm, I want more. These boys have spoiled me. I don't think just one orgasm will be enough ever again. Honestly, I don't think anyone could ever live up to the expectations I now have in my head, thanks to these two.

"It's best you keep one thing in mind." Kaine's voice sounds beside me as he walks into my line of sight. His shirt is off, but his pants are still on, the jeans slung low on his narrow hips, that delicious Adonis belt peeking out. "No matter what you see, no matter what happens here..." He continues to walk slowly, disappearing behind Maxen for just a second before popping up on the other side of him. My body is still tingling from the orgasm, but also craving more. He stops, lifting his head, and meets my eyes. "There is nowhere to go. You are at our mercy, and there is no God here to help you."

# CHAPTER THIRTY-TWO

## BEXLEY

If his words are meant to scare me, they don't. Not even close. Instead, a thrill crawls up my spine and goosebumps spread across my skin.

Maxen smirks before moving forward and I swear they can talk to each other in their heads or something. They work together too seamlessly.

"You know what we are," he says in a low voice. "Now all you need to do is admit it." Maxen drags his finger along the underside of my right breast, trailing it up the middle and then back down and around the underside of my left one. My skin prickles under his touch and I fight to keep my eyes open.

"Our world is different than yours," Kaine says, and I bring my attention to him, while Maxen's fingers brush along my ribs and around my backside, teasing me with a barely-there touch. "But not by much. Us, on the other hand? Well..." He huffs out a laugh. "There are quite a few differences, some of which I bet you will come to love."

Maxen moves behind me, his fingers sliding along my lower back. I give in and allow my eyes to fall shut as my body begs to lean into him, feel his warmth pressed against me, but before I get the chance, he's moving to my other side, and when I open my eyes, I know my life will never be the same.

Maxen is still Maxen, only he's different. His features are sharper, more defined, more primal. He looks a little taller too, his body more toned. Someone who didn't know him wouldn't be able to tell the difference, but I've seen his body so many times since being here that I'd be a fool for not noticing. But the biggest change in him is the two horns that sit on top of his head, protruding from that messy mop of black hair. They're thicker at the base, starting about an inch from where his hairline begins and they curl backwards and out in the smallest twist.

I have no fear as I look at him, even though it all looks wrong. Not wrong in a negative way, but wrong in the way I know it shouldn't be. This isn't how humans look, this isn't what I'm used to seeing. This is the stuff you read about in books and see on TV. The stuff you're told isn't real. Yet here it is, right in front of my face.

My eyes stay glued on those thick, black horns that I find more attractive than I should. Thoughts of what they feel like go through my head. Are they hard or soft? Cold or warm? Will he like me touching them, or are they off-limits?

My arm is lifting, wanting to reach out and find out for myself, but he steps back, and with the smallest shake of his head, I know I won't be touching them anytime soon. He stands beside Kaine, the both of them too fucking hot for words.

I want to ride him, feel each and every one of those piercings sliding in and out of me as I run my fingers up and down those horns. Are they sensitive? Or can he not feel them? I'm intrigued so I find myself staring at them, my mind filling with all the dirty things I want to do to him. Which is why I don't notice Kaine moving until he's gripping me and turning me, pushing me onto the bed so I'm bent over it, feet on the ground and ass in the air.

"Do you remember my promise to you before I left?"

*You're going to get fucked by something much more interesting than a knife.*

And I find myself wondering if he, too, has horns. A set that is shaped differently than Maxen's. A set that he can fuck me with because there is no way Maxen's can get inside of me without cutting me open. Which is a shame, because the thought of his *horns* being inside of me has me clenching my thighs together and wanting to come again. A moment later though, I know that isn't the case at all.

Kaine does not have horns that he plans to fuck me with. He has something else, something much different.

Both of his hands slide up my back, and he leans forward, gripping my breasts and tugging at my nipples. He pinches one too hard and I cry out, not understanding why I like it but also not caring.

"Answer me," he demands.

"Yes," I whisper.

His finger teases the nipple he just pinched, and the sting slowly fades. He leans up and the heat of his body leaves my back, but his hands stay planted on my hips, holding me in place. I wait, counting my breaths in anticipation.

In... out.

In... out.

On my fourth breath, I feel it.

Something sliding up the side of my thigh, but it isn't a hand, or a mouth, nor anything I've ever felt before. The material of it feels silky smooth, but I'm not exactly sure.

I hold my breath, the blood rushing through my ears is the only thing I can hear as I wait, trying to figure out what the fuck he's about to shove inside of me this time. What could he possibly have that he wants to use on me?

"Are you ready?" he asks softly, his fingers drawing little circles on my skin.

"Yes."

Whatever it is that's been teasing the outside of my thigh, moves around to the inside and slides over my clit. It's smooth and warm like his fingers, only softer.

So much softer and thicker too. It feels similar to the head of a cock, and I wonder if he has a second one?

But that wouldn't make any sense...

And then it hits me. Just as he wraps his arms around my waist and pulls me up, pressing my back to his chest, I know what it is.

It isn't a pair of horns and it isn't a second dick.

Kaine has a tail.

A tail that is slowly making its way around my belly, the tip slithering up my stomach and between my breasts. It's black, and the tip is thick, in the shape of a spade, only it isn't entirely flat.

My breath catches as it brushes over a nipple and then moves to the other. And just like with Maxen, I move my arm to touch it, wanting to feel it, learn what it is, make my mind realize this is actually happening and not just me going crazy. But just like with Maxen, I'm stopped.

Kaine grabs my wrist, pulling my arm up beside my head and pressing a kiss to my open palm before sliding my hand back down and resting it above my breasts, right above the tip of his tail.

"There is one rule here, do you understand? One rule, that is all."

I nod, unable to form words, mesmerized and trying to process everything that is going on.

These boys are demons. It's been proven to me now. Max has horns and Kaine has a tail.

"You do not touch this or Maxen's horns unless you are told to."

His voice is deep and firm, but he isn't being cruel, only laying down the rules.

Of course I don't want to listen, all I want to do is reach out and touch them, but I won't. I don't know why they don't want me to, but it could be something bad, right?

I don't know anything about demons and what they're capable of, if anything, so this time I will listen and without question.

"Okay," I say.

All in one motion, he moves me back towards the bed, pressing my head down into the mattress and resting his body over mine, his mouth close to my ear. "Do you know what a knot is?" he asks.

Of course I know what it is, I've been tying my shoes since I was five, but something tells me that's not the kind of knot he's talking about.

"No."

"Well, baby, you're about to find out."

He shifts, lines up, and slams into me. My back arches and I gasp as I ache at his size.

He's bigger like this. Or maybe I'm just sore and swollen from all of the sex.

He pulls his hips back and snaps them forward.

"Ah, fuck," I groan into the bed.

No, he's definitely bigger like this.

One hand stays on my head, firmly pressing me into the mattress and the other is placed on my hip, holding me in place as he thrusts in and out of me. My thoughts drift to Maxen, wondering what he's doing. Is he just standing back and watching? I like that thought. A lot, actually. Not knowing what he's doing is almost as appealing as watching him do it.

Kaine groans from behind me, his voice almost a growl and I know he's close.

His hands tighten on me, both in my hair and on my skin and his movements slow a little, turning into more of a grinding against me. Pressure starts to build inside of me to the point of pain. I grip the bed sheets, clenching my jaw, and what I assume is his tail finds my clit, brushing against it.

"Do it, Kaine," Maxen says from behind me, and I can't find it in me to care about what he's talking about because I'm coming again. Clenching around Kaine, the feeling of fullness has me not wanting to move, but I can't help it as my body jerks wildly, working through the pain of him growing bigger inside of me and the orgasm that's taking over every other part of me.

# CHAPTER THIRTY-THREE

## KAINE

All demons have a part of them that makes them who they are.

Lust demons have horns and Wrath demons have tails. They are the physical traits that make us different from one another. They're also a weakness, in a sense. They each make us go against what we're made to do.

Lust demons can control when they orgasm, it helps with feeding. The only time that isn't true, outside of being so high you don't know what you're doing, is when someone is touching their horns. It's like a magic button that turns off his ability to make the decision to come and just makes it for him.

For me, I'm filled with anger and hatred. I'm cunning and manipulative and don't care about hurting anyone who gets in my way.

My tail doesn't always go hand in hand with sex like an incubus's horns do, my tail is more about affection. A feeling that demons don't feel deeply to begin with, but especially Wrath demons. And even with someone touching our tail, it doesn't mean we'd instantly fall for them. It just means our walls are down and maybe we won't be as much of an asshole in that moment, which could then lead to stronger feelings.

I've barely been fucking Bexley for five minutes when the urge to come is there and I need to slow down. My cock is already growing, preparing its knot, and I'm eager to see Bexley's reaction. Clearly, Maxen is too, since he's standing to the side, just barely in my view, cock in hand as he watches me fuck her. Nothing new or weird. We've watched each other with girls numerous times.

I'm unable to fight off the pleasure anymore. My hips are barely moving, barely getting any friction around my cock and that need is still there. I don't expect her to come when she does, and that's what throws me over the edge.

The sounds she makes, her body tensing, her already tight pussy throbbing, squeezing, and contracting around me... My cock swells and I know the moment she realizes it because she panics. She jerks and a gasp leaves her mouth just as I groan out my release, my cock throbbing and pulsing, my cum pumping out, all the while the head of my dick is thickening into a bulb so big I won't be able to pull out of her.

And the pleasure just keeps coming.

Wave after wave of euphoria runs through me even after she calls my name.

The fear in her voice feeds me in ways her pussy never will.

The tremble in her tone fills me up with a different type of pleasure that only adds to this physical one her body gives me, and it's almost as if the entire word fades away, and all that's left is her and me and this wonderful fucking feeling she gives me.

"Kaine!"

"Stay still," I say calmly, trying to catch my breath, and brushing my fingers along her back. I shift my weight and move her hair, allowing me to see the side of her face, those bright green eyes frantic. "It'll go down, just wait a little longer and don't move."

She nods, agreeing, but her whole body is shaking, shivering, her fingers gripping the sheets tightly.

The thought of this will have me full on fear for years to come.

I've never shown my true self to a human before. Never experienced the fear my knot would give someone.

Most demons have them in this form, so the girls are used to it, they expect it. The only type of demon who doesn't have a knot is a Lust demon, no one really knows why, it's just how it is.

But this... the fucking beauty in her fear over this was perfect.

Fucking perfect.

After about a few minutes, it starts going down and finally, I'm able to pull out of her. She falls to the bed and curls up on her side, blinking up at me. I can tell she's fighting with herself; the urge to look down and see what it looks like is evident, but doesn't. She probably doesn't want to see it anyway. It's not anything pretty to look at, it just feels fucking good.

She'll get over her fear of it the more we fuck her. The more I allow myself to be in this form with her, to come inside of her, allowing not only my cock to fill her up, but the knot too.

And when she's ready, Maxen and I will fuck her together and he can enjoy it too. The extra pressure it gives him, feeling me through the thin walls of her pussy as he's settled in her ass.

I crawl onto the bed and lie on my side, propping my head up on my arm. "Are you okay?" I ask quietly, reaching out and brushing the stray hair away from her forehead. I blame the use of my tail on her, the stimulation it gave me, on my caring whether she's okay or not.

"What was that?" she asks, avoiding my gaze.

I grin. "A demon's knot. It's what happens in this form."

She looks up at me cautiously, and slowly she narrows her eyes at me, the fire coming back as her fear dissipates.

"You could have warned me."

"Where is the fun in that?" I grin even wider.

She rolls onto her back and closes her eyes.

"Hey," I say softly, and she opens them, finding mine immediately. "We're not done with you."

I think she's going to argue, tell me to go fuck myself, but she doesn't. Instead, she smiles and sits up, eyes on Maxen.

"Do you have one too?" Her words are slow and almost eager.

He shakes his head, hand still wrapped around his cock as he takes a step forward.

Bexley looks at me over her shoulder. "Good. I was hoping to get fucked in the ass tonight." And then she rolls over, lifting her ass high in the air, aiming it right at Maxen.

I raise a brow at her, impressed at her bounce back.

"I'd put your cock in my mouth, but I'd rather keep my jaw attached to the rest of my head."

Maxen crawls onto the bed and her eyes flutter shut as he sinks into her pussy. He then unsnaps the bottle of lube he grabbed from the bedside drawer and pours it all over her ass, rubbing it in with his free hand. I bet that's a lot better than the olive oil he used last time.

I take the moment to shift back to my human form, not wanting to miss the opportunity of getting my dick sucked. I push up and move, kneeling down in front of Bexley and she opens her eyes, grinning once she puts two and two together.

She opens wide and I slide in, the warmth of her mouth encompassing the half of my dick that she can fit inside. She sucks and licks, and I feel the exact moment Max stops using his fingers in her ass and replaces it with his cock. She freezes, biting down the slightest bit as she takes a moment to breathe, fighting the urge to bite down even harder as she handles the pain of him stretching her open. Once he's in, she lets out a breath and sucks me all the way to the back of her throat.

Bexley is a mystery to me on so many levels and maybe that's part of the reason I don't want to let her go, but no matter the reason, she's still a mystery that I need to figure out because at the end of the day, she doesn't belong here and getting caught will only end in disaster. I won't bother myself with it now, there are other things to focus on.

She sucks on the tip of my cock, pulling me from my worries and for a second, I consider shifting back and allowing her to touch my tail to make all of this bullshit go away, but I know that's stupid. It won't really fix anything. The only way I can fix this shit is to figure out how to keep her here safely, and I think the only way to do that is to figure out what August meant by what he said.

# CHAPTER THIRTY-FOUR

## MAXEN

The light slowly starts to peek in through the windows and I'm wide awake, lying in bed. When I'm this full, I don't need as much sleep. Same with Kaine, which is why he's also awake, lying down on the opposite side of Bexley, who is sound asleep and completely worn out from nonstop sex since she got here.

I've been expecting her to stop us at some point, tell us she needs a break, but the little champ just keeps truckin' on.

And fuck, does she know how to take a cock the right way. I don't know what Kaine's plans are for her, he still hasn't given the full details on the conversation with August or what his thoughts are on the matter, but if I know him, and I do, then he's already taking care of it, and I'm sure he'll tell me soon enough.

With that thought, I find myself thinking about Bexley leaving.

I look down at her, curled up on her side, facing away from me. Her hair is a wild mess, but still so shiny and soft. Long, thick waves fall around her side and partway down her back. Her skin is this light, golden color that can only come from genes and not something you pay for. I can't see her face, but I know exactly what it looks like. Full lips, dark eyelashes that girls would kill for, and a straight but—dare I say—cute nose that gives her a younger look.

I'll miss her when she leaves. Even demons of Hell don't fuck like she does, and it'll be difficult going back to what

I had. Like going back to drinking homemade coffee after tasting Starbucks... it's just not the same, but it'll have to do. She has to go back; she doesn't belong here. Her staying means nothing but trouble and that's what I need to remember.

I get up from the bed and go to take a shower. Kaine doesn't say anything so I know he's in one of his moods. I'm used to them, they happen often, but I've noticed he's always in them after sex and I'm not sure why. He should be happy, not fucking brooding around like a toddler who didn't get a toy from the store. I undress as I wait for the shower to heat up before getting in.

I wash quickly but stand under the water for a while, realizing I need to go back home and check in on things. Making that trip really sucks. It's not the actual trip I hate, I don't mind the traveling, it's just having to go back to see my father. Make sure he's still alive.

The toilet seat clacks against the tank and I assume Kaine got up, though I missed him walking in. As soon as he's done, and the toilet flushes, the glass door is sliding open and he's stepping in, moving to the other side of the shower to turn on the showerhead. He steps aside, allowing it to spray out for a few seconds—since the pipes are all connected and this side is hot, that side will be warm sooner than it would if I weren't in here.

I'm about to turn off the water and get out when he speaks.

"I don't think she's fully human."

I jerk in his direction. His head is leaned back and he's running his hands through his hair, getting it wet, as if he didn't just make a serious accusation.

"What?"

He runs his fingers through his hair once before lifting his head to look at me. He runs a hand over his face to rid it of water before opening his eyes.

"They never got an alert about her coming down here."

I raise a brow. "It must be broken."

He shrugs. "We'll find out soon enough." He grabs the shampoo bottle and pours some into his hand, then brings it to his head.

I huff out a breath. "Why do you do that?"

He starts to wash his hair, eyes closing once again as he asks, "Do what?"

"You offer up a bit of information, then withhold the rest. Like you want me to beg you for answers or something."

He smirks, squinting one eye open, his hair full of soap. "Would you?"

"Fuck no," I grunt out. And he knows I won't. I'm not begging for shit from him or anyone else. He shrugs again.

I pinch the bridge of my nose and close my eyes before taking a deep breath. "What do you know?"

"Not much. Marionette is getting information for me. She should have something for me later this afternoon."

"And you couldn't have just said this before?"

"I like being asked for things."

I roll my eyes. "You're fucked."

"Tell me something I don't know."

I turn off my side of the shower and step out, reaching for a towel and drying my hair before wrapping it around my waist.

"Have you talked to Davina lately?" I ask, gathering up the stuff I need to brush my teeth.

"Nope!" he shouts from the shower as I put the toothpaste on the brush.

"And that isn't causing an issue?"

The girl is a psychopath. I'm surprised she hasn't turned up here yet. She always pops in whenever she wants, thinks she owns the damn place. Problem is, Kaine's father loves her, for some crazy reason, cause the asshole hates everyone else. I think it's because he knows Kaine is going to need someone to help him rule and Davina is a ruthless cunt who will keep Wrath running the way he wants it too. So Tzalli should probably just ask her to do it without Kaine, since Kaine wants nothing to do with it. And I can only bet that's even more true now that Bexley has popped up. Just one more issue for the girl to cause. And to think, all this happened because I almost picked up some underage prostitutes outside of the bar. If I'd have just eaten before we went topside, we'd never had to have gone in search of food in the first place.

Never would have found Bexley or pissed off August.

She wouldn't be here and things would be... well, different.

# CHAPTER THIRTY-FIVE

## BEXLEY

The shower is going in the bathroom when I wake and that sounds so good right now but I can't bring myself to get up. The bed is warm and comfortable and as usual, I'm sore.

"And that isn't causing an issue?" Maxen asks, and I wonder if they always do stuff like this together? Is it normal for one to be in the shower while the other does... something else? Or are they in the shower together? Is *that* normal?

Is it a demon thing or do they have some other type of bond? Are they together or just really close? Their relationship is a mystery to me, but it isn't what I really care to figure out right now. I want to know about their lives as demons.

*Demons.*

They are demons.

The thought had been in my head after hearing about being in Hell but hearing and seeing are two different things. Seeing truly is believing because without seeing the proof, without seeing Maxen with a pair of horns, and a random tail slithering along my body, and feeling this giant, uncomfortable but delicious *knot* on the end of Kaine's cock, I'm not sure I'd have believed them.

It's hard to process. Not only because I realize I've slept with two demons but because this means so much more about life. If Hell exists, does Heaven? Are angels real? What about fairies? Vampires? The list could go on forever. Is there an end? Or is everything that's meant to be a fairytale actually real?

It's so much. Too much to process at any point in the day, never mind this early in the morning and before I've had food or coffee.

I bring my attention back to the conversation the guys are having. I'm being nosy and I'd love to know what issue Maxen could be talking about and if they're talking about me. They're hiding me from Kaine's father, that much I know, and it's probably because you aren't supposed to bring humans to Hell for the fun of it.

"Not yet," Kaine responds. "She was just someone to fuck to pass the time. I wouldn't care if I never saw her again."

My stomach turns sour and my entire body goes cold.

*Me.* He's talking about me.

My mind blanks, my brain full of fog.

So many things come flying at me all at once. I want to throw up and hide all at the same time. I want to punch him in the balls, make him hurt.

Everything I've brought myself to believe about them is all a lie.

I've allowed myself to accept the fucked-up things I learned about this place, about them, because I thought there was something here. Not only do I feel like I belong here, but I feel like I belong with them. Like something was going on between us. Now I'm just a fuck that he wouldn't miss?

This hurts. It actually fucking hurts. I thought...

It doesn't matter what I thought. In fact, those thoughts were really fucking stupid from the get-go.

Why would I allow myself to gain feelings for someone who can barely say two words to me and can only communicate with his cock? Someone who obviously *did* kidnap me because there is no way Kaine is saving anyone from anything.

I'm an idiot.

I allowed whatever crazy part of me that felt comfortable here to take over and convinced myself this could be a good thing. That I could stay here and there not be an issue... but again, I'm an idiot. I saw the signs, they were all there, and I ignored them.

A sharp pain jolts through the side of my head, and I hiss out in pain.

*"Where are you going?"*

*Daddy turns around to face me as he puts his arm inside of his jacket.*

*"I have to go, Bee."*

*"But you said..."*

*He sighs. "I'm sorry. I wish things were different."*

*"You always say that! You always say the same thing but you don't mean it. If you meant it, then you would make it true!"*

*I turn and run. Down the hall and down the stairs, right through the front door around to the backyard and into the tree house he built me when he was here the last time.*

*He always says the same thing when he's here. He always tells me he's going to stay, that nothing can take him away from me, but he always goes.*

*He always leaves me.*

*The signs are there, they always are, but I'm stupid and I ignore them because I don't want them to be real.*

I snap out of the memory and throw the blankets off me, getting out of bed in search of my clothes. The shower is still running so I should be able to sneak out of here and find my way out and back home. If I got here, there has to be a way to get home, and whatever that is, I'll figure it out.

Because if I've learned anything in the few days I've been here, it's that all guys are the same.

Every last one of them.

All they've ever done my entire life is let me down. It started with my father, then it was the boyfriends. Guy after guy... no matter how different they look, or how different they act, it's always the same outcome. Always the same thing. Well, this time, I'm not having it. I won't allow myself to get any deeper into this. I will not be hurt over one more guy. I refuse.

I quickly pull on my clothes, the outfit I was in yesterday, the one Rachel brought since I can't find my other one. My shoes are in the closet, and I put them on and hurry out of the room just as the shower shuts off.

I know I don't have long before one of them notices I'm gone, and I need to make sure I'm as far away as possible when that happens.

Kaine didn't explain to me how the stairs in this place work, but I sort of figured it out myself yesterday. There are two sets and I think I took the wrong one last time. So instead of going down the set we usually take to get to the breakfast room or the hot tub, I take the other and pray I'm right. I pray that this set is what will bring me to that main floor and towards the front door. And I only hope I do it without getting caught by anyone. As much as I don't want Maxen or Kaine finding me, I also don't want to be found by Kaine's father, or by any of the servants, the creepy fuckers.

I have no idea what I'll be up against once I get outside. I have no idea what it's like in Hell, how the people are, or what I'm even looking for to leave. I'll figure it out as I go. All I know is that I can't stay here.

Heartbreak is all I've known my whole life. Heartbreak and disappointment.

Not anymore.

I rush down the stairs and let out a breath when I see that first floor come into view, those large double doors just to the side of me. There is no one around so I rush across the foyer and push through them.

The air is warm on my skin and the sun is bright. I go back the way we came, thinking backtracking makes the most sense. At least I know a little bit of that area.

There is a path on the ground that I follow. I'm quick but cautious, wary of running into anyone. I have no idea what I'm looking for or how I'll get out of here.

Is there a train? A bus? Taxis? Can I get my ass Ubered out of Hell?

Staying on the path, it doesn't take long for that large brick building to come into view, the one I vaguely remember. The closer I get, the clearer the vision behind it becomes and I stop dead in my tracks.

"Holy shit," I murmur to myself.

I don't know how I missed this the other day... actually, I do. It's because I was heading in the other direction. I mean, I wasn't exactly looking out for bubbling, lava-filled volcanoes, either.

I'm frozen in fear, watching as the bright red and orange lava spits out the top in small bits, flying around and landing on the ground.

Is this normal or is it erupting and I'm about to become petrified in the fucking lava?

The only thing that gets me moving are the voices I hear coming from behind me. My heart is pounding loudly, and my limbs are not moving easily, but I dash towards some bushes on my left, duck down and hide in them.

Moments later, two people walk by, clearly demons as they both have tails...

Shit.

If it's normal to walk around in demon form, then I'm fucked. I can't even pretend to fit in. I don't have horns, or a tail, or whatever else these lying, scheming fuckers have.

I don't let it stop me though. I'm not giving up. I wait a few more beats before climbing out of the bushes and keep heading forward, in the direction the other two demons went.

If they're walking towards the explosive and terrifying volcano, then it must be okay. Normal, even... unless they're immune to it and can't burn because they are part of Hell?

Fuck, this is so frustrating.

How in the world did I get myself into this mess in the first place? I can't even answer that because I don't know. Rachel and I didn't have much alone time for me to ask what happened and how I ended up here. I didn't bother asking the guys because well, we rarely talk at all. And now I guess it doesn't matter. Unless it would have helped me to get back, that is. Which it could have, but now I'll never know.

I try to keep my head clear as I speed walk as far away from the castle as I can get. Once the path ends, I move towards what looks like a forest of trees with blood-red leaves. The trunks are black, not brown like I'm used to at home, and it helps me blend in. My hair is dark, and so are the sweatpants and shirt I'm wearing, so there's that. I keep moving forward for what feels like hours and I don't see another person at all. Yet, I find myself coming to another halting stop when the trees instantly go from being blood-red, to bright purple.

I have no idea what this means, but I have to keep moving forward.

I need to go home.

# CHAPTER THIRTY-SIX

## MAXEN

"Not yet. She was just someone to fuck to pass the time. I wouldn't care if I never saw her again."

"I doubt she feels the same," I say as I rinse my toothbrush and put it back.

The shower shuts off and Kaine steps out and starts to dry himself.

"I need to head home at some point. Check on that horny fuck of a father I have." Kaine reaches for the sweatpants he brought in and tugs them on. "Was thinking I should just go today and get it over with."

"Probably for the best. I need to find Marionette to see if she is as useful as she claims, but when I get back you can go."

I nod as I walk past him and back into the room.

As I turn towards the closet, I notice the bed is empty and I pause, looking around the room.

When I find it empty of Bexley, I pop my head back into the bathroom.

"Did you send Bexley somewhere?"

"The fuck? No. Why?" His eyes widen as he puts two and two together, taking long strides into the bedroom. He stomps towards the door, and I follow. He checks the lounge room, but it's empty of her too. "Fuck," he growls out, tugging at his hair.

"Well, this isn't good." I shake my head, hands on my hips.

"No shit!" he shouts as he walks past me. I hurry back into the room to find some clothes to put on. We both finish getting dressed within seconds.

"What's the plan?" I ask as we walk down the hallway.

"I need to find Marionette. The more info we have on Bexley, the better. If she isn't human, as I suspect, maybe she'll blend in a little better."

"And for me?"

"Find my father first, make sure he doesn't have her. Then start hunting. Call me if you find anything."

We split up and head in different directions. I make sure I have my phone in my pocket. We weren't exactly lying when we told Bexley we didn't have service. We don't actually have service to call anywhere outside of Hell, but we couldn't exactly tell her that at the time.

The phones work perfectly fine down here when needing to call someone who has the same service.

We aren't the most technically advanced, and it's mostly because we don't need to be.

Demons don't have friends to keep in touch with. They don't give a fuck if they have family to talk to. Phones down here are mostly only used for entertainment and for work. Head demons needing to make sure their employees—if you can call them that, since they're actually condemned to their jobs and not able to choose them—are doing as they're told. It's also a good way for people to hire hits—cause yeah, that happens down here. It's like a big thing. The demons who go topside make deals, get paid in whatever they want—no, it isn't always souls—then make deals with the demons down here who will go and complete the hit. There's a whole website for it and everything.

demonslist.dev

Hell is fucked up and the people in it are even more twisted.

As I make my way to find Kaine's father, I'm secretly hoping he was the one to find her, because at least we could explain and talk him out of doing something stupid. If she made it out of this castle and is wondering around... who knows what will find her. There is no way she'll make the same mistake twice and end up in the dungeons. If she makes it outside... she's in more danger than she can imagine.

Kaine

Moving down the steps quickly, I make my way to Marionette's room.

I don't bother knocking, just push through the door.

She looks up at me from where she's sitting on the couch with a bored expression. "Well, it's a good thing I didn't have male entertainment," she says, tossing down the newspaper.

"Did you do as I asked?" I step towards her, stopping only a foot away.

"I did."

"And?" I hold back the anger I feel for her not telling me this by now.

She removes her glasses from her face and puts them on top of the newspaper on the table in front of her. She pinches the bridge of her nose and rubs her eyes. Each second that passes I become more and more impatient and about to snap.

"And it was just as I said. There was no alert." I glare, my skin itching. "The system is fine, Kaine. Whoever you brought down here a few nights ago, is not human."

"You're s—"

"Yes, I'm sure. I'd bet my life on it." She gets to her feet and moves towards me, lowering her voice before saying, "Bring her to me and I'll figure out what she is."

"That's going to be an issue." She raises a brow. "She seems to have gone missing."

She lets out a frustrated sigh, and turns around, heading into the back room. "I don't know how you always manage to get yourself into this shit, Kaine, but I'm getting too old for it. I didn't move here to be your personal *cleaner*."

I try not to laugh at her use of the word. It's what Maxen and I always call her when she fixes our problems. She doesn't clean up dead bodies like a normal cleaner would, we aren't in the habit of unaliving people, but we do get ourselves into shit often. Especially with our trips to topside.

Though Maxen has been trying to be a little more aware of what we're doing, since we were caught by one of those Prideful bastards the time before last, and if it weren't for my father pulling some strings, both Maxen and I would be in the Pit right now.

"If anyone finds out I'm doing this, I'll be sent to the Pit without question."

I grin at her, trying to keep my demeanor calm even though I want to tear this place apart and go in search of Bexley. I have this sick feeling in my gut that it isn't my father who has her. "Come on, Mari. You know I won't tell anyone."

"There are other ways," she says through clenched teeth.

"Dad would never allow it."

"He isn't the only person who has pull in Hell. I think you know this by now." She takes out a key from the top drawer in her desk and opens a cabinet in the back of the room, pulling out a large tablet. Placing it down on her desk, she pushes the button on the top of it. The screen goes red before showing a full map of Hell. She's still mumbling under her breath as she navigates through the program, zoning in on the castle.

"When did she go missing?"

"About twenty minutes ago?"

She sets the time to twenty minutes prior and lucky enough, catches someone leaving the castle front doors and scurrying away. It doesn't show a picture like a camera would, it's more like a heat sensor, only each type of demon is a different color, and only a tiny circle and not the outline of a person. I don't know much about it, only what I see because she's very hush-hush about it. I know there are only a few select people who are entrusted with Wandering Tablets. All of the Kings have them, and a few others who help keep everyone in line, but that's it. And from what I was told, most don't use them because they just don't care.

It's easy to make assumptions when looking at this map based on the geography of Hell. Even though each area has their own distinct color, you can see all of them all over the map since no one is required to stay in their own kingdom but can travel as they choose.

Wrath has a load of red dots, Envy is a copper color, Pride is purple, Sloth is yellow, Lust is pink, Greed is green, and Gluttony is blue.

So when I see that the dot leaving the castle is white with a very pale outline of green around it, I know something is off. Especially since humans show up as orange.

"Well now, that's something."

"I thought people didn't show as more than one color?" This was something she actually explained to me before. There are some demons who breed with other types, so someone will come out not pure of blood, but they will always take on the attributes of who they are raised by. If a Lust and Sloth demon have a child, and that child goes to live with the mother in Sloth, then they will take on the attributes of Sloth demons, along with that color showing up on this screen.

"They don't..." she says softly.

"And why is she white?" I move my eyes from the screen, and lock onto Marrionette's.

"You need to find this girl immediately. If anyone finds out what she is, it'll start a war."

# CHAPTER THIRTY-SEVEN

## BEXLEY

The bright purple trees are more inviting than the red ones, so I keep walking. Not that I think anything in Hell can be inviting... well, except for those two sexy demons and their devilishly firm and tattooed bodies. Those are most definitely inviting...

*No, Bexley, knock it off.*

I should not be thinking about them. They're assholes.

Sexy, good in bed, nice-cocked assholes...

My god, I have issues.

Wait... should I be saying that in Hell?

I scrub a hand over my face and keep moving forward, still with no idea of what I am looking for, but I know I need to keep going and stop thinking about stupid things. Maybe I'll come across someone who looks friendly enough for me to ask for directions.

Directions on how to get back to earth? Back... topside? Is that what they called it? I think that's what I heard them say.

The deeper I get into this purple-treed area, the better it smells. I hadn't noticed it until now, but the smell of ash is lingering on my clothes, and I'm glad to be away from that area and into better smelling places. My shirt smells exactly as it would after spending the night by a campfire, and I hate it. Out here, though, these purple trees have a sweet, flowery scent to them. It's warm and welcoming and I find myself relaxing a little as I go farther in, the trees getting denser. I am worried about getting lost out here, in the woods of Hell, but the only way to go is forward. I have no idea what kind of animals I'll run into... but I'll deal with it if it happens.

The leaves on the trees surrounding me are as purple as eggplants, and the bark is a light gray. When I first reached them, I thought they were covered in flowers, but it turns out there isn't a flower in sight. It's all leaves. Odd, but this is Hell, so what do I know?

There is a distant gurgling sound I keep hearing, and because I'm feeling frisky, I walk in that direction. I have no idea what it is, but it has to be something...

I make my way through the trees quickly and carefully, hoping I'll find a road or person. Just one though, since that won't be a scary as running into a group of people.

A short time later, it isn't a road I come upon, it's actually a lake... or a pond or something like that. Only the water is black and boiling. Like a pot of colored water would look like on a stove. The weird thing is, it isn't any hotter over here than it is anywhere else. So maybe it isn't boiling from heat, but air trapped below?

I move closer to the edge, not wanting to get so close that I may fall in, but I'm a nosy bitch. I have no idea if that is actually water or some kind of skin-eating acid that would destroy my flesh in seconds. I'd rather not risk it so I keep a good ten-foot distance. It sits there with no waves, just bubbling. There is what looks like sand around the edges only it's also black.

It's very interesting. I bet it looks amazing from out there, like if you could go on a boat? The dark sand and water, with the bright purple trees. It would be a great painting.

"Hey!"

The voice sends me bolting ahead and back into the tree line.

Footsteps sound behind me and I know I'm being chased now. The voice didn't sound friendly, and I have no want to stop and find out if my assumption is correct or not. Yes, I wanted to find someone, but a *friendly* someone. Not someone shouting at and then chasing me.

I push myself harder, pumping my arms and willing my legs to move faster.

"Stop!" The voice sounds closer than it did before, which is terrifying. The fear gives me the extra adrenaline I needed to push even harder. I break from the trees, the water still to my left but to my right is a fortress of sorts. I don't slow down to get a good look, but I take a glance, making sure there aren't armed people hanging around and waiting to shoot me with something. Clearly, I am trespassing now, getting closer to somewhere people will definitely be, but as much as I wanted that before, I suddenly don't want it now. In fact, going back to the castle sounds like the best idea and if I can just get away from whoever it is that's chasing me, I'll turn around and go back.

"Gotcha!"

The wind is knocked out of me as a large, heavy body knocks into me, arms wrapping around my upper body and we both fall to the ground, landing on our sides. Sharp pain shoots up my left side as I land with a thud.

"Let me go," I snap, trying to fight off whoever it is that has me. They're behind me, holding me tightly. A large hand wraps around my mouth as I try to scream.

"Keep it quiet," they growl in my ear. The voice is deep and haunting, and something I won't soon forget. I do as I'm told. Seconds later, another person comes into view, hovering over us. I close my eyes, sure I am not seeing what I'm seeing, but as I open them, I realize I am.

The person in front of me is not only wearing nothing but a small loincloth, but they have wings. Big, black fucking wings, and I know this is not going to turn out well for me. Something about those wings just looks like a bad omen, bad luck, and every other bad thing in this world.

"Get her up," the one in front of me says.

The one who is holding me maneuvers themselves to get up without letting go of me nor removing their hand from my mouth. I'm breathing heavily, my nostrils flaring and lungs burning. My legs ache from running and I would give my left tit to be floating around in that hot tub right about now.

Without a word, the demon in front of me moves back towards the woods from where we came, glancing at the fortress one last time before entering into the cover of the trees. I think of fighting this one off of me, but he's really strong and carrying me with just an arm around my waist and the other around my mouth. It doesn't even seem like a struggle to him.

"Don't you know not to be hanging around Pride? They don't like seeing not a one person over here."

"Do you think they saw us?" the one with the deep and scary voice behind me asks.

"Nah, I think we is okay," the other responds. "But the girl needs to keeps it quiet."

"You hear that?" The warmth of the man's breath on my ear has me gagging, but I nod vigorously in response, not wanting him to hurt me.

"We gots to move or else they find us. Rounds soon." The guy starts moving deeper into the woods, but not the way we came. More off to the side and I have no idea where he is going. Not that I know where anything is around here...

The demon who is carrying me continues to do so and again, I don't bother fighting. I allow him to carry me and catch my breath, trying to get my strength back, hoping to take off when they let their guard down. If he's going to hold me like this I may as well take advantage of it.

I'm not sure how long it is we're walking for, but it seems like forever until we come to a stop.

"I thinks we good for a few."

The man who is holding me sets me down on my feet but doesn't move his hand from my waist. "Keep it quiet," he warns me again and I nod. He removes his hand from my mouth, and I lick my dry lips, the taste of salt and dirt on my tongue from his grimy hand.

I want to throw up.

"Who are you?" I ask, wishing this guy would just let me go. I hate being so close to him, it feels icky and wrong.

"Name's Fiasco and that's Gnome."

Fiasco and Gnome? What in the actual fuck...

"Who is you?" he asks, pulling a pack from his shoulder that I didn't even notice since it blended into his black wings, and starts digging through it.

"B–Bexley," I say.

He pops his head up and turns towards me. "Bexley? Whats a weird names that is."

I huff out a breath. My name is weird? This guy is named after a synonym for disaster and the other brutish one is named after a lawn ornament, and I'm the one with a weird name?

I don't respond and with a shake of his head, he goes back to digging in his bag.

It's hard to think *I'm* the strange one out here.

"Ah, gots it." He pulls out a rope and tosses it to the one behind me—Gnome. He catches it with his free hand, and I know what's about to happen.

"No, please. Just let me go. I just need to get back..." I plead with him, even though I know it won't work.

"Backs where?" Fiasco turns towards me again, crossing his arms over his wide chest.

"To the castle," I say, not knowing what else to say. I don't know if there are areas here, like towns or something. I have no idea where I was nor where I am now.

"Castle? What castle?"

"The one with the volcano," I say quickly.

He laughs. Literally throws his head back and laughs so loud animals fly from the trees. I'd say they were birds but those flaps sounded too eerie to be cute, feathery birds, so I don't even think about it. I can't, or I'll lose my damn mind.

"You wants to go back to Wrath? Of all the places in Hell, and that's what you wants to do?"

"I... guess?"

Gnome loosens his grip on my waist, but only enough to shift and grab my wrist. I work on instinct and use my free one to turn and swing at him, only he stops me, snatching that wrist in midair. He tsks and I look up, getting a good glimpse of him.

Holy hell.

This man... if he is a man, I don't know, looks like a fucking gargoyle. His features are so prominent, and his skin is an ashy gray and those wings... holy shit. I knew he was big by how he felt behind me but I didn't think he was that big. He has to be at least eight feet tall.

All of the air leaves my lungs, and my head gets dizzy.

"Not nice, little lady," Fiasco says, shaking his head.

I blink my eyes, trying to fight off the fog, and when I realize what is going on, Gnome has both of my hands bound behind my back, the other end of the rope in his hand like a leash. Like I'm a fucking dog or something.

My eyes burn with the need to cry.

I should have stayed where I was...

The devil you know, and all.

Even if Kaine and Maxen are dicks who kidnapped me and used me for sex, I could have convinced them to bring me back home, right? There had to have been a way. Why did I think leaving was a good idea? Especially after the first time went so badly... Or, I guess it didn't go badly, it was just unsuccessful.

I curse myself as Fiasco tosses his pack back over his shoulder and starts to walk again, his large wings pulled in tight to his back, the bottoms just about reaching the ground. Gnome shoves me on the middle of my back and I start moving, not wanting to see what he'll do if I don't. And of course, he even walks behind me, keeping the leash tight enough that if I walk too fast, my shoulders start to ache.

After walking through the trees for a while longer, I finally open my mouth to ask what the fuck is going on. "Where are we going?"

"Homes."

"Where is home?"

"Gluttony," he responds.

Pride. Greed. Gluttony.

It hits me.

"Are the towns named after the seven deadly sins?"

He laughs loudly and it throws me off guard.

"You must nots been here long if you is calling it that. But sure, if you says so."

I don't bother asking what he means by that because really I don't care.

"Can't you just take me back?" I plead.

"No can dos. Sorry."

"Why not?"

"Must bring you to the King. It's our duty. Finds people who don't belong, takes them to the King."

"And what does he want from me?"

He shrugs. "Don't knows. Guess it depends on his moods."

I'm going to die. I am definitely going to fucking die.

# CHAPTER THIRTY-EIGHT

## BEXLEY

The farther we walk, the sweeter the scent continues to get. My stomach growls and I wish I ate before I left.

Fuck, I wish a lot of things since being out here. Hindsight is twenty-twenty and all that jazz.

"Can we rest?" I groan just as I trip over a rock in the ground. Gnome pulls on the rope, which stops me from falling, but I scream as a sharp pain shoots through my shoulders.

"We must keeps going befores we are seen."

"Seen? Seen by who?"

I don't know why that thought hadn't crossed my mind. Sure, these guys have me now and I don't know where they're bringing me, but on all accounts, they haven't hurt me or been mean to me. Gnome is a pretty big and scary dude, but Fiasco looks like he'd get his ass beaten by a toddler. What if there are other demons out here who do the same thing they do? What if they find us and kill us?

There's always a bigger fish in the sea.

Always.

My stomach growls again.

"Shuts that up," Fiasco says over his shoulder.

I look up and glare at him.

"I can't stop it, I'm hungry."

"You make noises when you is hungry?" he asks, coming to a stop.

"Uh, my stomach does, yeah. That's what happens when it decides to eat itself when there is no food in there."

"You body is eating you body?" He takes a step towards me, and I step back, only there is nowhere to go because the giant of a man is there. "What kind of creature is you? Not demons. No, you not demons. We demons. Horns demons. Tails demons. Black eyes demons. But you? I don't know whats you are. Witches, maybe? With spells that makes you body eats itself?"

"What? No. I'm h—"

"Step away from the girl and you keep your wings."

Fiasco's eyes widen in front of me. He waits a beat before stepping back and raising his hands.

The rope drops behind me and I sense Gnome has moved too. The voice came from behind me—again—so yet again, I have no idea who it is. And this time I just about accept death.

"Where did you find this girl?" The person behind us asks. His voice sounds normal, like any average guy back home.

"We finds her trying to steal from Pride!" Fiasco spits.

"I was not!" I shout, turning to face the person behind me, only I regret it. Oh, how I fucking regret it when I'm met with a wide mouth full of razor-sharp teeth attached to a head that is the size of a fucking horse. I gasp and step back, tripping over another stupid rock and this time falling to my ass with a loud thud. I grunt as I hit the floor, and consider just lying there to wither away, but I open my eyes, figuring it's stupid to give up. With the distance, I now see what I'm looking at, though I don't have words for it.

There is a man, or who I assume is a demon, though he looks human to me, and he's sitting on top of a... well, what looks like a fucking dragon.

But not the cute dragons. No, this isn't fucking Dragonite or Toothless or Elliot. No, this is a fucking great white of a dragon. Like the shark leapt out of the sea, grew black scales, and learned to exist on land.

It's fucking terrifying.

*Terrifying.*

And if I'd eaten anything today, surely I'd have shit my pants by now.

The man on top of the beast looks down at me, studying me for a long moment before he speaks, aiming his words at Gnome and Fiasco.

"Get on your way. The girl stays with me."

Oh, no, no, no. I don't want to go with Jaws. Please, anything but this.

The man keeps his gaze on me as he hops off that monstrosity. "You're coming with me."

My lip trembles and I lose it. Tears fill my eyes, blurring my vision, and I lean forward wanting to hug myself, only I can't because my arms are still tied behind me. Sobs leave my throat, my chest burns, and I know this is the end of my fucking life.

I'm tugged up under my arm and spun around. It takes me a few moments to realize the man is untying me. When he lets me go, I wipe my eyes and realize it's only us left. Gnome and Fiasco took off quickly, not even a footstep can be heard.

"You're safe with me, no one will hurt you."

I turn to look at him. His irises are a bright green, an inhumanly shade of green, and I'd been so occupied by the all mighty dragon that I hadn't noticed.

"Do you work with Kaine?"

"Kaine?" he rears his head back, scratching his chin. "Tzalli's boy?" My look must say it all. He shakes his head. "From Wrath?"

I perk up and smile for the first time in hours. "Yes! Can you take me to him?"

He cocks his head to the side, studying me again as if I've just said something crazy.

"Why would you want to go there?"

"Because he—"

"Is he the reason you're here?" His tone has me cautious about what I say. I suddenly have the feeling that I shouldn't be telling him anything about Kaine or Maxen. Even if I am mad at them, I don't know anything about this place other than I shouldn't be here. I don't want Kaine to get into trouble for bringing me here when he wasn't supposed to.

"I... don't remember."

He doesn't believe me. I see it in the way he narrows his eyes, but he doesn't question it. Just nods his head. "Let's go then. There is someone you need to see."

The thought of running doesn't even cross my mind, not with those fangs being so close to me. That dragon-thing's teeth could cut a limb clean off. I doubt I'd even feel it, that's how sharp they look.

"Come on." He holds out his hand and looks up towards where he was sitting only moments ago, on top of Cujo of the dragon variety.

"Fuck no. I am not going anywhere near that thing." I take a step back, keeping my eyes on the evil beast. "I'll walk."

The man huffs out a laugh, shaking his head. "No, you will ride with me. Walking will take too long."

I shake my head and take another step back. His face grows more serious when he sees me not obeying his command.

"You will come up here willingly or I will tie you back up. It's your choice."

My mouth falls open as I look from him back to those rows of teeth and I swear that fucking thing just smirked at me. I close my eyes and pull in a breath.

How the fuck did I get myself into this?

# CHAPTER THIRTY-NINE

## BEXLEY

My pillow is soaked with tears.

It's been four days since Daddy has been gone and I have this awful feeling in my stomach that I'll never see him again. Though, I tell myself this is how I feel every time he leaves us. I never know when he's going to come back, if at all, but something about this time seems different.

The sun is only just coming up and I know Mommy will be in here soon to wake me for school. I've tried to think of ways to stay home, but I can't come up with anything that will work. She always knows when I'm lying. I've been trying every day this week to get out of going to school, but she won't allow it.

How is she always so okay after Daddy leaves? Doesn't she miss him too? I don't understand and I think that's why I yelled at her last night. How can she say she loves my daddy if she isn't even sad when he leaves? Why can't she make him stay?

And what makes me even more angry? I wonder if he loves us at all. He tells me he does and says he wishes things were different, but if you love someone, you do anything for them. Anything. No matter what. If he can't even stay here, then does he really love me at all?

My stomach growls and I remember that I went to bed last night without dinner. I got mad at Mommy right as we sat down to eat. Nana didn't say anything as I yelled at my mother, she just watched. She always tries to stay out of it, but I know I can trust her with anything, even if she doesn't like my daddy. She listens to me when I'm upset about him.

She has never told me why she doesn't like him, only that I wouldn't understand until I'm older. I don't like that she doesn't like him, but at least she doesn't lie about it. She doesn't pretend to be someone she's not, and she doesn't tell me things just to make me happy.

I really hate when Mommy does that. She treats me like a little kid even though I'm not a little kid anymore. Ten is big. That's two whole numbers now.

When I look at the clock, I notice it's past the time Mommy wakes me up, and with another growl from my belly, I decide to get up by myself.

I feel bad for being upset with her, so maybe I'll make her breakfast to make her feel better and show her I am sorry.

Whenever Daddy is here, he spends all his time with me and tells me it's important to not only tell the people you care about that you love them, but to show them too. Because a hug can be so much better than words. Maybe breakfast will be even better than that.

I get out of bed and go down the hallway and down the stairs, straight to the kitchen. Nana isn't awake yet either, which is weird, but maybe they stayed up late talking or something. Or maybe she went to the store. Sometimes she does that.

I get the eggs from the fridge and scramble enough for me, Mom, and Nana.

I'm very careful with the stove, doing everything just the way Daddy showed me. When I'm done, the eggs are a little brown but it's okay, I like them well-done. I toast some bread and then butter them, putting everything on a tray and place it on the kitchen table. I even pour some orange juice for the three of us and then clean up the counter where I spilled some.

*When I see the clock and notice that we have to leave in only a half an hour, I know I have to go wake Mommy up so I'm not late. At least she can come back home and go to sleep after she drops me off.*

*I skip down the hallway with a smile on my face. She's going to be so happy when she sees what I did. She'll accept my apology and maybe we can watch a movie later. Maybe she even knows when Daddy will be back. Sometimes she says she does, but mostly I know he comes and goes whenever he wants.*

*Her door is closed, so I knock. Maybe she is getting dressed.*

*When she doesn't answer, I knock again. "Mommy?"*

*Still nothing. I put my hand on the knob and turn it. It isn't locked, so I push the door open and what I see is an image that will haunt me for years to come.*

The ride to wherever it is we are going is quick. Much quicker than it would have been on foot. Surprisingly, even with the size of this animal we are on, it manages to weave its way through the trees like a damn snake. We popped out a while back and have been trotting down a barren road that reminds me of the desert, if only the desert were haunted.

My stomach growls continuously at this point and my head is starting to hurt from the lack of water and food. It's only been a few hours, but this bitch is used to eating her three meals a day, and it has to be close to dinnertime by now and I haven't had a damn thing.

We start up a hill and once we reach the top, I finally make out what looks like another castle far down the road. I know it isn't the same one I came from, and I don't know if this is good or bad, but I can't find it in me to care. If they're going to kill me though, I wish they would just do it.

With this man behind me, holding me close to him—probably so I don't try to jump off and run for it—I drift in and out of sleep or consciousness, I can't really tell, but soon enough we come to a stop, and I look up at a tall, shiny black gate.

It starts to open by itself, as if it knew we were here or something. The razer-teethed animal walks in and the gates close behind us. Ahead is a castle that is much smaller than the one I was in with Kaine and Maxen, and I wonder where I could be now. Which of the seven deadly sins will be the cause of my demise?

The dragon-thing walks us towards the steps. They're black marble with small flecks of green that you can only see close up. The man behind me, who hasn't said a word since he threatened to tie me up and force me onto Godzilla, hops off and then helps me down with his hands on my hips and mine on his shoulders. Thankfully, I didn't get any vibes that he's trying to sleep with me, he seems, weirdly enough, concerned for my safety on top of eager to get me to wherever it is we've just shown up to.

I keep wondering why he's being so nice to me. I can't decide if it's just to make the torture worse, or if he feels bad for wherever he is bringing me.

"Go on, Ezekiel, go take a nap." I raise a brow as the man speaks to the dragon beast who takes off like a dog, disappearing around the corner to apparently go take a nap...

The man then looks at me, a tiny smirk on his lips before he looks up at the black castle.

"Welcome to Greed."

# CHAPTER FORTY

## MAXEN

After realizing Kaine's father has no idea where Bexley is, I make my way out of his office without stirring up suspicion. Though, I'm not sure how well that worked out. I basically tried to make small talk with him, asking what he'd been up to and all he did was get annoyed with me.

If he'd have found a girl wandering around the castle, he'd be angry and annoyed and would most definitely have said something to me about it, knowing I'd have something to do with it.

When I leave his office, I head over to check the room with the hot tub, wondering if maybe she decided to have a soak without telling either of us. Not sure that makes sense, but maybe.

That room is empty too.

I search random rooms, thinking she just wanted to explore, even though I know deep down what happened.

She left.

There is a pang in my chest at the thought, and I blame it on anxiety over getting thrown in the Pit.

Why do I care that she's gone?

I don't know why she suddenly decided to leave, but it's what she did. It's the only thing that makes sense. She has no reason to be in any of these rooms I'm looking in. She isn't five so I doubt she's playing the best game of hide-and-go-seek ever. There isn't anything interesting in them to keep her there either, and she doesn't seem like one to be interested in the decor or history of the place. The last time she took off, it was to escape. Only she got lost and found some shit she shouldn't have. Kaine filled me in on that whole thing. She must have figured out how to get out of here because I don't think she'd risk the chance of running into something like what she saw in the dungeon again.

Only it didn't seem to scare her... yet, I don't think she'd go looking for it willingly. She doesn't seem like *that* kind of person.

She's good. Tinged with some darkness, definitely a smart-ass mouth, but mostly she's good.

My phone starts to ring, and I pull it from my pocket. It's Kaine, so I answer.

"Hello?"

He sounds out of breath. "Meet me outside, in the front."

"Be there in a minute."

He doesn't say anything else, just ends the call. Putting my phone back into my pocket, I race down the hall and back to the stairs. I get down them faster than I ever have before, bursting through the front doors.

Kaine is already there, waiting, with a cigarette between his lips.

"Well?" I ask, stopping beside him.

"She left and took off towards Pride."

"How do you know that?"

"Marionette is good for some things."

"Okay, so let's go." I start down the steps but stop when he calls my name. I turn and look at him over my shoulder.

"I need to tell you something first."

"Okay..." I say slowly. He meets me, stopping on the same step I'm at. He looks me in the eyes and looks almost worried. "What is it?"

"You know the Wandering Tablet?" I nod. "Marionette used it to see if she could figure out where she may be. There aren't many humans down here." He takes a drag from his cigarette before flicking it down the stairs.

"Go on." I don't know why he can't just get to the point.

"She's... uh, well, we know for sure now she's not human."

"Huh?"

"Bexley. She isn't human. Not fully anyway"

"Not human?" He shakes his head, which does not help me at all. Not human, okay, that could be good or bad...

He moves closer to me and looks around before speaking in a low voice. "She showed up multicolored."

"What? How is that possible?" He shakes his head again. "I'm gonna need more than a head shake, okay?"

"I don't know. Marionette didn't tell me. She just said we needed to find her and bring her back here, immediately."

"We should probably go then," I say, moving down the steps. He grips onto my shoulder, and I jerk back before stopping. I turn and glare when he doesn't seem to move with me to find Bexley. What is his problem?

"I can't lose her."

My eyes widen at his words. That was the last thing on the planet I was expecting to hear from him. Has he actually grown feelings for this girl? How is that possible? It's rare for demons to have feelings for anyone, and he and I already have a sort of bond. They never find more than one person they give a shit about. I don't bother asking questions. There has to be some sort of explanation for it, but now isn't the time for that. We need to find her first, then figure it out the rest later.

"Even more reason for us to get going then."

He stares at me for another moment before nodding, and then we rush down the stairs and around back to the stables. I can't remember the last time we used these demon horses and I hope it's like riding a bicycle because I don't feel like falling on my ass today.

We both have our favorite horses, who I'm sure remember us. These creatures have great memories and live for hundreds of years.

We both head to the back of the stable and find them side by side in their own stalls.

"Long time, no see, Ruckus." I reach my hand in to pet his warm snout and he chuffs at me, smoke billowing from his nose. "I know, it's been a while."

This horse has always been sassy and it's why I love him.

I undo the gate and get to work on saddling him up, talking to him, and apologizing the whole time, knowing it'll probably make my life easier. I lead him out once he's all set. Kaine is already there, sitting on top of his horse who is a great contrast to mine.

They're both the same size, from what I'm told they're as big as a full-grown male moose topside. Mine is pure black, so black he shimmers blue when in the right kind of light. When the sun is down, he blends right in, nothing on him able to be seen.

Kaine's horse, Ravage, is a deep red, matching exactly to the color of blood. His feet and snout are black, but fades into the red. His mane is pitch black, along with his tail. He's a very handsome horse, and also rare. Most horses down here are black or gray, it's rare to find any other color, but leave it to the Prince of Wrath to acquire a rare, blood-red horse... that he doesn't even use anymore.

Spoiled rich boy syndrome, getting all kinds of shit they don't need just because they can.

I hoist myself up and give Ruckus a pat on his neck. "Just like old times, Ruck."

Kaine and I both click our tongues at just about the same time to get our horses moving, and without hesitation, they do. We guide them down the trail at a quick trot and make it toward the main road.

"Are we just going to search around Pride for her?" I make sure my voice is loud enough for him to hear over the hooves digging into the ground.

"Marionette said she'd call me if anything changes, but when she saw her, she'd been sticking in the woods, following the water."

That's concerning. That water is fucking deadly. Worse than anything else down here. It's like acid, eating away at your skin, but it does so slowly. And even when you're out, it doesn't matter. It basically attaches itself to you and you're done. A fucking goner.

"You don't think she'd go in there, do you?"

He shakes his head. "No way. Shit's scary to even the demons."

That's a good point. I doubt she'd get the grand idea of skinny dipping in a boiling bunch of black scum.

It doesn't take us long to exit Wrath and reach Envy land, which is small, so we make our way through it quickly and soon enough we're in Pride territory.

There are no rules about staying off another's kingdom, people are free to roam where they want. They just have to respect property rules. You can't just head into Pride territory and walk up in their castle like you own the place, but you can roam around outside all you want. Just don't cause trouble, but that goes without saying. Though, it is Hell and there is trouble all over the place and Pride is one of the places you rarely see guards out. They think they're too good to be attacked, or something.

Yes, this is Hell, and shit is crazy, but it is never just pure chaos. The kings keep their kingdoms in order, guards wander about to make sure people aren't doing things they shouldn't, though, just like anywhere else, they still do.

There are still bad demons... which sounds weird to say since we're all bad, but I think you get the point. There are some who kill for the fun of it or steal because they can. Some areas around here are kill or be killed. It's no different than being topside, it's just much smaller down here and the jobs demons have aren't the same as up there. We have demons who are meant to go topside and murder. It's part of life. There needs to be bad to keep the good. Balance.

But they don't let just anyone do it because like I said, balance. Those who are appointed the job of Kill demon go through extensive testing to make sure they follow the rules and don't go wild. Though some are very good at hiding parts of them, hence some of the notorious serial killers that people just love. Then you have the demons down here who work off the hit list websites and go up to get shit done. It's a lot, but just like most other places, if you mind your business, you're fine.

Kaine veers into the Pride woods, slowing down, and I follow behind until I catch up to his side, and we move along at the same pace, staying side by side. We make our way towards the water and that's when Kaine's phone starts to ring. He pulls it from his pocket to answer.

"Yeah? What? You're sure? Fuck!"

He pulls the phone from his ear before aggressively shoving it into his pocket.

"Change of plan. Looks like we're going to Greed."

"Greed?" My eyes widen.

We turn back towards the main road.

"Seems she was picked up by someone. Made her way there pretty quickly."

"Well, that definitely isn't good."

"No. No it fucking is not."

# CHAPTER FORTY-ONE

## BEXLEY

"Where are we going?"

We've walked deeper and deeper into this castle and all I'm getting is more and more terrified.

I want to go home. I don't want to be here with this man or anyone else. Hell, just take me back to Kaine and Maxen... at least I was somewhat safe with them.

Or I thought I was anyway.

I mean, there was the good sex. And that hot tub. The food was good. Oh my God, the food alone... I don't even want to admit what I would give for a cheeseburger right about now.

"You'll see."

It's the same answer I've gotten the three other times I've asked him where he is taking me, and it's also going to be the last. It's annoying and adding to my anxiety, so I'm done talking.

After walking down an uncountable amount of hallways and up four flights of stairs, I'm good and lost. There is no way I'd make it out of this place. At least with Kaine's castle, it was a pretty basic layout once you figured it out. Sure, the stairs were confusing as fuck, but I knew where I needed to go. There were main hallways, then smaller ones off of those. This place? I'd die if I tried to get out on my own... and that thought... I don't like that thought. Not one fucking bit.

We turn another corner and we're met with a set of tall, wooden doors.

He pushes them open and walks in, so I follow behind, wanting to get this over with.

There is a man at the end of the room talking on a phone and staring out the window with his back to us. He's on the phone, but I can't hear his words.

Talking on the phone...

His phone works just fine, why the hell would that be? Maybe he will let me use it? If not, I'll come up with a plan to steal it and call Rachel. Actually, maybe I should just take it. Get it sooner rather than later. See if she can get in touch with someone to get in touch with Kaine? It's a long shot, but it's all I've got.

How I'm going to overpower this huge dude is a mystery, but I have to try. If I'm going to die anyway, I may as well fight to survive.

"I don't care how much it costs, just make it happen!" His words are perfectly clear now that he's shouting. "I want them all and I want them here within twenty-four hours!"

Well, he sounds like a peach.

We stop in front of the desk as the man pulls the phone away from his ear, sucks in a deep breath and lets it out. He turns around and I'm met with a pair of bright green eyes.

A pair of eyes that I could never in a million years forget.

All of the air leaves my lungs, and my legs grow weak. I reach for the desk to hold myself up and just barely make it. The man beside me holds me by my arm, but the man on the other side of the desk only stares at me, mouth wide open, clearly in as much shock as I am.

"How is this possible?" My words come out as a whisper, if they came out at all. This can't be real. There is no way this is real.

"Bee?"

He says my name and the word is like a dream come true. A voice that sends goosebumps across my skin and tears to my eyes. How I've longed to hear that name for years and years.

I nod as the first tear falls, then another, and I quickly lose count as my eyes fill and pour out.

My father makes his way around the table and pulls me into a hug without another word, squeezing me tight.

He holds me as the tears fall, and soon enough I am sobbing so hard my whole body is shaking. My throat is raw and my chest aches. It all comes out. Everything. The last seventeen years of being without my father, of wishing I could have done something more to stop him from killing himself... only he didn't, right? How else is he here? Unless he did and he was sent here... is that how this works?

Fuck, I don't know! So instead of asking the question, I just cry harder because for the first time in a while, I feel safe.

Even when I was with Kaine and Maxen, there was something in the back of my head, a worry about what would happen to me if I ran into Kaine's father, or if someone else who wasn't supposed to see me did. And today? Leaving, wandering around, being found by Fiasco and Gnome, and then this guy on the horse, being taken into this castle and not knowing a damn thing....

I can finally breathe... sort of. Through the tears I can, but it hurts.

After what must be at least ten minutes, I pull away, and my face is a disgusting mess, full of tears, snot, and drool, I'm sure.

My father picks up a tissue box from his desk and hands it to me. I pull a few tissues out to wipe my face.

"Let's sit."

He guides me over to a sofa and I plop down, fighting more tears that want to come. I blow my nose and wipe my eyes and end up needing more tissues. So many that they're now bunched in my hand the size of a baseball.

"How—" I clear my throat before I continue. I look up to meet his eyes and he looks just as confused as I feel. "How?" It's the only word I can think of clearly so it'll have to do.

He looks me over for a moment, almost as if he can't believe it's me. I know the feeling because I can't believe I'm looking at him, can't believe he's here, sitting on the sofa, less than a foot away from me. He looks exactly that same, as if he were frozen in time.

"I... Bee, there is so much to say." His voice is soft and calm, just the way I remember it to be every time he'd tell me he had to leave, and it makes me sick. "Why are you here? You're not... You didn't die, did you?"

I think about that for a moment. I don't know for sure, but I'm pretty sure I didn't come here because I died.

"Someone brought me."

"Brought you?" He rears his head back, eyebrows furrowing. "Who?"

"Kaine and Maxen." I tell him their names because why not?

"Kaine, Prince of Wrath?" His eyes are wide, but his cheeks are turning a shade of pink and I think maybe telling him who brought me here was a bad idea. But then...

"Prince? Kaine is a prince?"

He gets to his feet and starts to pace, talking to himself under his breath and ignoring my question. It's now I realize the other man left and we're alone. My father's pacing and mumbling goes on for at least a full minute before he stops and turns to me. "Did they say why?"

"No." But I know why. They were looking for a booty call. I can't tell my father that though.

"Did you speak with the king? Were they under his orders?"

"What? No. At least, I don't think so. They didn't want me near Kaine's father." He sighs before he starts to pace again. "Can you tell me what this is about?" I ask, feeling more confused than ever.

He stops again and turns towards me when someone bursts into the room. "Sir, there is someone here who demands your attention straight away."

Father's jaw clenches and he spins on his heel, leaving the room. I get up and hurry after him, only I don't get far before he stops me with a look that I know better than to question.

"You cannot come, Bee." My father steps closer to me and lowers his voice. "I have many enemies." He then turns to the guard who is standing by the door. "Call Grizen and Thulaz. Have them take her to my quarters and stay with her until I get there. She is not to be left alone under any circumstances."

The guard nods and then my father looks back at me, almost like he doesn't know what to say. "I'll see you soon, we can talk then."

I hear the words he says, but they go in one ear and out the other.

*I'll see you soon...*

How many times have I heard those words over the years and waited and waited and waited? Soon turned into weeks, then months, and sometimes years.

But he doesn't really have anywhere else to go this time, does he?

I want to argue, to ask him to stay or for me to go. I don't want to be without him again. I've only just gotten him back after seventeen years, how can I just let him walk away? Something tells me, like with most other times, what I want isn't going to matter. He has things to attend to, and I'll talk to him when he comes back to me.

He spins on his heel and hurries down the hallway.

I look to the guard who was ordered to escort me, and he ushers down the same hallway. We make our way up two flights of stairs before I'm brought into what looks like a large studio apartment.

"Make yourself comfortable." The guard motions to the couch and I move over to it and sit down. He then pulls out a phone and makes a call. Funny how all these phones seem to work without an issue. "The king needs you and Thulaz at his quarters immediately. I'll explain when you get here."

The king? Did he say king?

My father is a fucking King of Hell?

# CHAPTER FORTY-TWO

## KAINE

Our horses stop at the stairs of Castle Greed, and I hop off. Against Maxen's pleas, I burst through the door and am immediately met with seven guards. Of course, Greed of all places would have seven guards at the door.

"What can we do for you?" A portly one asks.

"You know exactly why I'm here. Where is she?"

"I'm sorry, but I have no idea what you're talking about."

I take a step closer. "Yes, you do," I say in a low, menacing tone. "Take me to her."

"Kaine," Maxen warns from behind me. "Can we speak to the king, please?" he asks in a nicer voice. My skin is crawling, and my anger is right there, ready to be unleashed and tear each of these pitiful guards limb from limb. They're playing dumb and it's annoying as fuck, doing nothing to help me stay in control. Of course they know why I'm here. They're guards standing at the front fucking entrance, they saw her come in!

"My apologies, but the king is on a strict schedule and—"

His words are cut off by my fist as it connects to his face. He flies backwards, slamming into another guard before tumbling to his ass. It takes only a second for the rest of the guards to react, reaching for me. I fight them off, throwing punches and jabbing elbows. I duck and push through them, but don't get far. One of them snatches me by the collar of my shirt, and it tears, hanging off my shoulder. Another one grabs me around the neck, and then someone has my feet.

Doesn't stop me from fighting though. They lift me up and I kick and try to punch them all the way to the dungeons, where I'm literally tossed in and land hard on my back, knocking the air from me.

"You're an idiot," Maxen grumbles as he walks in willingly, the cell door slamming shut behind him. Footsteps shuffle out of the room, the angry guard voices soon disappear and then it's silent, the only thing I can hear is my heavy breathing.

I lie on the floor, the chill from the stone bleeding through my exposed skin where my shirt is ripped. My chest burns with the need for more air and my limbs feel numb from the fight I put up. I keep my eyes closed and focus on settling down. My skin is still crawling but my anger will go nowhere. There isn't anyone here to take it out on besides Maxen and that's a mistake I don't want to make. He doesn't deserve that from me.

At least I can think clearly. That's the first sign of me gaining control.

"Why the fuck would you do that?" Maxen asks, but I don't answer him. I can't. I have nothing to say, other than I lost control, which isn't an excuse. I know it was stupid and got us nowhere, only in a worse position... but I have a feeling the king will hear about it. Hopefully, word will get to Bexley and maybe she'll put two and two together. No idea what that'll do but if she's looking for us while we're looking for her, that could be a good thing.

"Can you at least get your stupid ass off the floor?"

I open my eyes to find Maxen standing over me, his hand outstretched. I take it and he pulls me up. I let out a groan as I get to my feet, each of my limbs screaming in pain. I limp over to the bench against the far wall and sit, knowing I'll heal soon enough and be better than ever.

Maxen sits beside me and rests his head back against the wall.

"Maybe that wasn't so smart," I admit quietly.

"You think? They're probably going to leave us down here for days just to be dicks."

"Nah, I don't think so."

"Why's that?"

"Once the king learns I'm here, he'll want to come speak to me, or my father."

"Better hope it's you."

He's not wrong. If word gets to my father about this, it'll be a shit show I don't want to deal with.

"Why do you think they took her?" I ask him, though I'm pretty sure I know the answer.

"Hmmm, let me think about that. We're in Greed... the demons here are greedy fucks... should I go on?"

"Do you think they found out about her?"

He shrugs. "I guess it's possible. They could have someone watching their map too."

I groan and get to my feet, my body feeling a little better. I walk back and forth, stretching my legs with each step.

"If your dad finds out, we're going to the Pit, you know that?"

"No way," I say it, but I don't believe it, not for a second. My father is sick of my shit, and I wouldn't put it past him to bring us there himself. Even if he only keeps us there for a short time, he'd do it. And a short time there feels like a fucking millennium. No thanks.

"Pretty sure he'd send us there just finding out we came here."

Yeah, he's probably not wrong about that either.

"Whatever problem my father has with the King of Greed has nothing to do with me." I take a seat beside him again.

"And I'm sure that's exactly how they see it." He rolls his eyes.

He's not wrong. Demons don't care about that shit. Guilty by association is strong down here.

It's quiet for a few moments, but soon enough there are hurried footsteps coming down the hall. I turn towards Maxen and we share a look. I raise an eyebrow in question and he shrugs.

*A visitor already?*

The King of Greed himself walks in, alone.

"Why have you come here?" he asks, standing in front of the cells.

"No hello?" I grin and get an elbow in the ribs from Maxen which makes me groan. That spot is still sore.

"I don't bother with manners for people who can't seem to use them themselves. Tell me why you're here. Did your father send you?"

I clench my jaw and look up, meeting his eyes. "This has nothing to do with my father."

"Then what? You and your friend over there playing a game of truth or dare?"

I can see why my father isn't a fan of this asshole.

I smile, but it isn't friendly. "You have something that is mine."

"Oh?" he says with a slight tilt of his head.

He doesn't ask me to elaborate, which only irritates me.

I get to my feet, walking towards the cell bars. "Yep. Pretty little thing," I say, slowly making my way closer to him. "About five-foot-seven, curvy hips, plump ass, long dark hair, and striking green—" The last word doesn't get out as I reach the cell bars, and something clicks.

Something in my brain connects the very few dots I have, along with a whole shit-ton I wasn't even close to getting a hold of...

I take a step back, all the while holding his gaze. Those bright green eyes staring back at me.

Green eyes that look a lot like Bexley's.

The girl who is showing up on the map as someone who doesn't quite belong here or topside.

"What the fuck..." I say it under my breath but I'm pretty sure he hears me, and that's what does it for him. He knows I know. His eyes widen just a fraction, just enough to give away that my thoughts are correct.

"Enjoy your stay, boys."

He turns on his heel and hurries out of the dungeon.

"What was that all about?" Maxen doesn't sound any more annoyed than he did before the king came in here, almost like he was expecting not to be let out and is totally okay with it. "Kaine?" He calls my name when I don't answer, and I turn to take a seat beside him.

"I think... I think Bexley is the Princess of Greed."

"Are you high?"

I shake my head slowly, letting everything sink in. Does it make sense or is it too much of a stretch? Why else would she come here? Why else would she be showing up that way on the map? And those eyes... from the first moment I saw her I knew they didn't look human. I mean, they passed as human, but definitely questionable.

It's an unmistakable green, and for him to have the same exact shade?

"I wish I was," I mumble, and turn towards him.

He lets out a long sigh. "Doesn't seem like we're going anywhere, so I guess you have time to explain."

I don't have much and I assume he's just going to tell me I'm crazy, but I do it anyway. Give him all the pieces I have and when he doesn't look at me like I've grown a second head, I feel relieved. Maxen, though he's my best friend and I love him like a brother, we argue a lot and don't agree on many things. I was not ready to handle another argument today because there are so many things not making sense and so many new things I'm now worried about.

What does this mean for us and for her?

The King of Wrath and the King of Greed hate one another... So how can the Prince of Wrath and the Princess of Greed be together?

"So you're telling me this is more than sex?" I hit him with a glare. "What? I'm just asking." He holds up his hands, palms facing me.

"I don't know, okay? I have no idea what any of this is, all I know is that we need to get her back. I have no clue what he plans to do with her. She clearly has no idea who she is. Or didn't, anyway. Why? Is she in danger from him or from our world?"

He scratches his chin. "Either would make sense, I guess."

"You really going to act like you don't care about her?"

"I never said that."

"You sure as fuck act like it!" I shout.

"Just because I'm not willing to go to the Pit for her, doesn't mean I don't care."

"Forget it, it's not like it's even your fault," I grumble, crossing my arms and turning away from him.

"Excuse me?"

"You're a Lust demon. You can't help it."

"Fuck you, bro. Seriously."

I move to lie down on the bench and close my eyes. I have a feeling we're going to be here for a while, so I may as well get a nap in.

# CHAPTER FORTY-THREE

## BEXLEY

My father's space is pretty plain. It could pass as a show-case section at one of the downtown furniture stores. The furniture all matches perfectly; dark wood with brass knobs and trim. The cushions on the couch I'm sitting on are dark green, along with the rug underneath the bed. The entire wall across from me is a large window and all I can see out of it are mountains off in the distance. Dark, ominous mountains that creep me the fuck out.

The room isn't very bright even though the lights are on. It smells clean, almost as if there was someone in here cleaning it only moments ago.

The guard who brought me up here waits by the door and soon enough he's met by two more people who don't come in right away. I strain my ears to listen to their conversation.

"You go in and stay with the girl while I fill in Grizen." That's the one who brought me in here.

A tall, muscular man walks in, closing the door behind him and cutting off any chance of me eavesdropping. Such a bummer. He nods his head at me as he enters but doesn't say anything. He has on the same, green guard's uniform the other is wearing, only this guy fills his out in a more flattering way, hugging all the right places. He's nice to look at.

I'm not in the mood to chat so I'm glad he isn't trying to make small talk. After working in a café for four years, small talk is the last thing I want to do when I'm not at work. I pull my attention from him and continue looking around, noting the walls are bare, not a single picture or decoration to be seen.

Not even a photo of me. Not one. It evokes emotions in me I can't quiet explain. Is that an unrealistic expectation to have? Or am I right for being upset about it? Father said he has many enemies, but do they frequently visit his bedroom?

"Is there a bathroom?" I ask, getting to my feet. The man nods and points to the door that's just behind me. "Thanks."

I shut the door once I'm inside and make my way to the sink. I turn on the cold water and let it run over my hands before bringing it to my face and the back of my neck. The cool feeling calms me just a bit, and I do it a few more times, feeling a little better with each cool pass.

I shut off the water and grab the towel, drying my hands and face.

Looking around the bathroom, I note it's just as boring in here as it is out there. Not a single decoration. The shower, sink, and toilet are all white, the floors a dark brown while the walls are a lighter shade of brown. There is a small window that I move to and peek out of. More mountains.

Just as I reach for the doorknob to leave, I hear that heart-stopping, familiar voice again.

"Where is she?"

"Just in the bathroom, Sir."

I open the door to find my father walking towards me and he meets me with a smile, but it doesn't quite reach his eyes. He looks troubled.

"Is everything okay?" I ask.

"Of course," he responds. "Come, let's go talk." Motioning towards the other end of the room, I move in that direction. He leads us towards the large window, and we come upon a door to the right I hadn't seen before. He pushes it open and we enter a small lounge area. There is a full bar to the right, a table and chairs in the back corner, and another door that's closed, so I have no idea where it leads to. "My private eating quarters."

"Fancy," I say as I walk in and move towards the table, taking a seat.

I almost don't know how to act. Seeing him makes me instantly want to revert back to being a child. Running and jumping into his arms, hoping he'll make everything better. But I know that's how you act with your father when you're a child... I don't know how to act with him as an adult...

"Hungry? I can have the servants bring you something to eat."

"No, thanks." I was starving, now I'm not sure I could stomach anything.

"Drink?" I shake my head. "Are you—"

"I'm sure." He nods, taking the other seat. "I would just like you to tell me what's going on. This is..." I look around at the room we're in. It is also pretty boring. The most exciting thing about it is the bar, and only because it showcases numerous bottles of different colors. "So hard to believe."

His gaze follows mine before it lands back on me. I watch him from the corner of my eye, and I can tell he wants to apologize. I can see in his face that he's sorry. I've seen that look so many times. The slight frown, creased forehead, sad eyes... Only, sorry was all I ever got from him. Apologies, and promises that were always broken.

*I'm here to stay this time.*

*I'll be back soon.*

*Nothing will ever take me away from you.*

I'm going to give him the benefit of the doubt. Only because it's what my mother would want. My entire body is swirling with emotions, and I have no idea which one to latch onto. I'm happy to see him, but angry about him lying to me. Sad about missing so much time with him but excited he's here now. I'm also so fucking confused...

"Is Mom..." I say, turning to meet his gaze but he only shakes his head.

"I'm sorry, Bee."

"Please stop saying that." I blow out a breath and sigh before moving my attention to my hand as I pick at my nails.

"I've said it a lot over the years..."

"I don't want to get into all of that right now, I just want you to tell me about this." I motion around us. "What is this? How long have you been here? How is this possible?"

He gets up and moves to the bar, grabbing a bottle and pouring some amber-colored liquid into a glass before coming back over to sit. He stares at it, swirling it around before taking a sip. I can smell it from here and it smells like shit.

I'm a girly-drink kind of girl, and I'm not ashamed to admit that. I can't stand the smell or taste of alcohol.

"Well, to start, this is the Kingdom of Greed, one of the seven kingdoms in Hell." He looks at me, almost testing my response before he continues, and when he sees I don't have one, he goes on. "I've been the king here for sixteen years, just as long as my father has been dead."

"Sixteen?" I ask and he nods.

"I'll get to that but let me start from the beginning. Hell, Earth, and Heaven all work to exist together. You have the good, the bad, and then the neutral area, I guess you can call it. It all needs balance in order to sustain itself and that's where Heaven and Hell come in."

"So, Heaven is real too?"

"Unfortunately." He chuckles and then clears his throat when he sees that I'm not. "It's rare for demons to fall in love with anyone. We aren't known to have feelings or emotions, though sometimes we meet someone and that changes. For whatever reason, it just is. And your mother..." He takes a deep breath. "I loved your mother so damn much, Bexley."

My bottom lip trembles at the thought. I never questioned his love for me or for my mother, not really. No matter what happened, no matter how angry I was, deep down I knew he loved me because he always came back. Even if my anger made me think otherwise. He had other things he needed to handle, but he always came back. Except that last time...

"My father was the ruler here and I was the prince who loved to get away with whatever he could. I was young and dumb and enjoyed causing trouble. There are only certain types of demons who are allowed to go topside, and it's that way to keep the balance. I was not one of them, but I made my way up there often and it's how I came to meet your mother. I was smitten by her the moment I saw her. She was beautiful, Bee. Gorgeous. I knew though, that because she was a human, we would never be allowed to be together, but I couldn't stop myself when it came to her. When I had to come back here, all I could think about was her. I needed to be near her, touch her, love her. I felt like I couldn't breathe when we weren't together."

He takes another small sip of his drink, staring off somewhere behind me, a lost look in his eyes and I know he's remembering her the way I can't because it's just too hard. It's like I've forgotten about that entire part of my life because it's too much to handle, it hurts too much.

"I could never stay up there for long because it caused attention. I wasn't supposed to be there, and the older I got, the more my father wanted to prepare me for my duty of being king some day. A duty I wanted nothing to do with, by the way. I just wanted to stay up there with your mother. And then you came along, and it was almost impossible to leave your side."

Another sip and his frown deepens. My interest piques and I lean forward a little, wanting to hear more.

"I was honest with your mother, of course. I told her what I was. She believed me too. No questions asked, she just took it for what it was. We talked and agreed to keep things quiet until we could figure out how to be together. She didn't want me getting into trouble, and I didn't want any of the demons to find out who she was." He swallows hard, picks up his glass and takes another sip, looks at it, then finishes off the glass. He gets up and pours some more before returning to his seat. His bright green eyes meet mine, and he continues.

"Unfortunately, one day, they did find out. I'd told her I didn't want to come back here and I didn't care what they did. I would take her and you and we would move, go anywhere we could to hide from them. We'd live in an RV and travel if we needed, I didn't care. Only that didn't work. I was too late, took too long. My father found out and told me he'd kill you both if I didn't return immediately and I knew he meant it. I knew if I didn't come back here, you'd both be dead. So I did. I came back. As much as I didn't want to, I did as I was told and prepared myself to take the throne. But it didn't matter."

"What didn't?" I ask around the lump in my throat.

"Any of it." He looks away from me before speaking the next words because they're too hard. "He killed her anyway." His eyes lose all emotion, have this almost dead look to them. "I know I've said it a million times, Bee, but if there is anything in this universe I am sorry for, it's that. I'm sorry I couldn't stop her from being killed, I'm sorry I'm the reason your mother was taken from you, and I'm sorry I wasn't there when you needed me. But I had no choice."

"But... what..." I can't find words that I want to say. Don't even know what I'm trying to say.

"I was told if I took one more trip up there, they'd kill you too. So I knew I had to stay away. I couldn't risk it. I'd lost too much already."

"But you said your father has been dead. You said..."

He's shaking his head and I don't understand.

"It was his threat, yes. But he wasn't working alone, and he wasn't the one who killed your mother."

"Then who was?"

He glances at me, and takes a deep breath before saying, "The King of Wrath."

# CHAPTER FORTY-FOUR

## BEXLEY

"King... of Wrath?" I repeat the words. "But..."

There are so many things I want to say, and not all of them are to my father.

No, a lot of them are to Kaine. That lying sack of shit. He knew about this. He must have.

"If he finds out you're here, I don't know what will happen." I furrow my brows. "I promise you, Bee, I will never allow that man to hurt you. Never. I don't care what it takes. But in order to do that, I need to know everything. About how you got here, why you were brought here, and what you've been doing."

I narrow my eyes, getting the feeling he knows something.

"Have you been following me?"

"What? No! I only knew you were here when you set foot into my office. Jeziale has been a friend of mine for years; he's one of the only people who knew of your existence, and I'm thankful for it. Glad he was out in those woods today." He gets to his feet and moves to kneel in front of me, taking my hands in his and my heart aches for him, for me, for the life we didn't have together, and also for our future. Because what kind of future will we have in Hell? "I'm glad he found you, Bee. Who knows what would have happened if someone else did."

I don't tell him that's exactly what happened, and I assume Jeziale didn't either.

My father squeezes my hand before placing a kiss to the back of it. "I'd be lying if I said I wasn't happy you are here. I am thrilled. Never in a million years did I think I would ever be able to be this close to you again, but another part of me is terrified, Bee. I know what these people are capable of and it's scary. You have to be careful, okay? It's dangerous here."

I stare at him for a long moment, going back and forth in my head, wondering if this man is the man I always thought he was, or if he's the bad guy? Knowing I have to make a decision, I do. "O–okay. I'll tell you whatever you need to know."

He kisses my hand again before getting up and moving back to his seat. "Are you sure you don't want a drink?"

I glance at the bar and then back to him. "I guess I could use something." He smiles and moves to the bar, making me something that hopefully tastes good. Once he's done, he puts it down in front of me.

"It was your mother's favorite."

I pick up the glass and recognize it instantly. "Tequila sunrise," I say.

He nods, smiling. I take a long sip, hoping the tequila kicks in sooner rather than later. This is a lot to take in, all of it. As if I didn't have enough on my plate before, this just adds to it.

"What do you need to know?" I ask as I put my glass down on the table.

"You said Kaine brought you here? The Prince of Wrath."

"I didn't know who he was..."

"I know, Bee. None of this is your fault, I'm just trying to figure this out, okay?"

I nod, looking at my glass, running my thumb up and down the outside, watching as the condensation disappears, dripping to the table.

"I don't know how he got me here. I still don't remember that part. I just woke up in a sort of dungeon and found him and another guy; his friend, Maxen."

"Another Wrath demon?"

I shake my head and chew on my bottom lip. "No, he's a Lust demon." I look up at him and his jaw is clenched. I'm sure he knows exactly what that means because I'm sure it's as bad as it sounds.

"Did they say why they brought you here?"

"Not really, but I had the feeling they didn't want me to go home, even though they said they would take me. Kaine kept putting it off, and even brought my friend here to see me."

His eyes widen at my words. "A human?"

I nod. He sighs and pinches the bridge of his nose. "I guess I can't be too mad about that. As I'm sure you figured out, bringing humans here is not supposed to happen, but if I'd have been able to do it safely with your mother, I'd have done it too. Fortunately, for the Prince of Wrath, his father is out and about a lot, reigning terror over Hell and doesn't pay much attention to his son."

"I don't think he did this for his father." I've been thinking it and I have to say it. Kaine and Maxen give off a hundred red flags, and I'm sure they were lying to me about some things, but deep down, I don't think they brought me here to hurt me. My father needs to know that. He looks at me, trying to process what I'm saying. He doesn't believe it, but he'll take into consideration that I do.

"The king wasn't there when I first got to the castle, and when his father did show up, they made sure he didn't see me or know of me at all."

"It could have been a trick," he tries to argue.

"I don't think so."

"No offense, but I've been around demons a lot longer than you, Bee, and I know how they work. They're conniving, manipulative, and selfish," he spits the last words as if even thinking about someone like that being around his daughter is infuriating.

I meet his eyes, and say as nicely as I can, "You're not." He freezes, his eyes glued to mine before he nods, but only just slightly. "Look, I just..." I break the stare and look back at my drink. "I don't think Kaine wants anything to do with his father."

"What makes you think that?"

"Just a feeling, I guess. Something Mom said to me once." I look back at him. "You know what she told me about you?" He shakes his head, worry creasing his brow as if he doesn't know if this will be good or bad. My mother wouldn't have spoken an ill word about my father ever. "Villains in life and not in love," I repeat my mother's words that spoke to me many years ago. Words that have carved themselves into my brain for a reason I could never figure out. Not until now.

"Sounds like something she would say." He smiles.

"She told me you hung around with bad people and did bad things. She said you would be with us if you could, but it wasn't always possible. And she made sure I knew that just because people did bad things, didn't mean they were a bad person. That sometimes someone just hurts so much inside, they don't have any other choice but to make other people hurt too."

"That... wow." He blows out a breath. "Your mother could have been an angel, Bee. She saw good in people who didn't even deserve it, you know that?"

Yeah, I do know that. I nod, fighting back the tears the memories of my mother are bringing. I've barely spoken about her or Nana's death since it happened. When I was in foster care they had me in counseling, and still I wouldn't talk about it. It was just too hard. I wanted to process it in my own time. I did a lot of stupid and messed up things trying to handle it all, like sleeping with random guys, drinking, and partying... Then I met Rachel and something just changed. We clicked and I finally felt like I had someone again. She's the only person I ever opened up to about my childhood. The only one.

"I wish she was right. I really wish it was that simple, but it's not. Some people are just bad because some people aren't people at all. They're demons disguised as humans to do bad things, to keep balance in the world. It sucks, but it's life, and then there are the demons... Us down here who are just bad altogether."

"But there has to be some good, right? I mean, there's you. You loved Mom and... me." A tear falls from my eye, and I quickly wipe it away. He frowns but quickly turns it into a smile.

"I don't know how I got so lucky. I've done bad things, continue to do them on a daily basis because it's who I am, it's my duty. I'm a King of Hell and I have a kingdom to run. It's not only my job but my life. Your mother, though... she made me want to be different."

My thoughts go to Kaine and those moments I saw him soften when he was around me. The moments I saw Maxen caring about my well-being and how I felt and not just worrying about getting his dick sucked like I assume a Lust demon would worry about.

"Do you think there are others like you? Others who want to be different?" I ask cautiously.

He searches my face for a moment, almost like he doesn't know how to answer that. "I hope so." He looks down at his drink before picking it up and tossing the rest back. "Look, Bee, there is something I need to tell you, but you have to trust me on this, okay? I see you're feeling a little defensive over the Prince of Wrath and his friend, which is understandable. I, however, don't trust them as far as I can throw them. I may still look fit, but I'm old and I guarantee you I wouldn't even be able to pick them up." He cocks his head to the side. "I assume you understand why I am being cautious?"

"I... Yeah, I guess I can."

He nods. "You're safe here, okay? My most trusted men will be made aware of this, and the castle will be put on high security, and I'm going to get you comfortable in your own room." He gets to his feet.

"Didn't you have something to tell me?" I call out, wanting to know why he's just leaving me... I try not to think the word, but it pops up anyway.

Again.

Why is he leaving me *again*?

He pauses, turning to face me. "I think I'd rather show you." He holds out his hand and I look at it before taking it. Then he guides me out the closed door and we enter into a hallway. I'm still on edge about all of this. I feel that no matter where I turn, I can't trust anyone a hundred percent. Everything around me is unfamiliar and I can't be sure about anything. The only thing I can do is follow my father and see what he has to show me, hoping it'll quell some of those fears I have and answer some lingering questions.

# CHAPTER FORTY-FIVE

## BEXLEY

We walk down a bunch of stairs which I am quickly getting tired of. If I never saw a set of stairs or a hallway again, I would not at all care. When all of this is figured out, I want a one-story house with an open-floor layout.

I swear my ass must look five times better—which I guess I shouldn't be complaining about—since using all these damn stairs.

The lower we go down the steps, the darker and damper it gets, only instead of getting cooler like it would in a normal basement, it gets warmer and more humid.

We finally get to the bottom and turn left, which opens up into a room that isn't all that different from the one Kaine and I put a little show on in...

This dungeon, though, is bigger with more cells, and no cabinets full of surprise tools to be used as sex toys... thankfully, because that would be weird as fuck, considering this is my father.

"Why are we here?" I ask as we enter the room, which is when I notice movement coming from one of the cells.

"Bexley?" The sound of Kaine's voice has me turning quickly in his direction, my heart stuttering in my chest. He rushes towards the bars, standing only a few feet from me. I almost reach for him, almost. But I can't. He's in there for a reason... Why? What did he do?

"What is going on?" I ask, looking from Kaine to my father. I'm not sure who I'm even asking, I just want answers.

Part of me wants to go to Kaine, to hold him and hug him... and Maxen too. He's slowly made his way over and offers me a sad smile which I don't return. I'm too shocked to react any way other than confused.

Why are they here and locked up? Does my father know something I don't? Or is he just being cautious because of what he thinks?

"Bexley, tell him to let us go," Kaine pleads, though his tone still holds that bit of authoritative tinge to it.

"Dad?" I look to my father.

"I'll give you some time to talk; I'll be back in a few moments."

"But..."

He's already walking away and doesn't say anything further, just keeps going, so I turn back around to face Kaine and Maxen who are still locked behind bars. They look at me with a mixture of anger, sadness, and annoyance in their eyes. I can't blame them... I'm feeling the same way, if I'm being honest.

"Bexley..." Kaine sighs, his voice low. "Tell your father to let us out."

I perk up at his words. My father? How does he know that the King of Greed is my father? "You knew? This whole time you've known?" I almost shout but keep my own temper in check. My nails dig into my palms as I clench my fists, holding them back from swinging at his face—something I seem to want to do often.

His eyes widen and Maxen scrubs a hand down his face, shaking his head. "What? No! Not until like a half-hour ago," Kaine says, and everything in his voice makes me think he's telling the truth.

"Why should I believe you? You've done nothing but lie to me since I got here!"

"Bullshit!"

"Oh yeah?" I move closer to the bars, getting as close as I can, needing to prove that I'm not afraid of him. Needing to show him that even if I have been submissive to him, I won't back down from speaking my mind. "How many times did you tell me you would take me home, Kaine?" I look around. "Doesn't look like home to me."

He scoffs. "Well, I beg to differ." He steps back and crosses his arms over his chest.

This asshole...

I narrow my eyes at him. "You told me we were in Detroit." He smirks.

"Are you fucking serious?" Maxen asks, dropping his head back and groaning.

"It was a joke," Kaine growls, turning his head towards Maxen.

"Not very funny!" I shout. So much for keeping my temper in check...

"I thought it was." He shrugs and I swear if I could get to him, I'd knock his teeth in.

"You told me someone named August tried to take me and you rescued me, but that isn't what happened, is it?" He stares at me, not saying a word. His jaw ticks and I know I've got him now; know I've finally called him out on his bullshit. Maxen throws his hands up and moves to the back wall, taking a seat on the old bench that's there. "Is it, Kaine?" I demand, raising my voice even more.

"No," he says through clenched teeth.

"Then tell me the truth," I almost growl.

After a long moment of silence, Maxen lets out a frustrated noise. "For fuck's sake, Kaine, just tell her! What difference does it make now? Not only does she know where we are, she's part of it. You fucked up, so own that shit. Quit hiding behind your lies."

"Shut up," Kaine warns.

"No! This is completely out of hand. I told you from the beginning taking her was a bad idea. I told you you needed to bring her back when August told us to, I knew this would end in a fucking shit show!"

Well, it's nice to know they weren't in it together, that at least Maxen is kind of on my side?

"I said... shut up!" Kaine roars and I take a step back. His eyes start to glow a bright, neon blue. He closes them and takes a deep breath before opening them again and they're back to their normal shade. Back to their bright blue.

Maxen keeps going though, obviously angry over this entire situation, and I don't blame him for that. Seems he is the smart one out of these two. Or at least, the one who thinks the most clearly.

"This is bullshit. Fucking bullshit! All the years I've known you, it's always something. You always manage to get me into some shit that I have to get us out of."

"Better than hanging around with daddy though," Kaine mumbles.

Maxen gets to his feet, stomping towards Kaine. "The fuck did you say?"

Kaine turns around to face him, and they're eye to eye. This probably won't end well...

I watch, my entire body on edge. If they start to fight, I can't stop them. There's nothing I can do. Maxen seems pissed, and so does Kaine. A fight between them won't be good.

"I said, it's better than hanging around with your drunk, molesting father though, *isn't it*? It's all fun to hang around with the Prince of Wrath when it's good for you, but when I need something, it's fuck me, right?"

"Need something?" Maxen closes the distance between him and Kaine and they're chest to chest now. "Need something? You fucking have everything, you spoiled piece of shit! But it isn't enough, it's never enough. Nothing for you will ever be enough!"

"*She* is enough!" Kaine shouts, jerking his arm in my direction. "Don't you fucking get it? Haven't you fucking seen it?" He's screaming so loud his voice is echoing around the walls, piercing my ears from all directions. Kaine's shoulders shake from the deep breaths he's taking. Maxen glances at me and he blinks slowly, understanding taking over his features.

I don't know anything about them, about what they've been through, or about what Kaine's sudden proclamation means.

Yes, I feel something for him, something internal, instinctual, primal, I guess? I feel something for both of them, really. What I feel for Maxen is so very different than what I feel for Kaine, but it is there.

When I'm with Kaine, it's a whirlwind. Everything is fast and wild, burning furiously.

With Maxen, it's different. Slow growing and strong; secure.

Maxen looks back towards his friend, lowering his voice. "If she's enough, then tell her the truth."

My heart is beating wildly in my chest and as much as I want to hear this... I don't at the same time. Somehow, in the short few days I've been here, I've grown feelings for him. For both of them. I knew if I went back home, I'd miss them, but this is something different. What he's about to tell me, if it's something bad, it's going to tear me apart. It's going to break my fucking heart and that is so much worse than missing someone. That is something I never wanted to deal with again. Something I'm not so sure I can handle.

My whole life my heart has been nothing but broken. Over and over and over again by promises that weren't kept, and I finally got to a place where I was okay. A place where I was just a girl in her twenties, living in NYC with her best friend, and working at a job she hates. I accepted my parents' deaths, missed them like crazy, but I'd made peace with it all... I had to. But now? Those old wounds have been ripped open by my father's truth... by my mother's truth... by the truth this man I've fallen for is about to tell me.

If he knows about my mother... I don't think I can forgive him for that. If he knew this whole time... I can't let that go. No matter what words from my mother play in my head, I'm not that good of a person. I'm not her, I'm not that kind. I have a darkness in me, and now I at least know why. I know why parts of me call to Kaine and Maxen.

It's because I'm like them.

My father is a demon, and so am I. Half, anyway. However that works, I don't know, but...

I let out a sigh.

"Tell me," I say softly. He doesn't say anything right away, doesn't respond, just keeps his back to me. Like a coward... I didn't expect that from him. "Did you know about my mother?"

"Your mother?" he asks, turning around, brows furrowed and a frown on those perfect lips.

"What your father did," I grit out.

He meets my eyes and speaks his truth. "Bexley, I had no idea who you were when I first met you. You were just a girl in a coffee shop we were trying to pick up to get laid." He looks away, his gaze moving to the floor.

I bite on my bottom lip to stop the tremble. Why that hurts so much, I have no idea. All we've done since I've been here is fuck. Pretty much nonstop. I'd had a feeling this is what he wanted from me. I knew I was just a booty call. *I knew it.*

So why does that hurt? Why does that make me feel like a cheap piece of trash they picked up off of a NYC sidewalk?

Why did I think I was more? Like I was special. Even when the thoughts of them kidnapping me went through my head, I thought it was more than that. Thought maybe it was because I was *me*. How fucked up is that? How fucked up is it that I'm so broken I'd wished two men had been stalking me, watching me, wanting me from afar? So badly that they couldn't stop themselves and took me?

"Why?" It's all I can seem to say, though I don't think it matters. The why doesn't matter. I don't care why. Because he's a fucking demon on top of a man who loves pussy, that's why. Do I really need more than that? There is no further explanation, nothing that will ever change that.

"It was because of me," Maxen says, running his hand through his hair. He takes a deep breath before blowing it out. "Sex for me... I feed off of it. All demons feed off of something. We need more than just food to survive. We need sex or pain or fear."

Kaine meets my eyes at Maxen's last word, and I start to put more pieces together. The dungeon, the prisoners, the knife...

"We were at a bar, conning the stupid rich college kids, like we normally do, and I was hungry. We went in search of someone to fuck because I needed the sex," Maxen says, continuing his explanation of that night.

"What else?" I force the words out, knowing there has to be more. Of course there is more because that can't be it.

"We wound up in the coffee shop and instantly I was attr—"

"*We,*" Kaine interrupts. "*We* were attracted to you."

"Fine." Maxen lets out a sigh. "*We* were attracted to you. Not only looks, but that smart-ass mouth of yours." Maxen smiles and I almost do too. I want to, but I can't find it in me. "But then August came in."

"Is he a demon too?"

Kaine barks out a laugh. "Don't insult us." I raise a brow. "He's an angel. A sissy-ass angel who doesn't know when to mind his own damn business."

I look back to Maxen, urging him to continue his story.

"You, being exactly who you are, I've come to learn, did not fall for our bullshit lines and advances. Instead, you picked up on the tension between us and August and you decided to flirt with him instead. And the spoiled Prince of Wrath over here can't control himself when he doesn't get what he wants, so essentially he beat August to a pulp and then took you back to Hell."

"You hurt an angel?" I don't know why that's my first thought, or why I care, but it's what comes out of my mouth.

He scoffs. "Oh, please. We all have healing abilities. He was fine."

"What else?" I ask.

"What else?" Kaine echoes, moving towards the bars. "There is nothing else, baby. That's it, end of story. I threw a fit and took you because I was pissed you were flirting with that angel asshole."

"But your father..."

"What about him?" Kaine asks, his patience wearing thin, if his tone is any indication.

"He—" My words are cut off as my father walks back in.

"I think that's enough for now." I look to him and he gestures towards the exit with a jerk of his chin. I look back to Kaine, his eyes pleading. He wants me to believe him, and I want to believe him. It's just... a lot.

Maxen still looks annoyed, but he looks almost as if he feels bad too. Like maybe he's sorry for not saying anything sooner? Sorry for what Kaine did? But I can't fault him for not betraying his friend. Demon or not, Maxen is loyal. He's fun and carefree, but he's loyal.

I look back to my father and nod, and soon enough my feet are carrying me out of the dungeons, with Kaine yelling and shouting for me to come back and talk to him. I hear his screams all the way to the stairs, and each one is like a knife right through my heart.

# CHAPTER FORTY-SIX

## KAINE

The anger and fury I feel is like nothing I've ever experienced before. My skin feels like it's on fire, like I'm about to explode. I pace back and forth in the cell, not feeling any bit better for coming clean with Bexley about what happened. I should have done it sooner. I shouldn't have lied to her, but I didn't know I would grow feelings for her. Actual fucking feelings... Demons don't do that shit, so how was I supposed to know this would happen?

But I told her the truth now, so why did she still walk away? Why isn't she here with me, or better yet, why hasn't she told her father to let us out?

After Maxen telling me to calm down and come sit by him about a hundred times, and me ignoring each and every one of them, I finally sit to down, though it does nothing to make me feel better. My knee is bouncing, and my hands are clenching open and closed. I can't get a hold of my temper, and I need to or I'm going to go crazy.

"Maybe you should try to sleep." I know he's just trying to be nice, but what the fuck is sleep going to do? My problems will just be here waiting for me when I open my eyes. And that's if I can settle down enough to sleep in the first place. I open my mouth to tell him to fuck off, but quickly close it. I don't want to make this situation any worse, and we've argued enough today.

He's just trying to help. I tell myself that over and over again.

He's all I have at this point, so I need him to stay on my side. I'm pretty sure I'm on thin ice with him to begin with.

Days like today, I'm not sure why he hangs around me at all. Of course he doesn't have much of a choice right now, but all these years he's been here...

I try to bring my thoughts elsewhere to get myself calm, but every road I go down leads me to Bexley.

Bexley, Bexley, Bexley.

Those curves, her lips, those bright green eyes...

I growl and get to my feet and start to pace again, which soon turns into a jog. There's barely any room in here at all. It's maybe an eight by twelve cell, but I need to do something because sitting still is only making me feel worse. The jog soon turns into a run, with me slapping the wall each time I reach it and launching myself off. I start to time myself to see if I can get to the other side in less than a second. I never do.

I run back and forth until my legs feel like jelly. With my lungs burning and sweat dripping from my head, I take a seat once more.

Maxen doesn't say a word the entire time and he doesn't say anything when I sit down either. He could be sleeping for all I know. He hasn't moved in a while and his eyes are closed.

My chest heaves as I try to catch my breath, sweat gathering around my neck, dripping down my back and chest. My mind is finally somewhere clear. Clear enough that I can see through the fog and make a rational thought—I hope. I urge myself to sleep. It's something to pass the time. Who knows how long that asshole is going to keep us down here. I may as well sleep while I can.

I lie down on the bench, keeping my knees bent and feet beside Maxen and turn my head towards the cold, stone wall. I'm just about sleeping, my heart at a normal pace and my breathing slowing, when I heart footsteps. I shoot up to my feet and move towards the bars, gripping onto them, hoping to see Bexley. Hoping she came back for me—for us.

I deep growl leaves my chest when I see the greedy ass king himself, and not the woman I'd been hoping for.

I keep my mouth shut, even though I want to call him every name in the book. Curse him for eternities to come, if I could do that. I can't, but Marionette can, and it very well may be the next thing I order her to do.

"This is quite the situation we've found ourselves in," he says, tapping his chin in thought. As if he didn't walk down here with a plan? Stop putting on a fucking show and get on with it.

"Well, if you let us go, there wouldn't be a situation," I respond.

"I don't think that's wise just yet."

"And why not?"

Maxen stirs behind me, but he doesn't get up. He's never been the up in your face kind of guy, but rather lingering in the background, listening and learning. Seeing things I'm usually too worked up to notice.

"We have a problem," the greedy fucker begins, staring at me from a good distance. Probably because he knows if he gets close enough, I'll grab him by his collar and smash his face into the bars until he looks like a juiced grapefruit.

"There doesn't need to be, if you just let us go," I say through clenched teeth, my hands tightening around the iron bars.

He smiles at me, a sinister smile, one I want to punch right off his stupid face.

Only it isn't all that stupid, because *fuck,* Bexley looks just like him.

"Yes, I've thought of that. Only I think it'll cause even more of a problem, now that my daughter is in the picture."

"In the pic—" I squeeze the bars tighter, causing them to creak. I close my eyes and take a deep, steadying breath before choosing my words carefully. "She's been here for days and you haven't known, why do you suddenly care now?" I ask as calmly as I can.

He narrows his eyes slightly. "Why do you?"

"I've cared the whole fucking time!" I shout, spit flying everywhere, and I couldn't care less if it gets on the precious King of Greed. Fuck him and everything he stands for.

"You see, I want to believe you, I do. Only I know I shouldn't." He takes a step closer to me. "Has my daughter told you anything of how she grew up?"

"No," I grit out, realizing how stupid I sound. A demon—a Wrath demon of all demons—professing feelings over a girl he's just met.

"How do you care for someone you don't know?"

"How do you?" I snap back, my chest once again heaving. I steady myself, and this time speak more calmly. "It seems to me she has no idea who she is or didn't until she showed up here. So how long has she gone without speaking to you? When was the last time you saw her? How can you ask me the same thing that pertains to you, and expect a different answer?"

He huffs out a laugh. "You are smart, like your father."

"Don't compare me to him," I growl out. He raises a brow at my words.

"Touchy subject? Hmm..." He starts to pace, his thumb rubbing against his chin. "I loved someone once, you know. *Actually* loved someone. Something a demon shouldn't feel. I felt it and it was real and it was amazing. Yet, all it did was end in disaster." He stops and turns to me, I open my mouth to speak but he holds up his hand. "But out of that disaster, I was given something more than love. Something better. I was given a child. Someone who is a part of me. Someone I quite literally made."

He takes a step closer, stopping only inches from me. "If you have feelings for my daughter, *actual* feelings, I get it. But know that whatever you feel, I feel it times ten. That girl was brought into this world because of me. *Me.* She is part of me and always will be. If I thought I loved her mother..." He chuckles, shaking his head. "What I felt for her mother was nothing compared to what I feel for Bexley and believe me when I tell you I loved her mother more than you could ever comprehend. Demons aren't meant to love, we're meant to be cruel. To destroy, kill, and betray. Yet, for some reason, when we do love, we do it with our entire being." He keeps his eyes on me, and I figure he's done with his little pep talk, so I speak.

"What is your point?"

"My point is, Kaine, Prince of Wrath, that if you love my daughter, you will do whatever it takes to prove that."

"I never said—"

"The words don't need to be spoken," he whispers before straightening his shoulders and walking towards the exit.

"What do you want me to do?" I call after him, my voice weaker than I've ever heard it before. He stops and turns, a smile on his face.

"Well, I thought you'd never ask."

# CHAPTER FORTY-SEVEN

## KAINE

"I can't believe we're doing this," Maxen grumbles as we make our way back to Wrath on our horses, who were thankfully not harmed while wandering around the outside of Castle Greed. I'd have lost my shit completely if even a hair on Ravage's head had been touched.

It's late into the night, but the moon is full—as it always is—so we can at least see where we are going, but we stick to the tree line to make sure there is no chance of anyone seeing us.

"I know, Maxen. *She's not worth it*, I've heard it from you more than once. I don't care."

"That's not what I was going to say."

"Then what?" I glance in his direction, ready to fight with him—which seems to be our normal lately. But he only looks bored. Tired and exhausted. "You've done nothing but complain about her since I brought her here, have done nothing but argue with me and tell me I'm wrong."

"You are."

"No one is keeping you here!" I shout, pinning him with a glare. "Go home, then. Don't act like someone is forcing you to stay with me, Maxen. No one is doing that but you."

His jaw clenches but he keeps his stare ahead at the road. He doesn't say another word and I drop it for now. I don't have time to deal with his shit.

Maxen and I have a strong bond, but it's shit compared to what I feel about Bexley.

There was something about her from that first moment I laid eyes on her, right from the beginning. But something about her being kept away from me, from being in trouble, and then thinking I may never get another moment with her... it's made me realize a lot of fucking things.

And it's exactly why I agreed to do what the King wanted me to do.

I'd have done more. I will do more, if he asks. I'll do whatever it fucking takes to prove to him—or anyone else—what I feel for that girl.

I wish I could explain it, explain what she does to me and how she makes me feel, but I don't have the words to do it.

What the King asked me to do, it's simple and will no longer be my problem after the deed is done. He can handle the aftermath. That was part of the deal. Then he'll get what he wants, and I'll get what I want.

Win, win.

We reach the castle and veer the horses towards the stables and get them settled back into their stalls.

"Kaine..." I turn to find Maxen already staring at me. He takes a step closer, placing a hand on my shoulder. "You've been like a brother to me for almost my whole life. I stay around here because I want to, because I like being with you. Hopefully, it's the same reason you don't kick me out. I'm sorry I don't feel about her the way you do, and that I don't find any of this shit worth it."

"Don't apologize, Maxen." I grunt.

"Well, I need to say it, okay? I don't want to be without you. Ever. My home life is fucked, and you gave me a life here, one where I didn't have to watch my back. I'll admit that I like having her around and that there is something about her. I get it. I guess I'm just worried. The Pit is scary as fuck, you know? I heard what her dad said, every word of it. Do you... is that really how you feel about her?" I look up to meet his eyes and give him a curt nod. He blows out a breath. "Okay, then. That's all I needed to know."

"That's it?"

"Look, don't act like you're the most rational person. I've spent years cleaning your messes. You tend to go headfirst into situations. How was I supposed to know this was different?"

He's not wrong. I do do that...

"You weren't." I move to walk by him, but he grabs my arm and I spin back to look at him.

"There is one more thing I need to know before we do this."

"What?"

"Us, her... this? What is it?"

What is it? Do I have an answer for that? Do I need one?

"It just is." It's the only thing I can think of to say.

"I don't want shit to get weird with us..."

I let my head fall back and sigh. "Maybe I was adopted or some shit."

"Huh?"

"I may have the temper of a Wrath, but I've never fit in here. I think we both know that. I'm not what my father wants me to be, never have been. Me and you... we have this bond that's been there for years. Something I, of all demons, shouldn't be feeling, yet here it is. Whatever type of relationship we have, it doesn't have a name, it just is. We are us. Bexley came along and we're still us, just with her."

He opens his mouth to talk, but pauses, rethinking his words. "So you aren't gonna kill me for sleeping with your girlfriend?" He cracks a smile and I roll my eyes, huffing out a laugh.

"Not today."

It takes both of us to do what needs to be done.

I've lived in this castle my whole life and everything runs like clockwork. My father is exactly where I need him to be and so are all the staff. Maxen's job is to keep eyes on them as I make my way into my father's office.

"Damnit, Kaine. I've been looking for you all day. We need to talk," he grunts out as soon as I show my face. He doesn't move though, just continues standing behind his desk, looking over a file in his hand.

"Yeah, we do," I say, which surprises him. He looks up at me with his brows creased.

"Sit," he orders. I do, taking the seat across from his desk.

Patience. I need to be patient.

"What do you have to say?" I ask.

He narrows his eyes at me, obviously thinking I'm up to something. Can't blame him for that. "Maybe you should go first." He sits in his own chair, and I nod.

"Okay." I lean forward, resting my forearms on my thighs. "I was going to tell you that I'm ready to step up. I took a walk today, thought about it, and I think I'm ready to find out what ruling this kingdom means."

"You're fucking kidding." He stares blankly, not even blinking.

"Not at all."

He glances towards the door, then back to me before leaning forward on his desk. "If this is a joke..."

"It's not," I say firmly. "I realized I've been wasting my time doing nothing and that this kingdom deserves someone who will fill your shoes once you're gone."

His eyes bore into mine, clearly still not believing me and looking for any sign of deceit.

"Kaine," he warns, tilting his head. I get to my feet, clasping my hands behind my back.

"I understand why you don't believe me, but you will. I'm going to make up for lost time. I'm going to get myself on a schedule, find a routine. It's getting late now, but I needed to share this with you before I went to bed. I'll be here first thing in the morning, though. I think we can get a few days of training in before you have to travel again, right? I believe you're heading into Sloth for a week in only a few days?"

"Right," he says cautiously.

"I'd like to accompany you, if that's okay?"

"Sure," he says warily. I stand there and wait, allowing it all to sink in. Giving him the time he needs to process and to also make sure I'm not rushing this, even though my skin is crawling and my heart is threatening to beat right out of my chest.

This is the moment. The moment he accepts it or calls my bluff. It could go either way with him. Depends on his mood and how his day went. I haven't been here at all today to gauge it, so it doesn't help me in the least bit. But then a smile grows across his lips, and he gets to his feet, moving around to the front of his desk.

"I'm so proud, son. So proud." He holds out his hand and I unclasp mine, reaching forward. I grasp his firmly and shake it, all the while focusing on my left hand and what I hold in it.

He has no idea what is about to happen, that his life and everything he's built is about to crumble and die. And I couldn't care less. About him or about this kingdom and anything in it. I don't care about these people or what will happen to them after tonight. Hell, they've never cared about me. They're a bunch of angry demons who walk around on edge, ready to murder someone at the drop of a hat. Hating me because I was born a prince, like it's my fucking fault. The idea of being adopted is starting to make more sense, but maybe it's something different. Maybe I'm just an anomaly.

Someone like Bexley. Like Maxen. Like the King of Greed who, in the end, did still turn out to be a greedy old bastard, but not in a way that affects me, so what do I care?

I grip the blade tightly in my hand, waiting for the perfect moment, and when it strikes, so do I.

Right to his chest.

I sink the blade in deep, all the way to the hilt. His hands reach for mine, tightening around my wrist. My father's eyes widen, moving from me to the blade, then back to me. I let go of the blade, but he still holds onto me. His lips turn down into a frown, and everything happens in slow motion from there.

His last breath leaves his lungs.

His grip loosens.

His body falls to the floor.

The blood pools around the blade, down his side, and onto the floor.

I step over him, placing a foot on either side of his waist, bend down, and pull the knife free from his chest. The same knife I fucked Bexley with.

His eyes are dead, motionless.

His heart has stopped.

He's dead.

I killed King Tzalli, Ruler of Wrath, and soon enough this kingdom will belong to the King of Greed, all so his daughter can belong to me.

# CHAPTER FORTY-EIGHT

## BEXLEY

"Do you remember what we used to do when you were little?"

His voice startles me, pulling my attention from the TV and towards the door. I found a stash of movies and I've come to the conclusion that there is no cable down here. Something I'll have to get used to because I don't think I'm leaving. First it was Kaine who kept me here, and now it's my dad.

Now I know why I felt like this was home. In a way, this is my home. Part of me belongs here.

It's why I know it isn't my father keeping me here. Just like it wasn't Kaine either, not really.

All along it's been me. It's always been me. Those dark pieces I kept secret for so long were tired of hiding, tired of living in the shadows, lingering in the background.

"Stay up late, eat popcorn, and watch movies?" I ask with a tired smile.

He huffs out a laugh and moves to sit beside me on the oversized couch.

"Your mom always yelled at me. Told me I shouldn't spoil you just because I was home."

I raise a brow and toss a few pieces of popcorn in my mouth. It's the first "meal" I've had today and it's perfect.

"So she left out the part that she did the same thing at least twice a week?"

He chuckles, the sound reminding me of things long forgotten. "Why am I not surprised?"

He puts his arm around me, and I lean into him, like I used to when I was little. All those years ago and it still feels the same.

"This world is different than what you're used to, Bee. You need to know that. You don't fit in here and you never will. Now, that doesn't mean I don't want you here because I do, but I'll respect your decision, whatever it is, as long as you're safe. If you want to go back topside, I'll make sure you have someone to watch over you. If you stay here, then all my guards will be at your beck and call. Whatever you want."

"Do I need to decide now?" I ask softly, eating a few more pieces of buttery goodness.

He kisses the top of my head, brushing down my hair that is still as wild as ever. "Of course not."

So I don't say another word. I finish watching the movie until the bowl is empty and the credits are rolling. Which just so happens to be around the time I let my eyes shut and I fall asleep. Only to be just barely woken to someone carrying me into the bedroom that has been made to be mine, whenever I want it.

My father lays me down in my bed and tucks me in, running his hand over my hair the same way he did when I was little. I lie there, half-awake but pretending I'm asleep, the same way I did when I was little. And when he leaves the room, I fall asleep feeling safe and loved.

Something I've missed for as long as I can remember.

I'm startled awake to someone crawling into bed with me.

Not just some*one*, but *two*.

Their scent is what gives them away, and I whisper, "What are you doing here?"

Last I knew, they were still locked in the dungeon downstairs. How did they get out? My father will certainly kill them if he finds them here and I don't want that happening. He and I didn't get a chance to talk about the guys yet, and how I trust them and I think he should too. That I don't think Kaine or Maxen know a thing about what the King of Wrath did to my mother, and it's not just my stupid human feelings getting in the way, it's the truth.

I know it is.

"Shhh," Kaine says, sliding in behind me. He wraps his arm around my waist and pulls me close. My body molds against his, as if we were made to be together. It's perfect. Too perfect.

Maxen gets settled in front of me on his side and faces me. He takes my hand, interlocking our fingers and bringing it to his lips, where he places a gentle kiss along the back of my hand before resting them both between us on the pillow.

"My father, he'll—"

"Don't worry," Kaine says, pressing a kiss to the shell of my ear. "It's all taken care of."

"But—"

Maxen effectively shuts me up with a kiss. His warm, soft lips pressed against mine and all I can do is kiss him back. It's barely been any time at all since I've felt him against me, but its seemed like forever. I missed it. I missed him and Kaine. Their smell, their warmth, their firm and delicious bodies pressed against mine.

Kaine grinds against me, groaning low in my ear, his erection poking into my ass, hard as stone.

Maxen slides his tongue between my lips, long strokes against my own as Kaine's hand finds its way between my leg, rubbing my pussy over my sweatpants. I thrust against him, heat building in my core, the need to feel him on my skin urgent.

I need them like I need air to breathe. Here, in their arms like this, everything feels so right.

Kaine wastes no time sliding his hand into my pants and then a finger between my pussy lips, finding my clit instantly and circling it.

"So wet, baby. Did you miss us?"

Maxen bites down on my tongue and I whimper, trying to stay quiet so no one hears us. He pulls away with a soft chuckle. "Oh, I think she did."

"Let's see how much," Kaine says. "Let's see how bad this pussy wants to come." His teeth sink into my earlobe and he tugs. I bite down on my bottom lip, holding back the sounds that want to escape me. "Don't be afraid to let it out, Bex. Come for me so I can do it again." He lowers his voice before saying, "And again and again and again."

Stars burst behind my eyes as the orgasm ripples through my body, heat exploding between my legs as Kaine moves his fingers slowly, the euphoria going on and on and on.

I turn my face into the pillow as I cry out my sounds of pleasure, only turning my head back when Kaine removes his hand. I'm panting and my body is vibrating, but I'm not done with them.

"My turn," Maxen growls, shifting me so I'm on my back.

And clearly they aren't done with me either, but I didn't expect them to be.

Maxen tugs my pants down, tossing them to the floor. He settles between my legs, his tongue darting out and running along my slick entrance, moaning as he dives in for more, licking and sucking on my sensitive pussy. It doesn't take long before he's making me come again.

Then Kaine does as he said... I lose track of how many times they make me come, and I'm pretty sure every muscle in my body is on strike because by the time the sun comes up, I feel like a puddle of goo. Though, that may just be the soaked mattress we're lying on, full of a mixture of bodily fluids. I don't care though, I'm too tired to care about any-thing but sleep. So when the guys finally relent and allow me some time to rest, after having made me come so many times I barely remember my own name—even though they didn't come even once—I close my eyes and I think I pass out more than sleep.

# CHAPTER FORTY-NINE

## BEXLEY

If my body wasn't so sore, I'd think last night was a dream.

As annoying as it is, I miss feeling like this. The aching in my body—and most importantly, my pussy—is what reminds me what they put me through.

My bed is empty other than me when I wake, and it's still soaked.

Kaine and Maxen were definitely here with me last night, making me come over and over and over again, there is no mistaking it. They told me everything was taken care of, and I have no idea what that means, which worries me now that I'm awake and conscious.

I hope they didn't do something stupid like kill my father.

Fuck, I really hope they did not do that.

I hope to whatever God is out there that they didn't think I hated my father and wanted to get out of here.

The thought has me nauseous and jumping out of bed, only to realize I'm naked. I go to the dresser, the one my father said was full of clothes for me, and find a pair of black leggings that I shove on, along with a sports bra and a T-shirt—all of which fit me perfectly. I really should take a shower, but I won't be able to enjoy it without knowing my father is okay...

I race out of my room, only to run into that tall guard from the other day.

"Whoa," he says, holding up his arms. "Where you going in such a rush?"

"My father. Where is he?"

"He's having lunch in the dining area."

"Lunch?" I ask, glancing around. What time is it?

"That's what I said."

"Can you bring me there?" I'm thrilled he's telling me where my father is, but I'll feel better when I see him with my own two eyes.

"That's what I'm here for."

If I weren't in such a rush to see my father, I'd make a comment to this guy about his attitude and how he needs a new one. Then I remember he's a demon and if I stay here, this is probably what I'll be dealing with from most people. Especially since what my father said is true... I don't belong here and I never will. But is that true? Does it have to be? Maybe half-demons aren't a normal thing, but they have to fit in somewhere, right?

I'm not a full-blooded demon, which I bet means I'm not as good as everyone else.

Well, they can save it for someone who cares.

After what I grew up with, dealing will all kinds of mean shit from the kids I went to school with, I can handle just about anything.

There isn't a thing someone could say that would hurt me.

Not someone I don't know, anyway.

My father though... Kaine or Maxen... that's different. So much different. Any thought of rejection from them has my chest tightening.

I follow behind this tall guard, trying to rack my brain for his name that I can't remember. These demons have weird names. Even my father's name is weird. Growing up, I always thought it was Ethan. Apparently, it's not. Not even close. His name is so strange it sounds more like a random noise than a word. I don't think I could spell it if my life depended on it and thankfully, I don't have to worry about it, because I just get to call him Dad.

It doesn't take long to get to the dining area. It's on the same floor and only a few hallways down, much different than what I'm used to at Kaine's castle. Even though this place seems to be more of a maze, everything is closer together.

I hold my breath as I round the corner and almost choke on it when I see the three of them—my father, Kaine, and Maxen—sitting at a round table with mostly empty plates of food in front of them. Maxen is sipping from a green coffee mug. Kaine has his hands folded together, resting against his chin as he nods along to whatever my father is saying. My father who has his back to me but is—very much to my memory—speaking animatedly with his hands.

They seem so at ease in their conversation as if they're sharing normal chitchat. I watch them for a few moments, wondering what they're talking about and why the conversation is so easy, considering my father was holding them in a dungeon not too long ago. The guys never gave me an explanation last night, not that I'm complaining because I'm pretty happy with how the night went, but I'm still curious.

As if he can sense me or feel my eyes on him, Kaine looks my way. His bright blue gaze has my stomach fluttering. The smallest of smiles slides across his lips that I can just barely see behind his hands. He winks at me, and I just about melt before he turns his attention back to my father.

My stomach rumbles, pushing away the giddiness I was just feeling, and I decide it's time to burst in on their little get together because I'm starving. I walk over and round the table, sitting across from my father, between Kaine and Maxen.

"Good morning, Bee." My father greets me with a smile.

"Morning," I respond with a smile of my own.

"Morning, baby," Kaine says huskily as I take my seat.

"Sleep well?" Maxen asks, and I dart my eyes to him, shifting in my seat to find the most comfortable position since I've found myself rather sore this morning.

"Very well," I say, giving him a knowing look. He finishes off whatever is in his cup before placing it down. Someone walks over and brings me a plate of food, which looks like Chicken Alfredo—fancy for lunch, but it's one of my favorites so I don't care. I'd eat anything at this point, considering all I had yesterday was popcorn. I thank the waiter as he leaves and look down at my food, ready to dig in when I notice their conversation has stopped since I sat down.

I look up to find all three of them staring at me.

"What?" I ask.

"We need to talk," my father says, a humorous gleam in his eye.

"I figured as much." I glance at my food. "Is this a two-sided conversation or do I just need to listen? Cause I'm starving."

He smiles before nodding towards my food. "Eat up. We will explain."

I pick up my fork, twirl the pasta around it and take a bite. It's so fucking good. Creamy and cheesy, and the pasta is cooked perfectly.

"The guys here seem pretty sure you'll be staying here in Hell?"

I chew as I pick up my napkin and wipe my mouth.

"I've been considering it."

"Just considering it?" Kaine asks, dropping his hands and frowning.

I shrug and take another bite, chew and swallow before giving him more of an answer.

"Well, we haven't talked about much of anything. I don't even know if there is anything worth staying for."

"Unbelievable," Kaine mutters, leaning back in his chair, scowling.

"Well, I guess I'll just put it all out there, then leave you be. It seems you have much of your own things to talk about, but I'd like to say what I have to say first. If that's okay?"

I nod as I shove a piece of chicken into my mouth. It's soft and juicy, seasoned perfectly.

"I would love nothing more than for you to stay here with me, but as I mentioned, there will be difficulties that come with it. Things we can discuss, if you want to. For now, I'd like you to know that I feel these boys have proved their loyalty and I fully stand behind you being with them, if you choose to do so."

I raise my brows. "Is that so?" I pick up the glass of water that's in front of me and take a sip. He nods. "What made you change your mind? Yesterday you seemed to think they were just tricking me. That they lured me down here to finish off what Kaine's father didn't. You had them locked in the dungeons."

I catch Kaine flinching from the father comment, but I don't feel bad for it.

"I've changed my mind."

I smile. "I can see that, Dad. But why?"

"I did what any father would do. I made them prove themselves."

I huff out a laugh and look from Kaine to Maxen, before looking back to my father. "And what could they have possibly done to make you believe they aren't after me for his father's actions?" I nod towards Kaine.

"Because he's dead."

I whip my head in Kaine's direction. He looks as relaxed as ever, as if he didn't just tell me his father is dead.

"Dead?" I ask. He nods. "What? How—"

"I killed him." He says it so nonchalantly, like killing someone is an everyday task, as menial as doing the laundry or washing the dishes. Though to a demon... I guess it could be.

I lean closer to him and lower my voice. "You did *what*?"

"I told him to."

I'm going to get whiplash if these guys keep dropping bombs like this. It was my father who spoke this time and now I'm gaping at him. "What?!" I shout, dropping my fork to the table with a loud clank.

"It was the only way. The only thing that would make me believe you're safe with them."

I turn back to Kaine. "And you did that?" He nods again. Then I look at Maxen. "And you helped?" He also nods, fighting a smile.

I huff out a humorless laugh, letting all of this process in my head. I stare at my food, still starving but not so much in the mood to eat any longer.

"You killed your father... for me?" I glance over at Kaine.

"I'd do it again, too." There is long moment of silence where my mind is completely blank. I have no idea what to say to that. What *does* one say to that? Is he a complete psychopath or does he...

"I said my piece, Bee. I have a meeting to attend to." He gets to his feet but leans close, keeping his voice quiet. "Seems a king was murdered late last night and we must discuss what this means." And with that, he turns and leaves the room, and me alone with Kaine and Maxen.

I pick up my fork and poke around at my food, still unsure of what to say. My stomach is twisting with this new knowledge, but I know I need to eat.

"What are you thinking?" Maxen finally asks.

I shake my head absently, trying to find words to explain how I feel.

"What does this all mean?" It's what I decide on, hoping it may settle some of my thoughts.

"It means that we want you to stay," Kaine says.

"With us."

"Where?" I ask, looking from Kaine to Maxen. "Here? Back at Kaine's castle? Where do we go?"

Kaine scoots closer to me, taking my chin between his fingers, and turning my face towards him.

"Does it matter?" Something in his eyes tells me all I need to know. Without thinking, I lean forward and press my lips against his, not caring that my breath probably reeks of sleep and cheese. He doesn't seem to care as he kisses me back.

I pull away, the giddy feeling back in my chest. "No. I... don't think it does." I smile and chuckle. "It doesn't matter one fucking bit." I kiss him again, this time longer, deeper. It's like I can't get enough of him, can't get him close enough to me even as I tug on his shirt. I pull away briefly. "Take me back to my room," I say softly, and look up to meet his eyes.

"Both of you?" I form it as a question because I still have no idea what the hell the three of us are doing. Are we going to be a throuple? Is that what we've been doing this whole time? Is this okay?

He rests his forehead against mine, but turns slightly to face Maxen before saying, "Yeah, both of us." And then he picks me up and carries me to my room. Maxen is right there too, shutting and locking the door behind us, and joining us on the bed just as Kaine plops onto it with me.

My life has been full of disappointment and heartbreak, but maybe that can all stop now.

Maybe I needed all of that to be who I am today, to be the kind of person who can allow two demons, two people who aren't meant to love a single person, into her world.

Into my world, and into my heart.

Because just as my mother said...

A villain in life but not in love.

Kaine and Maxen are certainly villains, but that doesn't matter. Not to me. Because I don't get that part of them. I don't get the cruelty and the pain. I get their darkness in the form of rough sex and a loyalty so unbreakable they'd do anything to prove it. A darkness that calls to me in the form of nightmares and sin so delicious I can't ever say no.

No matter what.

# CHAPTER FIFTY

## BEXLEY

*One year later...*

"Green looks good on you." My father's smile can be seen from the mirror behind me.

"It does," I agree. "But I still prefer the red one."

He strains not to roll his eyes, I can see it in his face, and I laugh.

"At least I can say I tried," he grunts, moving to the back wall and pulling off the blood-red dress. I knew from the beginning it was the one, but I wanted to humor my father and try on the green one he liked. As the King of Greed, and green being the color of his kingdom, he'd love nothing more than to see his daughter be married off in *his* color.

Not only do I prefer the red one, but my future husbands would too. It's the color of Kaine's kingdom, after all.

And yes, I did say *husbands*. As in plural. Because this is Hell and we do whatever the fuck we want down here. Especially as the Princess of Greed and the King of Wrath. Seems those titles give us a bit of leeway around here.

It's rare for demons to marry. Very rare, but it does happen. The fact that our wedding is the first one in five years is a little unnerving but that doesn't really matter. No to me. It's also the first time in almost two hundred years that someone has officially married more than one person at the same time... but again, fuck it. This is my life and I'm going to do whatever the fuck I want.

"I appreciate it, but you know even if I wanted to, I could not marry the King of Wrath in a green dress."

"They would understand." It's his last go at trying to convince me.

I roll my eyes and do nothing to hide it. He huffs out a breath and brings the red dress over to me, hanging it on the hook by the mirror in front of me.

This dress is beautiful. Made of satin. Shiny and soft. Corset top with a flared bottom. It's gorgeous, but it's just not the one.

After Kaine's father's death, it took a while to figure out who would take the throne in Wrath. Plenty of people thought he was responsible for it, claiming he couldn't wait until his father's death to do so. But that idea was quickly thrown away when plenty of others made a point to prove how disinterested Kaine had been in that position for his entire life. Which isn't wrong, as far as I know.

It was the perfect cover. And just one more thing that proved how loyal Kaine is to me. He never wanted that throne, wouldn't even take it for his father. But he took it for me. Because it was part of the deal he had with my father. Sort of...

Not only did Kaine have to kill his father, but he had to get that kingdom to belong to my father too—King of Greed, am I right?

The simplest solution was to take the throne himself, since no one trusted anyone else to do it. This ultimately gives my father reign over Wrath, but without anyone really knowing, though I'm sure they suspect it.

The Princess of Greed is marrying the King of Wrath... it's actually kind of obvious, isn't it?

Of course that isn't why I chose to do it, though I'm glad it helps. I never thought I would marry anyone, never mind two sexy, tattooed demons who worship my body on the daily. Multiple times on the daily, I should add.

I have absolutely no argument over this situation. Though I did have one request.

Rachel needed to be here and I needed to tell her every-thing. It was the one and only thing I asked for.

The guys and my father didn't seem to care, and weirdly enough, neither did Rachel.

She took the information as if I'd told her we were in France, not the Seven Kingdoms of Hell.

Actually, the only thing she was upset about was the fact that I'm marrying two people. She called me a man-hog. Which made me laugh really hard, and then even harder when I realized that I probably can't help it. It's in my blood to be greedy, isn't it?

This last year hasn't been easy. For a while, it was a little scary as the Kingdoms were on the verge of war while trying to decide who would take the Wrath throne. When word got out I wasn't a full-blooded demon, well, things got even worse, but then they eventually got better once the kings made deals and figured their shit out. Everyone wants some-thing, and once you figure out what that something is, they usually bend pretty easily.

Envy, Pride, and Gluttony were hard against us. It was easy enough to get Envy on our side though, all we had to do was promise them more of pretty much everything. More land, more resources... It wasn't easy for my father to give it up, but he did.

For me.

Gluttony was almost the same. We dangled a few wants in front of them and they took it. Pride on the other hand, well, you can imagine how difficult they were. And I think the only reason they finally caved was because they realized they were the only one left, and if they didn't agree, they'd essentially have nothing left. And still to this day they maintain they do not agree with this but have chosen to drop it solely for the fact that they don't want a war. So yeah... keeping their pride intact, of course.

"You sure you want to do this?" I turn to find Rachel walking in, a grin on her face.

"Where have you been?" I ask, placing my hands on my hips.

"I'll leave you two..." My father steps onto the dais, kisses my cheek, and then leaves.

As soon as he does, Rachel waggles her eyebrows. "Finally got into that hot guard's pantaloons."

I bark out a laugh. "Fuck, Rachel, you are ridiculous."

"What? You won't be giving up either of your two guys, so I may as well get at least one of my own. You know he's got all kinds of tattoos under that uniform?" She whistles. "Not as many as your guys, but hey, they're sexy as fuck. And he's toned as fuck!" She bites her bottom lip, eyes going a little glossy.

"You're too much. Can you unzip me?" I turn my back to her and she does. I let the dress fall and reach for the other as Rachel picks this one up and puts it back on the hanger. I'll use it for something, I'm sure. It was specially made by a seamstress my father hired, so I can't just get rid of it.

I reach for the red one and pull it on. Neither of these dresses looks anything like a wedding dress, but this one... wow, this one just feels so right.

It's made of silk, tight from tits to hips. There is a long slit up the left side that will show the goods if I move the wrong way. The straps are thin, and the back is low with crisscross ties.

"Girl, you look so hot in that thing." I glance at Rachel, before looking at myself in the mirror.

"Yeah, I fucking do. Kaine and Maxen are going to love it."

I turn to my side to get a good glimpse of my ass.

It looks fucking good.

"So, marriage, huh?"

I sigh and shake my head. "Yes, Rachel. Marriage."

"It's not too late..." She tilts her head to the side, planting her hands on her hips.

I turn to her. "Will you stop?"

She holds up her hands in innocence. "I'm just saying."

"Well, so am I. I love them. They fill all these holes I didn't know I had."

"Pretty sure we all have assholes and mouths, Bex." I swat at her, but she moves out of the way too quickly, giggling. "Okay, I'm sorry!" she shouts through her laughing.

"This is where I belong, Rachel. I know it's weird as fuck, but hey, this is my life."

"Better you than me." She tugs at her shirt. "This heat is not for me."

I roll my eyes and turn back towards the mirror, running my hands up my sides, the fabric soft under my fingers.

The only thing that could make this day better would be to have my mother here.

Dad is convinced she's in Heaven. There's no other place she could be. He can't ever go there since he's a demon, and I probably can't either. All I can do is hope she's looking down on us, so far down that she can see us all the way in the depths of Hell, and she's smiling, knowing that her decision to trust a demon of Hell was the right thing to do.

You like demons... how about a snarky God?
https://books2read.com/KaiosintheBlackSea

Let's keep in touch!

www.quelltfox.com/newsletter
(You'll get four free books, too)

# BLOOPERS

Sometimes when in writing mode, authors type some pretty funny things.

I've added a few I came across when self-editing this book and thought I would share for your entertainment.

Hope you enjoy... I sure did.

1. He said punishment and punishment is what I expect. I don't want him to go easy on me, though I've never been punished before, so I don't even—

"Ah!" I shriek when a sharp sting spreads across my right ass cheese.

2. Kaine shifts and a moment later he's filling me with his fingers and sucking his clit into my mouth.

3. The trunks are black, not brown like I'm used to at home, and it helps me blend in. My hair is dark, and so are the sweatpants and shit I'm wearing, so there's that.

4. Those who are appointed the job of Kill Demon go through extensive tasting to make sure they follow the rules and don't go wild.

# THANK YOU!

Thank you for your support ♥

I truly appreciate you as a reader and as a person—because you clearly have good taste!
If you want others to fall in love with these characters too, do your friends and fellow readers a favor by leaving a review.

# About Quell

**USA Today Bestselling Author**
Quell T. Fox brings you all things spicy!
From RH to MM and fantasy to paranormal... she never stops writing.
Quell loves animals, rainy days, soft blankets, and loud music. She's an introvert at heart but is passionate about her readers and friends.

Made in the USA
Middletown, DE
15 August 2023

36225225R00170